i Contents

Editorial

Gutter is on holiday in Venice and spots Roman Abramovich's 553 foot super-yacht, The Eclipse, moored on the Lido. It also features in a fresco at Jeremy Deller's art installation at the Venice Biennale, where it is being hurled out to sea by a titanic, morally outraged John Ruskin[1], the Victorian critic.

The rich like their playthings, be it yachts, charitable trusts, football clubs or, believe it or not, literary magazines. Art has always had a conflicted relationship with patronage, regardless of whether it comes from the church, state or aristocracy. Over the centuries, much of the world's greatest literature, painting, sculpture and architecture has, to varying degrees, been instigated or paid for by patrons.

Get it right and you can end up with the Sistine Chapel, *Las Meninas*, *King Lear* or *Gulliver's Travels*. Get it wrong and the consequences can vary from larceny by the artist (Richard Wagner famously had a series of stinkers before gaining the inspiration for his first hit, *The Flying Dutchman*, storm-bound in a Norwegian port after fleeing his angry patrons) to cultural vandalism by the benefactor (the Catholic Church in Scotland's reputation as one of the great patrons of modernist architecture is tainted by the abandonment of the world-class Gillespie, Kidd and Coia St Peter's Seminary at Cardross just fifteen years after its completion).

As editors of a literary magazine, we'd be lying if we said we hadn't fantasised about a Russian oligarch or former investment banker inviting us onto her or his private gin palace to make us an offer we couldn't refuse. Despite consistent and hugely appreciated support from Creative Scotland, we're ambitious and would love to give *Gutter* contributors the chance to rub shoulders with the very biggest names in Scottish, UK and international literature. Imagine a *Gutter* roadshow of Scottish live literature touring the campuses and salons of Europe and North America. Wouldn't we all benefit from the reinstatement of a national or international short story competition to rival if not surpass the late and lamented Macallan / *Scotland on Sunday* prize? As some Swedes once said, 'All the things we could do, if we had a little money...'

But we must be careful what we wish for. What gains patronage brings in scale and scope are lost in independence. Patronage is the crack cocaine of the arts; its effect a glorious initial high followed by years of dependency or, in the worst cases, a premature death. We were sad to see the beautifully produced Edinburgh-based *Arts Journal* with its *Gutter*-like supplement, *Scottish Pages*, fail after two issues. *Arts Journal* was instigated by cultural behemoth, Summerhall, who also provide support to Belfast-based literary journal, *Irish Pages*.

Also in the news recently has been the minor meltdown at *Granta*, bankrolled by Tetra Pak babillionaire, Sigrid Rausing. Editor John Freeman, deputy Ellah Allfrey, associate editor Patrick Ryan and art director Michael Salu have all handed in their notice, causing a flurry of chatter amongst the metropolitan twitterati.

Although she bought the magazine in 2005, Rausing only took control this summer after, one can only assume, ongoing and eye-watering post-crash expenses. Rausing told the *Guardian* "publishing is going through rocky times – we are lucky because I can afford the subsidy... The magazine I don't think will ever be profitable, but I am certainly hoping that the book side will make money." In justifying the haemorrhage of

---

[1] *Gutter* remembers that our favourite quote from Ruskin is from *The Lamp of Beauty*, where the critic states emphatically, 'the only morality is taste'. We wonder if Jeremy Deller's intention was that Ruskin hurl Abramovich's boat into oblivion because of the staggering opulence in the face of Third World poverty – or because Ruskin would clearly have thought it the height of naffness.

↦

senior staff, she said, "The economic realities of small imprint publishing today has made it obvious that we need the magazine and books to be a single entity to exploit the synergy between them."

While we sympathise with her scepticism over whether magazines can be profitable or not (anyone who thinks otherwise needs their heads examined), we suggest that the rest may have been code for "I can't bloody believe I've being paying four full-time staff to produce four magazines a year when other publishers with half that resource are generating triple the number of titles/editions."

Undoubtedly *Granta* magazine will survive, with staff on its sister imprints, Granta Books and Portobello, picking up the slack. But had Rausing been less enlightened it could easily have been another casualty of the vagaries of patronage, where the money tap is turned on and off at will. Just look at what the same model has done to the likes of Heart of Midlothian FC, football being the other favourite playground of the dreaded super-rich benefactor.

*

We are currently reading the first instalment of *Gutter* contributor Fiona Rintoul's beautiful translation of Arnold Zweig's 'lost' Great War masterpiece, *Erziehung vor Verdun* (literal translation: 'Education before Verdun' – although it'll be given a more meaningful English title in due course). It has never been available in the UK before and Freight Books will be publishing Rintoul's brand new translation in 2014 to coincide with the centenary of the outbreak of conflict.

We believe that readers have grown bored with the Barker-Faulks style World War One epic. This road has been travelled so often in recent years that it's hard to know what a contemporary writer could now bring that would be different. Zweig's novel was written in 1933 and is a first-hand account based on his own experiences at the front. If nothing else it is utterly and convincingly authentic, and where others grasp for poignancy, *Erziehung vor Verdun* is soaked in it.

What has surprised us though is just how political the book is. It is as much an examination of the social injustice, institutional incompetence, self-interest, anti-Semitism and political aspirations of the time as it is of the Great War themes we are more familiar with. Zweig examines with forensic intensity the hierarchies, jealousies, oppression and brutality that keeps the Imperial war machine running.

We have to admit that our initial response to the description 'political novel' is too often a sinking feeling. This is because so much politicised fiction can be leaden-footed agitprop, lacking characterisation and narrative. But it is a surprise, as Scotland hurtles towards the Referendum, that there is a distinct lack of political prose coming *Gutter*'s way (with a few notable exceptions).

Political writing is often best presented to the reader as a mailed fist in a velvet glove. Too often we revert to the default dystopian future (yawn!) to examine the present rather than letting our imaginations truly run riot. With *Gutter* approaching its fifth anniversary, we exhort contributors to send us some outraged but sophisticated explorations of our political choices (or lack of them).

Arguably, in recent years, a great proportion of the literate class have eschewed direct political involvement in a way that would have been unthinkable in the 1980s. We're all happy to go on the occasional demo, but actual participation in the political process beyond voting is seen as juvenile or Machiavellian. While this disenchantment is understandable, by leaving politics to odious hacks and apparatchiks, it is no wonder we are therefore disengaged with both the system and the individuals who allegedly represent us. A common complaint in relation to Scotland's ability to self-determine is the lack of political talent in Edinburgh – and by political talent we invariably mean 'normal people' able to communicate with integrity and inspire a degree of confidence.

Politics is such a dirty business that direct party activity is maybe too much to expect from anyone who is sane. But as writers we surely have a responsibility to engage with and comment on not only how things are in that big wide world out there, but also how they could be.

*

This issue contains much fantastical braintertainment that we are sure you will enjoy. We are particularly delighted with the bumper selection of poetry, and honoured to have contributions from Jen Hadfield and John Glenday, two of the UK's finest contemporary poets. There is also new work from Gutter regulars including Ross McGregor, Rob A Mackenzie, Graham Fulton, Marion McCready, Jim Ferguson and Mandy Haggith.

Many poets are making their *Gutter* debuts including a Beckettesque brace from Rody Gorman, Nikki Magennis (a previous prose contributor) with her wonderful poem on Polmont Young Offenders Institution, and the topical Harry Giles with his inventive, witty, poignant 'Drone' series about remote-controlled warfare.

Following the last issue, in partnership with An Lòchran, we gave a call for contributions in Gaelic and were pleased to receive a small but excellent selection of work. Included is a triple Spanish-Gaelic-English poem by Martin MacIntyre as well as two bi-lingual poems by Peter Mackay and Niall O'Gallagher's translation of Christopher Whyte's wonderful 'June In Vác'. The Scots language is also well-represented with poignant poems by Fran Baillie and Andra McCallum and others, plus George T Watt's response to a story by Jorge Luis Borges.

In prose we are delighted to include a short story for the first time from novelist Andrew Crumey, author of amongst others, *Mr Mee, Mobius Dick* and *Sputnik Caledonia,* while his latest novel, *The Secret Knowledge,* is discussed in the review pages. We also include a story from best-selling children's and young adult writer Gillian Philip, author of the hugely successful Rebel Angels series, amongst many others. We are thrilled to welcome back Ron Butlin who provides two extracts from a novel-in-progress, and Regi Claire, a regular contributor, who offers a cutting take on how physical power can corrupt.

As always, we feature an exciting range of fresh, new work from emerging writers, with this issue including a funny and poignant novel extract from Kate Tough, an insightful short story from Vicki Jarrett, and a haunting look at biotechnology from Jane Alexander. And we also provide an extract from the much anticipated third novel by Elizabeth Reeder, whose debut, *Ramshackle*, published by our own Freight Books, was short-listed for the Saltire Scottish First Book Award.

We may not have a rich benefactor but we have our independence and we're proud to publish such quality and breadth of writing.

FRIENDSHIP ACROSS THE SOCIAL DIVIDE

Four New Words For Love
Michael Cannon

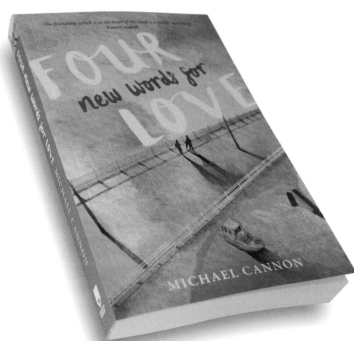

'There are all kinds of love in here. Gentle, dignified and beautifully wrought, the friendship which is at the heart of this book is a lovely, rare thing - as is Cannon's writing.'
Karen Campbell author of *This Is Where I Am*

RRP £8.99
Publication date:
5th August 2013

Praise for *Lachlan's War*
'A dark tale that manages to offer hope. He is not only an appealing writer but an extremely good one'
Sunday Herald

FREIGHT BOOKS

Order now from:
freightbooks.co.uk

Extract from *Learning to Fall*
Kate Tough

I GET UP, I go to work. I'm hit on the ear by scrunched-up paper.

The boss has left for her holiday ('Last chance of sun before another bloody Scottish winter') – and the others appear to be doing as little as possible.

A cheer goes up when I roll my seat over to join them. One explains that I got in the way of the target. I look over to where I came in and there's a printed photo of the boss tacked to the door. 'Ten points for her nose,' he says.

A joy on Monday, by Wednesday, the inanity has back-fired to the point where I want to kill myself. At midday, I say that I'm taking a long lunch-hour, '...because I can, ha ha ha,' but actually because I need to do something, anything, with a point to it. What I have in mind is the shops: stocking up on toiletries and replacing the gloves I couldn't find when I looked for them. What occurs is a split-second decision to board a bus which comes to a halt as I'm passing its stop. *As long as I don't stay on it for longer than half-an-hour, I can be back from wherever I am by one-thirty.* My luck is in; the traffic is light and after twenty-five minutes I disembark in a village that would have been quite isolated before the suburbs came out to greet it. There are a few shops up ahead. I wander towards them.

The woman behind the bakery counter is from the generation which considers it a female's duty to herself, and everyone else, to take pride in her appearance and look as groomed as she is able before leaving the house (even if it's to serve sausage-rolls to pensioners and off-course office workers).

Observing her, I can only conclude that her generation is right. The care she has taken over setting her hair and tying her neckerchief extends to the way she has the Empire biscuits arranged; the way my sandwich is placed into its paper bag and the corners twisted with a dainty turn of manicured fingertips. She can touch nothing without nurturing it.

Handing over my money, I wish I'd made more of an effort this morning. 'Is there somewhere nearby I can eat this?' I ask.

She thinks for a second. 'There's a viewpoint behind the park,' she replies. 'Don't go into the park, mind. Go up the track at the back of the cottages. You'll see the signpost. It's a climb to the bench but the views go all the way to the reservoir.' For the length of time she smiles at me, I forget to speak.

'Will you be warm enough?' she asks.

'Be fine,' I say, making a "tipping my cap", "good day to you" gesture with my sandwich bag. This excruciating display of masculinity bewilders me. I make myself leave though what I want to do is wait there till her shift is over, go home with her and live in her house.

At the bench I imagine how bakery-lady might sit and I do my best to emulate it. Gulls and crows are fussing in the distance: each group determined to claim a field as its own but neither getting to settle on the churned earth for more than a few seconds.

Watching the black-and-white rough-and-tumble, I stand to sweep crumbs from my coat then sit down again, quite content, wondering, *Does the bus go as far as that loch? Could I get*

➤➤

off there another time?

Edging in from around these musings comes the sense that something, somewhere, isn't right. It accrues momentum. Things are not fine. But what isn't fine? The feeling swells till it's loosened my moorings. The sandwich is on the ground and I am bent forward in a gaping-mouthed, perfectly silent howl.

I can't hold him. I don't have him.

Spit trails from my lower lip.

...All the things I've lost.

I don't know how long I'm like that – seconds? Minutes? – before I manage a drink of water. Thank God no-one could see me. Thank God it happened here. It can happen anywhere; the acute, occasional human pain that stops your stride, robs your breath and sends you into the nearest alley, the nearest toilet, because you can't cry in the street. Who in their right mind cries in the street?

*

At the base of the track sits the village war memorial, a chunky granite needle engraved with names. I quash the usual curiosity to see if my surname is among them; it's too high a risk that I'd see his and the heavily carved permanence of it is not an image I need to carry back.

Disco music builds inside my bag, signalling the life I have away from this place. The screen says, Tania. She's been in touch more regularly since I ceased to be a 'smug married' (her words).

When I open the phone there's scant chance to offer greeting.

'Jill? Thank God you answered. Where are you? Can you talk?'

Tania's grasp on the timetables of regular people is slight. She doesn't seem to need to work but none of us have been brazen enough to ask why. We assume her grandparents left a few bob. If someone at a party asks her what she does she says 'freelance' and excuses herself to the bar.

I tell her I'm on my lunch break and ask if she's okay.

'I need surgery.'

'When, now? What?'

'It's shooting out my nose, Jill. Oh it's horrific.'

'Put your head back.'

'Not *blood*. God. If only. I found a hair. A bionic one. It's hanging right out my nose and I don–'

'And you think you need surgery?'

'To cut out the follicle or something, so it never grows back. And I'll need hormone pills too. I'm turning into a man. I must be.'

She's turning into something... Let's see if I can coax her back. 'Tania, everyone gets a rebel hair now and again.'

'I don't. I think I should get it checked.'

'I wouldn't bother the doctor. *Really* wouldn't do that.'

'What am I supposed to do?' she whines.

Get a job? Do a bit of voluntary work? 'What do you think?' I say. 'Set to it with nail scissors.' After a short pause I add, 'And don't look at your big toes.'

Cruel, maybe, while she's still in shock about her nostril but she'd have found out sooner or later.

*

On the journey back (me, three OAPs and a Chihuahua in a jacket) my conclusion is, *I am not taken seriously enough at work; they have lost respect for me.* Musing on when this might have happened, I can conjure no evidence that they've ever had any. Not in two years of compiling their rotas, reconciling their wages, making good their customer service blips and not telling the boss when their call-times were out. If I stay any longer I'll be in danger of a personal best.

My desk isn't overlooked by anyone so I spend the afternoon updating my CV and surfing job websites because things can't go on like this ('It's not fair on either of us.').

I get up. I get to work at five to ten; within the bounds of flexi-time (just) but I've to get to the sixth floor, still, and put my computer on.

The lift doors close behind me and the guy who's already inside says, 'A'right?' It's a rhetorical question. An awkwardness-easer. He doesn't need an answer. Doesn't *want* an answer. Why do I feel compelled to answer?

If the lift hadn't stopped on Level

Three, if he hadn't got out, I'd have told him.

'Yeah,' I'd have said, 'all right. Though I woke up alone, again, to come to work which has descended into a zoo this week, with me as the performing seal. I know what you're going to say and, don't worry, I'm already looking. Where d'you work? Do they need a Section Manager?...If I could just shake this pervasive malaise... Everywhere I go, there it is... *Plus* I'm going to be logging-in late 'cause I was in my pyjamas for an hour googling a cervical procedure. My appointment card arrived. Colposcopy – heard of that? I'll spare you the details but I don't fancy it. At all. I didn't have time for breakfast in the end. I don't feel right without breakfast. So, yup, it's going all right, thanks for asking. You?'

*

Hilary and I laugh behind our hands like Japanese women, shielding each other from the food that may be lodged in our teeth. I'm telling her about the Facebook account the guys at work set up in the boss's name during her holiday – and the insulting (or plain insane) messages they sent to the old school buddies who "friended" her.

'You should've seen the replies these people were sending back, after hearing from her,' I continue. 'Outraged and full of personal stuff; what she's supposed to have done in the toilets in 1978.'

'That's awful,' says Hilary, settling down. 'I wish I hadn't laughed. Is she married?'

'To a German Shepherd, in a humanist ceremony.'

'Not her "relationship status", Jill. Married in real life.'

'...how can you marry a dog in a *humanist* ceremony?'

'I wouldn't like to be there when her bloke finds out.'

'...unless they meant an actual German, who keeps sheep...'

Hilary claps her hands in front of my face.

'There's nothing to find out,' I tell her. 'They've taken it down.'

She looks at me for a second before reaching into her bag. She brings out her diary, clicks a pen into 'ready' mode and hovers it over the open page. 'Note to self,' she dictates. 'Email Jill's boss with details of Facebook prank. Suggest Jill is sacked.'

'Me!'

'I can't believe you joined in with that,' she says, laying the pen down (but not un-cocking it).

'I didn't know they'd done it! Until the replies started coming in and the hilarity went up a notch. You don't realise what it was like in there. I was tuning it out most of the week, trying to concentrate.'

Hilary shakes her head in slow-motion. 'You lost command,' she says. 'Never lose your authority. If I taught you anything I thought it was that.'

I raise my glass. 'A toast to October half-term and Miss Marshall being out on a weeknight.'

'And to you, Ms. Beech, for being single and free to come out anytime.'

'Every cloud...'

*

I get up.

At work, I remember to block off a morning on my calendar for the colposcopy clinic. Try saying that when you're drunk. Whispering it to myself over and over (with mixed success) a text interrupts. Hilary's message says she wants to make the most of having no homework to mark and do I want to see a film this evening?

Top hole, I text. Shall we meet somewhere first?

At six o'clock, there she is, in a hangar-like bar close to the cinema. As I approach, she gets up from her seat and turns in a circle, drawing my attention to her shorter hair.

'Classy,' I tell her. 'Very nice. Suits you.'

'Spur of the moment decision in the shower,' she says. 'I phoned up and there was a three o'clock cancellation. This new do is *destiny*.'

I pick up her empty glass. Buying two large wines at the bar, I remember what she said last night and sitting back down I ask, 'Did I never come out midweek, when I had a bloke?'

'Made no difference to me,' she says. 'I

➡➡

don't go anywhere on school-nights.'

'Tania must have commented on it, then. Did she?'

Hilary's expression doesn't change.

'If I went straight home during the week,' I tell her, 'it wasn't to snuggle up with Angus.'

'Tania doesn't understand six o'clock exhaustion,' she says, which suggests she may have defended my corner when Tania was moaning about me.

'I looked forward to getting home,' I say, re-experiencing that congruent sensation between where the body wants to be and where the body is. 'Now I take as long as I can to get there. And I can't even cook a meal because serving it onto one plate makes me cry.'

'Still? After how many months?'

Two (and-three-quarters) but to say this would be evidence of counting. I'm supposed to be beyond the counting stage.

'If I can't get used to being alone, maybe I'm not meant to be by myself,' I say, to appear solution-focused; less of a wallow-er. Hilary's expression doesn't change. 'I could meet someone else and then I'd feel normal again.' I don't mention that I got this idea from browsing a dating website.

'Do whatever you think you need to.' She's not looking at me; she's primping her hair in a metallic wall-panel by the table.

'But?' I offer, because there is one.

'But...' she concedes, 'a man would smell you a mile off. Why would he take you on, in such a fragile state?'

'Are you saying I'm tragic and needy?'

'I'm simply saying that maybe you don't have enough to give, yet, and that wouldn't be fair on someone who *is* ready.'

'What does that mean, *ready*? I hate being alone, therefore I'm ready for a boyfriend.'

Hilary draws away from her reflection to answer. 'It's because you hate being alone that you're *not* ready for a relationship.'

'I hope you don't teach this to impressionable children.'

'I think it makes perfect sense.'

'What? That if I'm a couple-y person, who feels happiest with a boyfriend, I've got to transform into the kind of person who is

happier with my own company and that's how I become ready for pairing-up again? Plus, if I went to all the trouble of becoming an ecstatic loner, why would I bother getting into a relationship at all?'

'It's the conundrum at the heart of romantic love.'

'Or you're drunk.'

'On a Wednesday! Praaaise Jeeesus.'

'The conundrum at the heart of love,' I say, 'is that losing it is harder than grieving a dead person.' She can scoff at this, too, if she wants but I will say it. 'When someone dies, there's no ambiguity. You can't talk to them ever again and you have to accept that they're gone. The person I want to speak to is still alive, but I'm not allowed to make contact. I have to *act* like he's dead when he's not. The pain of that, at times, is indescribable.'

'You only think you want to speak to him,' Hilary says.

'Ease off, teach'.'

'Jill, it's time for a hard-line approach. If I'd realised you were still at the ugly-mess stage I'd have intervened sooner. The pain you're playing with is heady stuff. It's as addictive as love, in fact. You have to nip it in the bud.' Her Rioja-fuelled fist presses on the table, annihilating the 'bud'. 'You want to speak to Angus again. Explain it to me – what purpose would that serve?'

'We might get back together and I could stay at home on weeknights, not be out getting abuse from a drunk school-ma'am.'

She emits a whoop-screech, leans across in a fumbled hug and carries on. 'Habituation? Mmm? Over the years, you got into the *habit* of existing as part of a couple; of having him around. But that twosome habit will fade... when you make more of an effort to replace it with new habits.'

'How long are we talking?'

'There's no set length of time to get over a break-up. You haven't been single for what, a decade? It'll take as long as it takes.'

'I need figures.'

'Welcome to my world. Sometimes you exist as a solo operator, sometimes as an 'other half'. You need to learn to move between the two, to survive.'

'If you're suggesting I could be single for years, Hilary, I don't have years. I'm already past the beeps; I'm on the long continuous tone before the burglar alarm goes off. I need to shut the front door.' This bamboozles her. I will clarify. It's worth saying. 'You know what I realised this week – and I can't believe I never thought of it *before* waving Angus off to Canada – I realised that any guy my age wanting a family, has no interest in starting to date me, at 34, then trying for a family at 36 or 37. And what's more, any older guy, in his 40s or 50s, would go for a dolly-bird. A proper 'younger woman'. A pert one. I am already surplus to requirements and you're suggesting I wait however long it takes to be *ready*?'

Hilary doesn't have a response to this. I thought it was quite revelatory, myself. After a substantial sip of her drink, she speaks. 'Tactful as ever. We're the same age.'

And both single.

'That's true,' I say, 'that *is* true. But *you're* ready. That's the difference. If you meet a nice guy tomorrow, you can get on with it. Plus, you have been eating dinner every night since July. You're a lot more fertile than I am. You, Hilary, have the eggs of a 22 year-old. You'd get pregnant from a blow-job.'

Ladies Day
Vicki Jarrett

A WET, GUSTY wind barges across the race track and slaps the crowd for being daft enough to have pictured this day as sunny.

The women, the *ladies*, are woefully exposed to the elements in thin dresses that flick and snap around goose-bumped fake tan, not a coat to be seen, clinging on to head gear, reinserting clips and pins, trying to hold it all together against the odds.

Three of us from the baby group – me, Kaz and Ashley – shelter behind a bookies booth.

'Remind me again why we're here,' says Ashley, leaning on my shoulder for balance as she picks a wad of muddy grass from the heel of her stiletto.

Kaz glares at her. 'We're here to have a day off. Away from the kids, the husbands, the housework and everything. We're going to have fun, right?' She scowls at the two of us until we nod agreement. 'Anyway, the tickets cost a bomb so at least pretend like you are.'

Ashley examines the muddy streaks on her fingers. 'I need a drink,' she says.

I give her a baby-wipe from the packet in my bag.

I should've stayed at home, phoned Kaz and said I'd got a cold, or Sean's shifts had been changed at the last minute. Something. Anything.

Sean had come up behind me as I fiddled with my hair in the hall mirror. 'Mmhmm. Looking good,' he said, wrapped his arms round my waist and pressed in against my back. His hands travelled upwards as he nuzzled into my neck.

I steadied myself against the wall. I'm not used to heels so my balance wasn't great to start with. I peeled his fingers off and wriggled out of his grip.

'Thanks, that really helps.' I tried a laugh to soften the sarcasm in my voice but it came out bent. I don't know what's wrong with me. I'm angry all the time these days and it's not his fault. My reflection frowned at us both from the mirror. It's not anyone's fault.

'What?' The mirror-Sean raised his open palms behind me. 'Well, you look sexy,' he pretend huffed, stepping back.

'No I don't. I look like someone's mum.'

The dress was bought for a wedding last year and was supposed to be *floaty* to blur the edges of my post-baby figure but it just hung on me like a worn-out flowery dishcloth.

Sean smiled. 'You *are* someone's mum, pet.'

'I know that.' There was that irritability again, showing through like a spot under too much concealer. 'I meant someone older. Someone… else.'

A moment of silence opened up and out of it poured this sadness, like the sky had just emptied straight down on me. The anger washed away but I was drenched, the stupid dress drooping and dripping. I jerked in a breath and blinked a couple of times. Sean squeezed my shoulder and for a second I thought maybe he understood but I didn't have time to find out because there was a cry from upstairs. We both froze and tilted our heads to listen. A couple more whimpers and then silence. We looked at each other and nodded.

I went back to jabbing at my hair clips. I

had no idea if I'd done them right. We were all supposed to have hats for today and I did try but hats make me look fake. I even tried a few of those feathery things Kaz showed me. 'It's a *fascinator*,' she said. 'Like I'm not fascinating enough already,' and laughed that loud laugh she's got, daring anyone to contradict her. All the time, this phrase, *morbid fascination*, kept pushing into my head and the fascinators, the *morbid* fascinators, started to look like exactly what they were: bits of dead bird. So, I compromised with these tiny enamel flowers, three of them in different purples. Hopefully they're enough to show I made the effort.

We make our way to the line of bars and food stalls strung out behind the betting ring, backing on to the red brick pavilion. Two plastic cups of fizzy wine pretending to be champagne and a double vodka later, the weather isn't so bad.

'Another?' I wave my empty cup at the others. I'd be feeling quite relaxed if it wasn't for these heels.

'Nah. Those prices are ridiculous,' says Kaz. 'Ashley, phone your Barry and get him to pass something over the fence for us.'

When the rumour had first gone round about security guards at the gates searching handbags and confiscating any alcohol, the options were discussed at our Tuesday afternoon baby group.

'You know if you open up boxes of wine, they have plastic bags inside?' Kaz had said. 'I could get a couple of them, strap one to each leg, up high so they couldn't be seen. They're not going to actually frisk me, are they?'

The other mums looked sceptical but cracked up laughing when Kaz stood up and waded around the hall like a fat gunslinger.

Liz, an old hand on baby number three, came up with another scheme. 'Those blue bricks you freeze for coolbags? Empty them out, fill them with whatever and stick them in with the picnic. You'd get a fair bit in that way.'

In the end, we didn't put any of the plans into action. We did get our bags searched though, which was just rude.

The Barry plan is a good one. If we keep buying drinks in here, I'll run out of cash before I manage to place a bet. I wouldn't bother, but it's not, strictly speaking, my own money.

Sean lifted his jacket off the banister and pulled his wallet from the inside pocket. 'You got enough?'

'I took some out of my account,' I muttered, looking at my shoes.

He knew as well as I did there's nothing left in there. I've not worked since Tom. That was the deal and it isn't like what I do at home, looking after Tom, cleaning, cooking, all that, isn't work. We both agreed. It's fine. It's only times like this, not that they happen often, when there's something just for me and it takes money. I can't ask. Cannot force the words out my mouth. I'd rather go without than have to ask. It's humiliating. I know it shouldn't be, and Sean does nothing to make it that way. But it still is.

'Take it,' he said. 'Put a few bets on for me.' He was trying to make it okay by turning it into something I could do for him, like a favour, or a job. He understood that much. 'I'll expect a share of your winnings when you get back.'

He pressed the money into my hand and I took it, said thanks and shoved it into my handbag. There was an awkward silence and I turned towards the stairs. 'I'll just—'

'You'd best not,' Sean said. 'Don't want to wake him.'

'I'll be careful,' I whispered, already half-way up.

Tom lay on his back, arms thrown up above his head, as if the afternoon nap had taken him by surprise. His sleep breath snuffled in and out in a steady rhythm. I leant over the cot and felt that familiar desperate lurch in my stomach. Despite the satisfaction of seeing him grow, I can't help wishing he'd never change, that I could protect him from time and everything it'll bring, even though I know it's impossible and I've already failed. I reached a hand out to brush his curls but stopped short. Leaving would be much harder if he woke.

I stepped slowly backwards towards the door, in the pattern dictated by which

➥→

floorboards creak and which don't. Almost there, my heel came down on the soft toy from hell. It started up, high-pitched and insistent:

It's a small world after all

Christ, bloody thing. I hear that tune in my sleep.

It's a small world after all

It's become the soundtrack to my life. I snatched it up,

It's a small world after all

and fumbled with the off switch.

It's a small, small—

Finally!

Tom turned his head and raised one arm, like he was waving, but his eyes were still closed and he puffed out a sigh and settled back to sleep.

Me and Kaz stand near the paddock, waiting for Ashley to get back, watching the horses being led in circles, snorting and stamping, manes knotted in bumpy braids, tails wound up tight. Women drift in and out of the betting booths and bars, carrying drinks and fluttering betting slips. The rain has gone off and a weak sun is making the grass sparkle. The scene looks almost like it was supposed to.

'That one!' Kaz shouts. 'We should bet on that one.' She's pointing to a brown mare skipping nervously around the paddock. The horse's skin looks tight and thin, every sinew and vein visible, eyes rolling, nostrils flared. As she goes past I catch a sharp whiff of sweat and earth and hot grassy breath. She's making a horrendous sound, chewing at the metal bar between her teeth. Flecks of white froth collect at the soft corners of mouth.

'Why that one?' I ask.

'It just had a shit. I heard they go faster if they have a shit first.' Kaz folds her arms and looks knowledgeable.

'Well, less weight I suppose.' She might have a point.

'Perhaps we should try to scare another one,' she says.

'What for?' I asked, looking at the other horses, bristling with trapped energy. 'Why would you want to do that?'

'So they, y'know, *go...*?'

Sometimes it's hard to tell when Kaz is joking. But for once we don't have to stop and explain, or apologise. We're both crying with laughter, holding onto each other's arms, when Ashley arrives carrying a rolled-up cardigan.

'Guess what Barry says to me?' she demands, but doesn't stop for an answer.

Me and Kaz straighten our faces.

'He says, "*Talk about special treatment. You get to have your own day. Blokes don't get anything like that. We don't get Gentleman's Day.*" Can you believe that? Poor you, I says, all you get is every other day.'

'What did you get then?' Kaz interrupts, plucking at the edge of the cardigan to reveal the red top of a vodka bottle.

Ashley steps away, pulling the wool back over the bottle and giving it a pat, cradling it like a baby.

An hour later, Ashley sits cross-legged on the tartan rug, one strap hanging off her shoulder, talking about her Barry and how he's great with the twins but the house will be a bombsite when she gets back because he can't multi-task. When she starts talking in circles, Kaz takes over about her dad's cancer and how her brother's no help at all since their mum's gone and she has to drag the kids backwards and forwards to the hospital. She talks fast, eyes wide, lips wet with vodka and coke. I think she'd like to stop talking because now she's rounded the last turn and we can all see what's waiting on the finish line. She stops abruptly and stares off across the track then knocks back the rest of her drink before clambering to her feet and swaying off to find the Ladies. I start talking about Sean and Tom and how I'm thinking of going back to work, which surprises me. I hadn't realised I was seriously considering it. None of us are used to talking without constant interruption from children. Combined with the drink, it's like running too fast downhill.

The horses thunder past, throwing up crescent-shaped clods of turf high into the air, the jockeys hunched on their backs in bright colours like parasitic beetles. The ground shakes, like drums from underground working their way up.

Kaz arrives back waving a race programme. 'Right! We need to pick which horse to bet on. I think we should go for Liberty Trail, but I like the sound of Blue Tomato too.'

I pour more drinks and Ashley blows her nose.

'So, twenty quid each way?' Kaz pauses but gets no answer. 'I've no idea what that means either so don't look at me like that.'

I watch the horses as they loop back round for another circuit. I think I can see that mare from the paddock. She's out in front and my heart starts beating faster as I watch her straining ahead, a hurtling mass of muscle and sweat. She's tearing through the air, ripping it apart. It's like she's trying to tear a hole in front of her and escape through it, to some other place where something else, something more is waiting, a place where maybe she can stop running. It's always that bit further ahead. The promise of that.

Heritage
Paul Brownsey

**Find out who YOU are at *Everyone's Heritage* visitor attractions.
Their story is YOUR story.**

SO WILL THE middle-aged mother, harassed and straggly-haired, her wee boy at this moment clambering onto a plinth on which stands a stuffed bear, find out who she is? The squat man in track-suit bottoms and a T-shirt saying *46 YEAR OLD PORN STAR* – is Ardluncart Castle's story his story? The three Chinese tourists, two men and a woman, among the nineteen people here in the Great Hall waiting for the tour to begin – its story is theirs?

The guide emerges in full regalia: kilt, sporran, skean dhu, the lot. No doubt he changed out of T-shirt and denims ten minutes ago. He wears his uniform with a young man's curly-headed conscientiousness.

As he waits for us to get into attentive mode, two plump smiling ladies, each wearing an anorak, one mauve, one floral, exchange glances. They'll be enjoying little trips together to interesting places now they're retired. One whispers, 'We're not getting the Earl, then,' but they still smile.

'Right, everyone, my name's Rabbie. Welcome to Ardluncart Castle, I'll be telling you its stories.' He has a gruff monotone like Andy Murray's.

A dry well-spoken female voice is heard: 'I expect you were told you mustn't tell *Stories*.' It seems to have been uttered to the small boy, who's now trying to climb up the bear, by an elderly lady (*old woman* isn't the phrase for her). She's white-haired and a little frail, but she's powdered and lipsticked, smart in a navy-blue coat and skirt, silky grey blouse and pearls.

Rabbie continues, 'We're starting here in the Great Hall, part of the original L-plan tower-house built by Orlando Hay in 1513, the year the Scots were defeated at Flodden by the English invaders.'

Climbing boy says, 'Boo,' and we laugh, even those of us who are English. His mother says hopelessly, 'I don't want you climbing up there, Josh.'

The walls of the Great Hall display rows of ancestral portraits: wise but baleful Jacobean stares, haughty late-Stuart ladies inviting you to notice their breasts, uniformed chaps brandishing a sabre for an artist encountered in Rome on the Grand Tour. Rabbie asks what we think of two rows at the top, little paintings all of the same size, head and shoulders in identical poses.

At the front of the crowd there's a squat woman in tight denims that emphasise her large behind and tight black boots that say she's a contender. She's with *46 YEAR OLD PORN STAR*. They'll be *having a relationship* and have roughened swollen red faces – they met at an Alcoholics Anonymous meeting, perhaps? She shoots her hand up as though in primary school. 'All the faces are the same.'

'Yes!' For that one word Rabbie's voice rises like that of a quiz-show host triumphant on a contestant's behalf. She smiles bashfully at *46 YEAR OLD PORN STAR* at having got something right, while Rabbie, back in his monotone, explains that great families would want a complete set of ancestor portraits and for long-ago ancestors might get them done in a job lot, all from the same face.

'He's so like my sister's boy, the one in Canada,' whispers one of the anorak ladies, still smiling.

...The laird's business-room is stone-flagged, cheered up by a trompe-l'oeil painting on the surface of one wall: a serving-girl with a tankard leans through a hatch. The sturdy plain wooden chair in the middle of the floor is, Rabbie tells us, 'the famous Lady Helen's chair.' A thin shaven-headed man asks no-one in particular whether it's Lady Helen or the chair that's famous.

Once upon a time, Rabbie replies, the Hays were hard up and planned to get money by marrying this Lady Helen to someone called Dugald Cheyne, who'd made a fortune in the Aberdeen fishing and wanted to up his status by marrying into an ancient family.

'But all families are ancient,' says a tall girl with a sort of lioness ruthlessness about her.

What she says is true, of course. But not *really* true.

She's still a schoolgirl by the look of her, but you can see the strident politician in the making. In a minute she'll be saying Ardluncart Castle should be turned into flats for people on benefits.

Rabbie ignores her, delivers his shocker. 'Lady Helen was sixteen, he was sixty-two.'

There is general laughter and grueing, and lioness girl says, 'So forced marriage is not alien to western culture.'

'Well, there was a lot of pressure on her, certainly. There was a formal meeting to settle the wedding. This was the chair Lady Helen sat in through all the talk with the lawyers and so on about money and so on, and then a young servant called Jamie McKenzie carried in a portable desk for signing documents on and she caught hold of Jamie's arm and said' – Rabbie reads from his plastic folder – 'Here is the man my heart takes for my life. My heart shall not change, nor shall I move from this chair until my resolve is allowed.'

'*Downton Abbey*, Lady Sybil and the chauffeur,' says one of the anorak ladies.

In this very room, Rabbie tells us, father was raging over the Cheyne money disappearing, mother was wailing and flapping, brothers were trying to manhandle McKenzie

from the room, Lady Helen was holding tight to his arm so she and her chair were dragged about, too.

The loves and griefs and quarrels of the Innes-Hays are different from what happens in our own lives. They are like those in mythological tales about heroes and heroines, gods and goddesses: they have real beginnings and ends and what's going on is definite.

'And she had her way. It was a long and happy marriage. They died within three days of each other because she literally could not live without him.'

Awww!

Still, if our little lives were blown up large, they would be like that, too, for we are all Jock Tamson's bairns, and the rich aren't really different, so we are learning about who we are. We've learned that any of us could have married into the Ardluncart Castle family, become one of the rows of ancestor portraits. We're almost part of the family.

Since then, continues Rabbie, all Innes-Hay females, whether born into the family or marrying into it, sit in Lady Helen's chair when they get engaged and repeat, 'Here is the man my heart takes for my life,' and there has never been a divorce among them, never an unhappy marriage.

As we ponder this, thinking of our own divorces and so on, we hear the dry well-spoken female voice again. 'Countess Elinor spent all those years in Nice for her health?'

Rabbie's serious young face strives for joviality. 'So if there's anyone here who's engaged, getting engaged, and would like Lady Helen's good luck, you can sit in her chair and say it, too. I'll give you the words.'

Some of us smile, and squat contender woman looks hopefully at *46 YEAR OLD PORN STAR*, but he's clowning away, pretending to be taken in by the trompe-l'oeil painting, grabbing at the tankard. The painting was there before we were born and will exist after we're dead. Stately homes, by taking you out of yourself, can make you think of death even while you're joining in the laughter at *46 YEAR OLD PORN STAR's* antics, and then we realise

➤

that a guy with nerdy black glasses has plonked down in Lady Helen's chair and taken the hand of the shaven-headed guy and is saying, 'Here's the man I take with my heart for life.'

One or two people laugh at the send-up, but we then realise it's not a send-up because of the way they are looking at each other. We laugh again, in a different way – of course, we are all tolerant, but it was a sweet old story, and one or two people glance anxiously towards climbing boy (*There are children here!*), though his mother looks too much a *Guardian* reader to worry.

Rabbie says, 'Uh,' and stops. He has definitely blushed.

Lioness girl tells him, 'It's a valid relationship.'

Ooh!

But then her earnestness carries her on: 'Also, what you said about the Battle of Flodden: actually, Flodden is in England and it was the Scottish army that invaded England!'

That allows us to move on, both metaphorically and literally. The dry well-spoken female voice is heard saying, 'An old chair from an estate cottage.'

…After several poky rooms, we emerge from the old part of the castle, walls and furniture all drab and dour and damp-feeling, into a shining wonder of magnificence, luxury, opulence. As we *Ooh!* and *Aah!* Rabbie tells us that this drawing-room, of which we can hardly see the far end, is part of the eighteenth-century enlargement, when peace and aristocratic wealth turned castles from defensive structures into country houses.

'But Ardluncart Castle has always been as well an ordinary family home.'

An ordinary family home! We laugh as we contrast this grandeur with our own ordinary family homes. This huge ornate settee wouldn't get into some of our living-rooms.

Rabbie has steered us to a stand of framed photographs on a grand piano. Nor do our *ordinary family homes* get visitors like this – Churchill, Tony Blair, Elton John, Tiger Woods and is that Jackie Kennedy? In the front there's a signed one of the Queen.

'The Queen sat here with her feet up watching soap-operas on the telly,' says shaven-head.

'But there's no telly!' wails nerdy-black-glasses, surveying the grand room. We laugh.

There's a harrumphing noise and then the familiar dry voice again. 'She was never here. My – *He* tried hard enough to get himself invited to Balmoral. Somehow the invitation never arrived.'

Who is she? It's like a tennis match, the way our eyes swivel back and forth between her and poor Rabbie. There's the thrill of conflict, but also a little wave of sympathy for Rabbie. Nice young chap. *Let him do his job!* Sometimes he walks with legs wide apart, like he's impersonating a rough cattle-stealing highlander, and sometimes he takes sedate little steps,

'Uh – well, thank you, I'll have to take that up with, uh, the castle manager, but...' He gives us lots of historical data about clocks and chairs and an escritoire from Versailles acquired by an Innes-Hay who fought at Waterloo. Are the Chinese learning who they are?

Someone asks about a lovely painting of five happy smiling children, two boys and two girls sitting on a low branch of a tree and another girl standing behind; she's rather shadowed by leaves. The boys are in shorts and long socks and jerseys, the girls in pretty striped dresses, and they look so nice, dappled by sunshine, that they become the ideal children we imagine our own kids being.

'Uh – the four on the branch,' Rabbie tells us, 'were the children of the Sixth Earl and Countess Elinor. The one in the background was a sort of cousin who was here for lessons and holidays and things. They had lots of adventures together and were known as the Famous Five and were the inspiration for the Famous Five in Enid Blyton's stories.'

Lioness girl says, 'But Enid Blyton's Famous Five were four children and a *dog*.'

Rabbie seems at a loss, but help comes from an unexpected quarter. 'The five siblings *were* called the Famous Five,' says the voice with the pearls.

…In what Rabbie announces as Countess

Alexandra's Bedroom, nerdy-black-glasses asks, 'Didn't her husband sleep here, too?'

Some of us know better. Unlike us ordinary folk, who make a virtue of necessity, aristocratic husbands and wives have separate bedrooms, like the Queen and Duke of Edinburgh.

Rabbie replies that the decor, which is plain but sort of curvy, too, is called Art Deco, then points at a painting next to the huge four-poster bed and says, 'Follow his eyes. He's looking at his own monument.'

We follow them, the eyes of a gentle-looking young man in early-twentieth-century army uniform, and find we are looking through the window at a grassy knoll on which stands an obelisk with, on top, a globe with tendrils – meant to be the sun, perhaps? We murmur, for little people don't have portraits painted that gaze out on their own monuments, and we take a moment or two to enlarge ourselves and imagine ourselves doing this.

'He's Countess Alexandra's younger son, Gavin Innes-Hay, the Scottish War Poet.'

Rabbie adds, 'When people hear of war poets they automatically think of people like Wilfred Owen, who was English.'

Yes, we do; squat contender woman and *46 YEAR OLD PORN STAR* and climbing boy and shaven-head and the anorak ladies and the Chinese.

'But Scotland has its war poet, too, and that's him.'

We learn that after being wounded at the Somme when only 19, he was brought home to die but against expectations lived on as an invalid at Ardluncart Castle until 1969.

Some of us are thinking that that wasn't just against expectations but also because the Innes-Hays could afford top medical treatment for him, unlike our families for their soldier menfolk, but that definitely feels mean and grudging. His having had top medical treatment kind of retrieves something for all the soldiers and for all of us. He stands for *all* the poor devils and the hell they went through. Wounds are wounds, whoever you are.

'And when he died it was discovered that while bedridden all those years he'd been writing wonderful poetry about his experiences in the First World War, in the trenches and so on.'

Outside the castle some of us think poetry isn't for us, but in here, especially in the presence of Chinese people, who are known have a high regard for poetry, we are reverential. Squat contender woman asks what his poems were like.

'Well, I think I have one here.' Rabbie leafs through his folder, recites:

'I fought by popular demand.
I fought for race and God and land
And peace, that sad bedraggled dove,
And home and, more than all, for love.
Justice grants to me command
Of nurse's cold bed-bathing hand.'

Is that good or bad? We don't know. But then, it's poetry.

'And actually,' says Rabbie, 'you can buy his poems for yourselves because the family has had them printed and the book is on sale in the Castle shop.'

Would we want to take poems home with us? As we ponder this, the dry well-spoken voice says to no-one in particular, 'The *sort of cousin* wrote those poems as she kept him company while the others were doing more exciting things.'

Ooh!

She says, 'Oh, he would have *liked* to be a poet. But he could never stick at anything. Not just because of his wound, either. What fun it was to write the poems he couldn't and leave them typed up among his papers!'

'Uh, well, this is very, uh, interesting.' Rabbie's hand moves to a button on the wall and soon a door that was previously invisible opens in the panelling. A distinguished-looking man with a confident mouth and thick creamy-white hair emerges.

'Tim,' he calls, in the hailing voice which means: "you wanted me?"

Rabbie – Tim? – motions him over and as we fall back to allow the newcomer, who's very stout, to make his way through us, he says

➤➤

sincerely, 'I'm so sorry to interrupt your tour,' his smile taking us all in, making us feel we're aristocratic guests, not tourists. He says '*Héllo*' to squat contender woman as though she were an old and valued friend, the one person he'd have hoped to encounter, and pats climbing boy on the head while giving his mother a lovely congratulatory smile, before conferring inaudibly with Rabbie.

One of the anorak ladies nods to the other. 'That'll be the Earl.' Yes, he must be: he has the assurance and grace our own better selves aspire to, a model for us all.

Now he goes up to the elderly lady in pearls.

'Look here,' he says, not minding us overhearing, 'if you want to see the old place, *you* don't have to join a tour.' He has taken her arm, only, one might think, to assist her in her frailty. 'Come and have a cup of tea with Gordon – you remember Gordon? – and later we can have a private look at anything you want to see.'

'But it is a most interesting tour,' she says, in a very refined way, but even while saying it she's allowing herself to be led through the previously-hidden door, which then closes, invisible again, so that we feel prevented from asking what all that was about, even when during the remainder of the tour Rabbie asks if there are any questions. Even lioness girl doesn't dare.

The *sort of cousin*, she said she was, didn't she?

But that could have been a fantasy and she's just crazy. True aristocrats, like the *Downton Abbey* family, are proud and self-sufficient and always courteous: they'd never make sniping remarks dragging down the family in front of inferiors, like this old woman. Look how nice the Earl was to us as well as to her. She's probably something like a bitter ex-governess or a maid sacked for pilfering, sneaking around years later trying to avenge a grudge. You saw that sort of thing in *Downton*, too.

When we get to the shop it's the end of our sixty-minute escape from ourselves into a world that could so easily have been ours if history had been different, and we make lots of purchases, including no fewer than eight copies of Gavin's poems.

Gates
Jen Hadfield

Q. What empties itself out speaking?

A. Gate like a chapped mouth,
that the wind picks and peels,
gate that droops outwards like a broken wing
and cries until it's empty,
giving and giving.

Q. What fattens itself listening?

A. Clenched pink gate
in the soupy, winter pasture.

Q. What gathers all it owns in a desperate passion?

A. Sun-gate on the sea, foreclosing.

Q. What dry gate itches like a ghost limb
between ghost dykes
covered with ghost lichen?

Q. What gate returns you to friends forgotten?

A. Gate you open guiltily, fastened with a fanbelt,
admitting you to an assembly of graves.

Q. What is frantic to be touched?

A. Gate whose wooden latch is so melodious—
like a xylophone—
that it persuades you to close it three times.

Hydra
For D, S & F; A & L

Jen Hadfield

Were we like a plough, ancient or modern,
or a plough like us

as we laboured together along the rows
and down the yard,

straining to turn the chunked soil,
and intermittently fell into a genius rhythm:

in unison trod
the spade-heads, and teetered

while you cut
the corner of the clod;

and raised our blades
in the fissure to turn the dead

weight of it together
and then, impelled by momentum

and gravity, struck
the same, rolled clod in unison

with spades honed over the years
to a thin, ragged edge,

as cobra-heads with hoods spread
dash from the same knot

of muscle; three dull eyes
blanking the sun?

Just as often I whacked one of you

with my hip or arse
or our hat-brims cymballed

or the spade just missed the hand
that darted into turned earth

for lim or plumped mandrakes
of docken root,

or we eyed Foula
distant in blue haze

and panted, or hosed the pig,
who shuddered the bright drops

from her curling bristles
and her ears like cabbage leaves,

and in an eruption of the spirit
tackcd about her park.

Or we filled our hats at the tap
and worked on with earlobes dripping

while the dryness washed down
from our first row,

the turned roots
parching in the sun,

until it was done,
in the cooling of the light.

Blütenstrasse 9
John Glenday

All that awful mess still lies ahead of him of course:
the silly posturing and bombast, those terrifying
stylish uniforms, the sticky end. For the time being

he's sitting by his mother now the cancer has finished
its work. The sickroom carpet ankle-deep in his mediocre
sketches of her, endlessly rehearsing every incidence

of light – all those angles and shadows suffering
worked into her, as if somehow one loss might be lost
in many versions of itself. The traffic on Blossom Street

dims to a reverential hush. Echoes whisper in the stairwell
then the impatience of a single knock. Yes. Now it is time
to put the pencil down. From this day forward

all pages will be blank pages, with never a trace
of what he has grown from, or where he will go from here.

X Ray
John Glenday

So this is outer space,
this filmy sheet of black
blemished with stars?

That grinning moon
is balanced on a milky haze
of cloud, snagged in the thousand

branches of a bare
white tree. But these
are nothing – nothing's marks,

pauses for thought,
the interstices, the junctures
at which something slowed

and thickened as it made
its way through her. Surely
this speaks of a wilful

hesitancy – interest even?
For want of the proper science
we should call that love.

2 poems from *Sweeney: An Intertonguing*

Rí-rá

Rody Gorman

When Sweeney heard the *rírá* buzzclamourtalk
Of the communityhost and fondletumult
Of the exaltgreat fairyarmycrowd he rose up

From the sacredscionbordertree to the showerabundant trancenebulae
Of the firmaments above the rooftops of every place,
Above the ridgepolerooftrees of every quarterland-domain.

For a melancholylong moonspacetime he *Robin-sonnered*
Throughout Ireland, transient-visiting and rush-searching
In rock-hard spelldefilesodshelterclefts in the Scalp

And in dronebushthickets of tall ivy penismast-trees
And in kyle-narrow covehollows in Coose among
The isleshorecastletesticlestones from estuaryspit to estuaryspit

And from sweetcliffgablepeak to sweetcliffgablepeak
And from smoke-cloudhollowglen to smoke-cloudhollowglen
Till he came to the eternally delightbeautiful Glenbalkan.

There the grazingnakedwoodlunatics of Ireland
Would hauntgo after a fullsafe year of grazingnakedwoodmadness
For it is a place of eternal delight for grazingnakedwoodmadmen.

Glenbalkan
Rody Gorman

Glenbalkan is like this:
Four dooropenings to the estuarywisewinds
And delightbeautiful mildpleasant castrationscrubcoppicewoodheadlands
And clean-sided wells and balneary springs coldspringy and sabulous
Clearcleanrainwater greengrey boglandstreams
And greengreycroptop blood-tracewatercress and faint
Brooklime long-trailing on the groundcentre.
And lots of sorrel too and rivetmutterwood-sorrel
And herbage viands and shavegrass
And glowingsheepberries and garlic growing wild
And atriplex and esculent sea-breezedulseintoxicant
And darkblack glandsloes and Jovenobletimberbrown eyeberries.
The woodloonies used to hammerpummel
Each other for the best pick of the fool's watercress -
Kapow! Vronk! Zwapp! - and for the choicest bed
In that smoke-cloudhollowglendale.

A Brief History of Time

Kevin Williamson

An hour in the morning with Robert Frost
is worth that extra slice of toast.

An hour in the sun with Norman MacCaig
is worth the tidal traffic wave.

An hour in the dusk with Louis MacNeice
is worth eight hours of screen & glass.

An hour in the day with such poetry
is worth a day in prose you see.

I Was a Designer Existentialist
Rob A Mackenzie

Even if you, from an angle, are all
I might desire, I am the angular priest
fearful of your hair, mouth, obstinate
rightness and flowering unattainability.

Twenty-five years ago I married you
in my head, certain you could never
exist. And now, I imagine your bed,
I lurk in the shadows of your bed.

I met your black dress in cafes among
espresso, wine and other existentialist
frisson: exorbitance before essence,
all I misunderstood from the opening

pages of *Being and Nothingness.* I read
Sartre's novels. Where were the constant
feminist beauties like Simone in my life?
I bought *The Second Sex* second-hand,

I read *The Big Sleep.* I slept my small
thoughts away until you came thinking
me awake. Like an alarm bell you rang
and ring out my desire, my bad faith.

Bolzano, 1998, an extract from *an untitled novel*

Elizabeth Reeder

FROM WHERE HE stood, with one hand on the desk to steady him, Alonzo Trianelli turned the clock face down on the desk and only then did he realise it did not need batteries; it needed to be wound. He pressed one hand into the desk even harder and gave the rest of his weight to the other hand and to the walking stick that stapled him to the floor. He took his time, as he'd been told to, feeling the edge of the chair's seat on the back of his thighs so he knew it was there, and managed to sit back down with a tender precision. He moved the clock towards him with one hand curved like a scoop, his fingers knotted and no longer able to obey smaller commands and then used the tips of his fingers, of both hands, to turn the handle that was too delicate for his thick old fingers to grasp. Now he remembered doing this before, yesterday, and the day before that. His granddaughter's doing, some sort of task that in her youth she thought would be good for him.

She was a good housekeeper and she went to the market nearly every day and followed his recited list to the letter. She had a different, small list of her own needs, which she'd let him see; he nodded approval and it was assumed she would never take liberties. His list never altered and it never held any excess. She bought just what he'd need and he needed the same things every day. Every few weeks they'd discuss items like soap and tissues and these were bought only when a low supply warranted the purchases. He kept nothing spare.

Every night he used to eat pesto and linguine, with a handful of salad leaves and tomatoes from the garden, and bread from Leon's bakery in the village. Or was it Leon's daughter who made it now? Or granddaughter. The shutters of the house were closed against the heat of the day and it was dark in his favorite room, his office, and his eyes had trouble fixing on the key to the clock, or on the desk before him. This old desk he'd picked up for free, some time ago. And the picture too, from a house sale of sorts as he recalled, an abandoned house is what the men said, when they arrived with an open bed truck, that had traveled a few days to get to him, through some rough landscapes and weather, he could tell, but he could take anything he wanted. Keep it, sell it, it was his now. He'd had a new office to furnish, employees to take care of and he kept it all. Had a few of his employees sand it all down, re-stain it, to get rid of the watermarks. Much of the furniture was heavy and awkward but well made, expensive once, and they'd put it in a cart and it was only a few blocks to the premises they'd taken over. The business was growing, so fast.

His granddaughter Sarah was quiet in the house and he couldn't hear where she was at any one time. She would steal up behind him with a cup of tea or a glass of cold water or with his medications. There were many of those and he'd started to have trouble swallowing them. These aches in his legs, ran into pain really, and deep, and the quack couldn't find a thing wrong with them, It's just old age, he said. But old age he could deal with, but this pain, this constant fight to stay upright, was something else. He kept losing that battle, to stay standing, to be the last man standing. This was decay, decrepitude, and would not end well. The pesto tasted wrong, he told Sarah so. But she said, 'No Papi, it's fine, it's Mari's, as good as always. I just had some, same as you. Licked my bowl clean.' That was a week ago but he complained again and Sarah had started to make it for him, in that fine large pestle and mortar his wife Maura had used, while he watched on, on some days.

Big enough for a baby, his wife Maura had said. She hadn't meant it, but she'd bought it because it would allow her to make the things they needed for the huge family they'd planned to have around them. But people kept dying, their people, other people, babies, and they only ever had what could be considered a modest, and fairly foolish, family. Always a modest family. His dad's sister hadn't had any luck during the war and her clan had all died, except one child and he hadn't lasted long after. Alonzo felt that those who died so easily were stock the world didn't need, to be so easily waylaid from life. He never said this out loud. Of course not. There's what you think and what you say. He knew that.

His sister never believed that, didn't live like that, and look where that got her.

His dad survived the war, but his mother had not. A broken heart, they said. She was too old to see these changes; these places she knew had changed so much, these people she knew who were lost so easily, and so many people, well it was as if they didn't notice, they certainly didn't disrupt their own comfort to help others and make it a world still worth living in. She hadn't been able to look at the neighbours who remained with their heads down in the same and she hadn't done enough, hadn't done anything really and her daughter was gone and there was nothing she could do about that. Before she'd died, she took down all the mirrors in their house and she keened; he remembered hearing her keening and it was a sound he would never make, he promised himself. A sound she made until it stopped quite abruptly like snapping the neck of an injured bird. Such things. Here this desk, with a wood surface and metal legs, and drawers soldered to the legs, like they were filing cabinets and each drawer was a specific size, and they didn't fit the things his secretary had needed, nor him now, after his other office had been dismantled, moved and domesticated.

His son, Gio, had married too young. Trianelli men certainly did love women and foolishly involved the State and God way too early. Although, clearly, his son had forgotten God when he chose that woman and this was something Alonzo couldn't abide. But his son ignored him, such love, he'd said, such true love. She was a beauty and hadn't known what she married into, how could she, a foreigner from America, he couldn't remember from where, it could have even been Canada or Brazil, and when she found out about the family there was such trauma, such fights. A woman should never yell, it is not her place, and his son was much too weak to teach her this lesson. Alonzo had tried to temper his son's shortcomings but his opposition had only served to unite the lovers who had three children too far apart and then Gio was out on his speedboat, rather than working, coasting because Al was still at the helm of the business and it couldn't be wrestled from him, Gio had tried, but Al couldn't be bested, and why not, until he dropped dead no one could do it like he could, even now with these clubbed hands and sore hips, even as he'd become the figurehead he knew he now was, all but forgotten about, and back then he'd been younger, fit, and his stupid son was out on the fast boat trying to beat his own speed record, that he'd set the year before, so fast, already bald at 45 and the windswept hair in the photos were the locks of his mistress. They both died in the crash.

He lost his daughter-in-law too, that day, with her haughty eyes and suitcases stuffed full, but he wasn't sad to see her go. Her sons were old enough to make their own choices and they chose him and the company. No fools, half-caste perhaps, but not fools, they denounced their mother and he hadn't even asked for such loyalty, but it showed initiative. And the girl, she was young, clinging to her mother's skirts and taken away to Chicago into the auspices of the mother's family. Until she came back. A year ago, when he'd asked her to, to look after

➻➻

him. He could save her, he knew. Bring her back into the fold. She had a degree from Harvard, was unsure of what to do next. She had a good head for numbers, he saw that as soon as she'd arrived, and he wasn't chauvinistic, not like they said, he wanted the best person to run his company and within days of her arrival he knew she was the best person. And the delicate cross that hung from her neck proved to him that she had broken free from the talons of her mother. She was her own person. The papers were drawn up, signed, notarized and no one knew what was coming, most specifically the girl knew nothing. She had chastity and grace and a kindness that gave everything and asked for nothing.

Outside in the early morning she walked him to a chair and he watched as she worked the garlic and oil together in the mortar, the salt, and it was a paste. He watched and sipped at the sweet milky coffee she brought to him in a bowl and even then, now, too bitter. He added two more spoonfuls of sugar. 'Papi,' she said softly meaning to temper his excess. He waved her off. She tasted just a touch of the paste, too soon, before it was worked together it could be bitter, and her lips puckered, unkissed, and with such garlic on her lips, she'd remain so. And then the basil, more oil and she worked the pestle and mortar. 'For you papi, for you. This one will taste just like you like it.'

'The heat's rising,' she said, 'would you like to go in?' He gripped one arm of the chair, her arm with his other hand and she leveraged him up. To be so pitiful, but you have to allow yourself to be weak with some. With one. He couldn't pretend, not now. She walked him to his desk; there were messages, but he couldn't focus. For the last week, he couldn't see what he wanted to see. And the clock had stopped, again. When she brought lunch the pesto tasted of sawdust and he left it untouched. He pinched his thigh, to be awake, but his fingers didn't have the strength in them. She had the flush of the day on her cheeks, 'But it's delicious papi, if I say so myself. Mami's recipe is flawless.'

When she helped him stand to take his daily constitutional, his legs buckled, again. 'Like yesterday,' she said. He didn't remember,

except there was tenderness on his lower back, his knee, his elbow bruised if he looked, if he could see it. 'You fell papi, yesterday too. What are we going to do?'

'Take me to bed,' he said. And she called to the gardener, a dark boy who didn't speak Italian that well. 'Where did you find him?'

'He's the grandson of Michael, who used to take care of the gardens. I thought you'd want to keep it in the family. But his Italian is no good. It's okay, he has English, he was raised in the US, like me papi, he's good people.' And the boy and the girl laid him down on the daybed, the old man, because he couldn't hold his own weight. And when he shivered, she brought a blanket.

It was always dark in this room, with the shutters closed. Day and night and day and night. Dark and cool. He closed his eyes, opened them. Sometimes she was there, sometimes not, or maybe asleep in a chair out of sight she was quiet and he was tired and he couldn't move. Such pain. As life left it was excruciating. He wanted it to move faster but he was old and his body couldn't take him there any faster. Each breath became harder, and sounded so loud, like it scratched along his ribs, in and out, so hard to make room for it all, his ribs were heavy, his bones had not become lighter but denser and heavy and his hips his legs his ankles, he felt them against the bed. Laboured, so laboured.

In the dark, the cool, her voice. 'You can go now papi, you can go. The boys can take care of the company; I'll take care of you,' she said. 'I'll carry out your wishes.'

He'd put those in a box, along with his lawyer's number for the other papers, he'd shown her where not long ago, the key, she'd have to search for the key. She knew his wishes already, he wanted to be put in a box in the ground, with somber blessings and prayers, and he was to be buried beside his wife and his parents. In a mixed cemetery but that was not to be helped, he raised his finger to his forehead, brought it in a shaky line to his chest and there it rested. He could do no more and it was enough.

Sarah sat by his side and left him, in turns. She

held his hand, put a hand on his chest, listened for his breathing to change. Natalie, Jake the gardener's grandmother, came to help her care for him, but he wouldn't last long, no more than a few days. Sarah let her go home when it became clear she'd be able to take it from there. He was no longer himself. That iron will of his couldn't remember itself and he muttered and drifted and had no reserves.

She did not wait until he was gone to find the box. First she searched his drawers and found the key, hidden in a nook under the corner of the desk, part of the original structure. Amazing. She found it with a flashlight and by slipping her finger nail beneath a thin overlaid piece of metal and a compartment, a tiny drawer really, slid down. The box held only a few papers about the service: he wanted a somber funeral, and burial. Familiar songs; boring prayers. No surprises. It'd be like every funeral she'd ever been to over here, of his friends; she'd taken him to a lot of funerals in the last year.

She phoned Theo, the local coffin maker and undertaker, as soon as he died. 'It's over,' she said.

'I'll come and get him.'

'I'll meet you there in two hours. Is that enough time?'

'Yes,' he said. 'I'll call my son, he knows what to do.' Sarah went out back and down to the wood shed. She'd been coming here each evening and breaking wood with the axe. Jake had watched her grandfather while she was down here, but out of sight of the old man, because a day gardener would have no need to be inside, nor indeed, in her bed. Today he watched over the body and waited in case Theo came too quickly and then he'd call to Sarah and she'd walk up the hill in her jeans and t-shirt and he wouldn't reach out to her when she walked past him, as he stood by the door.

She'd been wearing a cross since she arrived and he'd asked her about it and she told her it was a small symbol to give peace to a dying man.

'It is deception?'

'It is a story, and there's good in this story.'

'And if I asked you to take it off.'

'I will take it off.'

'And this too,' he said, touching the top, small button of her shirt.

'Quid pro quo.'

He assented.

Beneath the Skin
Paul McQuade

TWO BEDS ONCE pinstriped: pale blue and white, tattered. The social worker notes their misshapenness, the uneven bumps made by a series of different bodies: dog-shapes, cat-shapes, man-shapes, bird-shapes. There are small tears in the fabric from claws and beaks and she makes a note of this too. I eye her sheet of paper as best I can, but I am not a good reader. I don't trust shapes that stay still.

The Mojave. Afton Canyon sees the river burst its bonds of dry earth. It rises from below, as a kind of a resurrection, and the dead land is there made green. A jackal skulks warily through the sparse colour before lying in the shade of a railway bridge. Its ribs press against its skin as if demanding release. A train rackets over its laboured breathing.

Everything in the desert is death, they say. A place where the earth will not give. Here no corn stalks, no carrot flowers, no apple swelling red as blood drops. Only the bones of silver aircraft lined up in tombs near Mojave City.

The desert has its own relief. In the skin of cacti, in the soft pulse of aloe. At night the desert is pure silver. Lizards mine it. Snakes slither and cool bellies stewed all day in rock caverns waiting. Eggs crack in the dark.

Two coyotes meet on the desert plain. Black clubs of cactus shield them from the night wind. There they meet, two wanderers in the land of death. They circle each other hungrily.

Not pain but pressure. The body contorts. The head at the centre displaced, moved forward as the shoulders course in one great wave. There is a point, an instant, a moment of indecision. Then slowly, slowly. Slowly the bones come to a form. The skin moves like elastic, pulled as far as it will bend, then snaps into something new.

This is how a woman becomes a spider,
how a frog becomes a prince,
how wolves take human form
and discard it in the light of the moon.

My brother's skin writhes. He is not good at being human.

The social worker does not see. She sees two children, meek as mice, shoulder to shoulder on a ratty bed. She is also adept at transformations. She transforms us into words: hair (clean), skin (no sign of violence), teeth (some decay), weight (on the thin side, but not malnourished).

She does not write: *Alice and Munroe are two happy children who like living at home. They have no toys because all their pleasure is inside them: tail-chase, claw-dig, balance of a lizard leg on the sofa edge. They do not need school or words or other people. Theirs is a world closed off to others. The formation of a pack. Cease investigation. Burn the files. Let the wind take the ashes.*

She writes: *Cause for concern.*

Two coyotes sniff each other. They have each travelled strange ways to get here. One from the eastern side near Arizona, the other from the north down from Nevada. They knew the Mojave from the Joshua trees, the stink of their white flowers, the star-splays of the fruit as it rots and the seeds dig into the earth.

Two coyotes circle each other. Eyes glow, moonlit, fiercely yellow. A growl rises in the throat. Paws trace a circle in dirt. Two heads shoot up to the sky and a high sound pierces the night. There is understanding.

Two coyotes come closer. One knows the other. They share something like kinship. One moves muzzle to the other's neck. The other flinches, expecting the hot crush of fangs. Then neck on neck, fur to fur, and bone to bone, they speak without language.

Two coyotes step back from each other. Something has been decided.

Not pain but pleasure.

Needles, California, lies at the edge of the Mojave Desert. It is named for a group of grey rocks that rise on the eastern side of the Colorado River. Jawbone of a giant, the teeth form a falling ridge down to the city where what is left of the Mojave people lingers. They are a distant cousin of the Navajo. They do not practice the Navajo's skin magic. Their power is in plants and communicative trance. The sacraments of datura.

The datura is death. The root is powdered then placed in the eyes, so as to blind, so as to make visible. It is the burning of the veil.

What is seen is forgotten. Only a part of wisdom remains. This is what makes Mojave boys men. The datura tells them this: Nothing is ever truly lost. There is only everywhere the endless process of transformation.

The Mojave dwindle.

They will one day leave nothing but a trace.

A buckskin jacket, fragment of a clay owl. Half a cusp of jawbone.

The social worker comes round on Thursdays. It is always the same questions, same notes, though I'm sure it is all leading somewhere. I am not sure I like where.

When she leaves my brother is a dog. He is at that stage. He leaps about the house yipping and yapping and dad tells him to be quiet while looking out the window. He wants to make sure the woman is gone. The Department of Social Services have no record of us having a dog.

They have records of me and my brother. But none of dad. Mom has paperwork but no birth certificate.

When the social worker's bug-green car is gone dad is a coyote. This is the form he is most comfortable in.

Munroe nips at dad's heels playfully. Dad snaps his jaws. The two spar then collapse.

Of the three of us, I am the most comfortable in human skin.

The social worker will be back. A Thursday. Maybe next week, or a month from now. When we see the car we will know. Dad's pretty bad with time. He can't understand the division of words. He focuses on sun and shadows and the days melt into each other. My brother takes after him.

The social worker will be back.

I am ready.

Two coyotes lie down in the desert and transform. They start out as one, then become two. They start out as eight legs then become four. Shins rub shins. Toes curl in the chill of packed earth.

The body makes decisions while the mind is blank. And it settles on this: a man and a woman, human-bodied, breath misting. Each thrust is bond and each tenderness avowal, and each pant would yield a name, but there are no names between beasts, even ones in human form.

Sun rises pale ivory. Two coyotes walk. The desert grows hot beneath their feet.

They go looking for walls.

Yee Naaldlooshii. He who goes on all fours. The Navajo know skin magic.

There are different witching ways: cursed objects, corpse powder, spirit possession. To combat these: a gathering, a song lifted like a shield. A diffusion of pollen.

The skinwalkers remind the people of something forgotten. It is harder to breathe with them nearby. As if the sky is too close, as if something about themselves is too tight. Doors are locked. Blood turns against blood.

From each tribe the skinwalkers walk.

➻➻

They travel high and low, as bird, as wolf, as snake, as jackal. They are no longer welcome among humans. But humans are everywhere. They cannot be outrun. Even in the high passes of the Rockies, they come. Deer scatter. The sky is a shattering of crows.

The skinwalkers walk. It is their nature. Home to their backs, they are searching for each other. For their own bondage of sameness.

When the West is young, people come and settle the land. Some strive to the coast, others settle for less. The bravest make walls in the desert.

In their hands they feel the hot fury of it – the Mojave. It is not the softly cupped palm of cultivation, not the gentle slowing down to stand still, at last, in a place now home. The men and women who work the desert come for strength, and patience, and the toil of the earth. They come to live at the edge of life.

It is a matter of dominion.

But the desert suffers no master. The arid air robs the walls of moisture. They buckle, breathe inward, collapse. The little people inside scatter to the wind. The seeds of the Joshua trees bury themselves in the earth.

The people collapse and leave white husks. The houses are ribcages. Nothing moves inside.

Joshua trees grow around them. Columns of white flowers like tongues of pale fire.

Mom and dad are not used to being human. There are so many things to do, so many numbers that pile up month after month. But this is what they walked for, what they fought so hard for in exile. Mom gets a job waiting tables and dad works in a factory. Without the numbers to prove they exist, they can't work legally. They have bodies but no numbers. Numbers are more important among people.

Munroe and I go to school. The first thing they notice is that we cannot read. The social worker comes round after our first day. She is concerned.

The factory poisons dad. Chemicals settle in his lungs. The men he works with die. Dad does not. But he knows too much. He gets money every month so long as he doesn't sue.

Dad doesn't understand, not really, but signs anyway. The lawyers cannot make out the scribble but assume it is his name.

Mom dies when I am eight and Munroe six.

A man follows her to the alley behind her cafe. She has a bag of coffee grounds and cone filters, scraps of steak fat and stale crusts of bread. He has a knife. He presses the blade to her throat and tells her to undress. She does so.

First her baby blue uniform. Buttons of unnatural pearl catch the streetlights dimly. She folds the fabric on the ground behind a dumpster.

Naked, she stands before him, and takes off her skin.

An adobe house. The walls are stained the colour of pollen.

It remembers the family that built it. How they brought furniture of solid oak, a stove of black iron, and a dream of mastering this, the last expanse of the untamed world. This the frontier's frontier. This the very limit of life.

The house remembers them and mourns.

Two coyotes find it. They crawl inside and lie down on the floor, roll over the ground to disperse the heat that has gathered in their fur. They are not alone.

A rattlesnake coils in the corner, behind the frame of a bed whose straw mattress caved in long ago. Only a pile of dust and insects remains. A spider hangs on to its web, lifted by the unfamiliar breath of mammals.

The coyotes smell strange. They are not of the desert, not truly; neither is the house. It belongs to them as nothing has ever belonged to them. They share with it abandonment and persistence.

The snake and the spider and the insects leave. Two coyotes lie down on the floor. The house stirs with forgotten gladness. Two skinwalkers find home.

A knife lies on the ground. The asphalt glimmers damp with dumpster runoff. A baby blue uniform is stained at the edges.

The man on the alley floor has no throat. His wrist is bitten clean through. He lies on the ground like a sad marionette, waiting for someone to pick up his strings. The police officers standing over his body cannot do this. Instead, they place him carefully inside a bag. The black plastic rises over his face like dark water.

A police officer is phoning animal control. 'No rush,' he tells them. 'We already shot the coyote. Yeah. Yeah, Allans was having a coffee when one of the waitresses down here heard a commotion. Came out and shot it. The guy was already dead, through. Looks like he pulled a knife on it, too. No use. He's on his way to the coroner just now. Yeah. Okay. Think we'll be inside getting a coffee. Okay. We'll shout you one when you get here. All right. Thanks Jim. Bye.'

The social worker is concerned about mom's disappearance. She has no faith in dad. She is convinced he has killed her. When she visits on Thursdays she raps on walls when she thinks no one is looking. The walls refuse to speak.

The days close over the death of a mother. The children have no body to mourn. A coyote carcass is burned in a state owned facility. The bones are ground up and used as fertiliser. Joshua trees grow in the Mojave.

Dad stays home with us and spends his poison money on groceries. The grocery store excites dad. Its abundance. He was weaned on bone-dryness, on desert air. He remembers the thinness of dog bodies. He buys steaks in packets, blood sliding side to side, pale beneath the cellophane. By the time we get home he is deflated, as if something is missing.

'Good, innit?' Munroe asks him. We sit human-shaped for dinner. I insist.

'Yeah,' Dad mumbles.

He is forgetting why he came here. As if only in twos does our kind feel any sense of grounding. Dad wants to roam. Munroe is happier as a dog. The social worker tells me it's up to me to keep the family together. The boys need a woman's influence.

The Colorado River rises east of the Never

Summer Mountains. From there it travels south, forgetting. It was once called Rio del Tizon. It had other names, too, by other peoples. But the people are forgotten. The names are forgotten.

The Colorado River twists and bends, sheds itself across the land, rises, falls. It takes on many shapes and then forgets them, as if everything must be cast off in order to be present. By the time it reaches Needles, California, it has forgotten La Poudre Pass, it has forgotten east of the Never Summer Mountains. It has forgotten once upon a time.

—The children are too wild.

—It's not the father's fault. I really think he loves those kids.

—The wife? Can't rule it out but he doesn't seem the type.

—No idea, seems to have just disappeared. Five years back. They were a mess at the time. Think they've got a better handle on it now.

—Yes, I checked the walls. Nothing. No weird smells, no echoes, nothing out of the ordinary except a bit of dirt.

—What do I recommend? Hard to say. The children are

—Yes, yes, I am aware of that. I take my duties seriously.

—No they're not in danger.

—Thriving? In a way.

—In the way that they seem happy. They could be cleaner, more present at school.

—Partly.

—Gun to my head? Yes. I think they would do better in foster care. But the father

—Yes. Yes I know. But I can't help feeling

—Well, responsible.

—Thank you. I'll file my report by the end of today. Uhm, if I may…

—When do you think they'll take the children?

—It's just that I usually go round on Thursdays.

Three coyotes walk south along a jawbone, to a town in the shadow of stone cuspids. One of them is smaller than the others. As they approach human settlement, something

➤→

kindles. A memory. They imagine return, togetherness, being bound tight as knots.

Dad starts to pack up our things then shakes his head, realising that we have nothing and need nothing.

'Been here too long,' he says.

Munroe jumps around excitedly, pawing at the furniture, wagging his tail.

'Munroe, you know you can't do that. We have to leave as humans.'

When he is boy-shaped he asks why. He squirms in his skin.

'Remember what happened to Mom,' I say.

'Will the new house be like this one?' he asks.

'I don't know,' I say. I take him by the shoulders. 'Munroe, you're going to have to be good for Dad, okay? And it's going to be dangerous. You can't go running off. And no more dogs. Coyotes. You need to be tougher.'

'It's okay, I've got you to protect me,' he says.

I clasp a hand over my mouth.

'We should get going,' Dad says. 'Alice, you coming? Alice?'

The social workers come round on Thursday.

An empty house, wind rattling an open window. The smell of the desert mingles with the fading scent of bodies. The social workers smell nothing. They note the misshapenness of two mattresses, once blue and white pinstripe, tattered.

A large woman turns to another large woman and asks her a question.

'No, they didn't have any animals in the house.'

Question.

'Of course I didn't tell them we were coming. Do you think I'm stupid?'

Two coyotes walk into the desert.

They carry with them the memory of home. Of being among people, of what it means to have been people. But they are not people. They have outgrown the skin that clings to other skins, that relies on numbers, that orders the world in unalterable forms. They walk toward change.

They will find an adobe house with pollen-stained walls.

It will belong to them. It will share with them abandonment and persistence.

A girl watches two coyotes walk into the desert. The city is at her back, a river courses before her. She does not remember its name. Two coyotes walk on the other side, their shapes becoming smaller and smaller. She cannot follow. They walk too far from something that has become her.

At the edge of the Mojave, in the shadow of the Joshua trees, a girl digs her feet into the earth and sheds something heavier than skin.

Tinker Bell
Juliet Conlin

ON THE DAY they auction me off, I start my periods for the first time. I wake up that morning with a twinge in my lower belly; during the course of the morning, it turns into a stronger pulling feeling; then a little later, pain that comes and goes in waves. They've given me a fairy costume to wear – Disney, I think – and though it's a bit tight around the chest, I like it. It's pink and sparkly, with a feathery trim on the skirt and sleeves. There are two wings attached to the back. If I weren't feeling sick, I think I would enjoy spinning around to see the skirt fly up around my waist. I'm not sure if they'll let me keep it, or whether this is the dress they give all the girls my size to wear.

As soon as the woman has finished fussing over me – brushing my hair hard until my scalp feels red-raw, picking fluff off the front of my dress – I wait until she has walked onto the stage. Then I make sure no-one is looking and quickly slip my hand under the dress and down the front of my pants. It's wet and sticky down there, and I think uh-oh, I hope I don't have to sit down because I'll get the wetness all over the back of the dress. I pull my hand back out. I have blood on my fingers. I don't want to wipe them on my dress, so instead I shove them in my mouth and suck them clean. They taste dark and meaty.

I suddenly spot Tarik in the opposite wing. He catches my eye and winks at me. I try and smile back but I'm not sure if he just saw me stick my fingers down my pants and then put them in my mouth. I look away.

Tarik came to pick me up from Granny's

yesterday. Granny had been waiting for him all morning, in and out of her chair a hundred times despite her arthritic knee, to twitch back the curtains every time there was a sound in the yard. Tarik finally arrived in the village in his battered orange car at around two o'clock. He parked right outside the house, knocked on the front door and came in. He's quite big, but his shoulders are very round and his head seems to fall forward slightly, like it's too heavy for his neck, or maybe he's embarrassed at being so tall.

'Not easy to find,' he said. His t-shirt was damp with sweat. Then he looked at me. 'This her?'

Granny had made a huge pot of tea and some *Baklava*, but she didn't offer him any. She was angry because he was late, I could tell.

'Yes,' she said. 'You have something for me to sign?'

Tarik pulled a folded up piece of paper from his back pocket. 'You in a hurry?' he asked.

Granny just tutted and took the paper. She glanced quickly at what was written there and then signed her name at the bottom. Tarik handed her an envelope. Granny looked inside. She nodded.

'I don't have an address for you now,' Tarik said. 'But the foster parents will be in touch as soon as she gets there.'

It's Besnik's turn to go on stage first. They haven't given him anything fancy to wear; he's still wearing the same clothes she gave him

➻

yesterday: grey trousers that are too big for him and a dark green shirt. He was really filthy when he arrived last night and so she made him take a cold shower.

The pain is back. I try to take a deep breath, but the bandage she wrapped around my chest this morning is so tight, it's like I can only fill half my lungs. Gentijana and I have been told to stand well back from the stage, deep in the wings, so the audience can't see us. But I have a good view of Besnik from where I'm standing. He's Roma, of course – anyone can see that – but he's actually quite nice. His skin is soft and brown with silky black hairs on his forearms. I think he's about the same age as me.

When I got into the car with Tarik, I tried to fasten the seatbelt but it was broken.

'I'm Tarik,' he said, 'and a safe driver, so don't worry.' He started the engine and we drove off. I didn't look back at Granny's house.

'So,' Tarik said after a while, 'you're what – eight? Nine?'

'I'm twelve,' I said.

He turned to look at me. I could tell he was staring at my chest and I had to stop myself from crossing my arms. I didn't want him to know I knew he was staring.

'You sure?' he asked, still looking at me.

I lifted my arm and pointed straight ahead. He'd taken his eyes off the road for so long that he'd veered onto the dirt track to the right.

'Shit.' He jerked the steering wheel to the left, sending clouds of dust up on either side of the car.

'Of course I'm sure,' I said.

He frowned, as though he didn't quite believe me.

'I'm just small for my age,' I added.

Tarik shrugged.

Someone in the audience says something. I don't recognise the language. It's not English, because I've had that in school for two years now, and I'm one of the best in the class. The woman on the stage smiles a really fake smile. She's wearing dark red lipstick. I can tell the smile's fake because the bottom part of her face starts trembling as she tries to hold it. It looks like her face is about to crack. She says 'Go on, go on,' to Besnik and he begins to unbutton his shirt. But he's quite slow and even from here I can see his hands shaking as he tries to push a button through its hole, so the woman grabs the shirt by the collar and pulls it over his head. Then she touches his bare shoulder and tells him to turn around. He does a full turn with his head down. He is very thin. Then he looks up and I can see that he's crying. I hope I don't cry when it's my turn. The woman sighs, like she's really bored, and tells Besnik to take his trousers off. Now he only has his pants on. Like me, he isn't wearing any shoes.

Tarik and I drove in silence for the next hour, stopping off only once to empty our bladders. The countryside we were driving through – further than I'd ever been in my life – was dry and bleak. Miles and miles of dirt and stones; now and again we'd pass a couple of trees that looked black with thirst. But eventually, the flat ground began to take on some shape; stones turned to rocks; rocks turned to boulders; until we were driving through huge red-brown rock faces on either side. Tarik pulled over and switched off the engine.

'Got to piss,' he said. Then he pointed to a large grey boulder a few metres away. 'You can go behind there.'

I was dying for a pee, and I was glad he wasn't making me go in front of him.

There is coughing from the audience. A man, the same voice as before, calls out something. The lipstick woman frowns and says something very quickly in response. Maybe it's German, or Dutch. Then I hear a different woman speak. A man's voice answers. The lipstick woman puts her arm around Besnik. He turns his head to look at me and I give him a smile. His eyes are so dark, they are almost black. If we're really lucky, I think, we'll both go to the same foster parents. I've always wanted a brother or sister. But I don't want to hope too much, just in case.

When we were back in the car I asked Tarik, 'Will I be going to school straight away?'

'What?'

'The summer holidays are over next week.'

He breathed out in a rush. 'Yeah, I guess so.'

'I don't have any books,' I said.

Tarik drew his hand across his forehead and then wiped the sweat on his jeans. 'I don't know. I don't know anything about school, or books. You'll just have to wait till you get there.'

He sounded annoyed, so I didn't say anything else.

After a few moments he asked, 'So you live with your Grandma?'

I nodded. Then I said, 'She's not really my Grandma. I just went to live with her when my parents died.'

'When was that?'

'When I was eight. They were killed in an accident.'

Tarik reached across to the back seat and pulled a beer can out of a bag. He handed it to me. It was warm.

'Open that, would you?'

I cracked the can open and handed it back. He took a long sip.

'Never knew my dad,' he said. 'Killed in the war.' He looked at me. 'You know nothing of the war, do you?' And he sounded angry.

The wire where the wings are attached in the middle is cutting into the skin on my back. I wriggle my shoulders a bit, but that only makes it worse. Once, a girl at school had her ears pierced, and because she forgot to twist the studs every day, the skin behind her earlobe started growing around the back of the earring until it was completely covered. A doctor had to cut the earring out. I wonder whether, if I had to wear the wings for a long time, the same thing would happen. Whether my skin would grow around the wire. The lipstick woman claps her hands and tells Besnik to put his clothes back on. Then she speaks a few words in a sharp, clipped voice and leads Besnik towards the front of the stage, out of my view. I wait for him to turn and look at me again, so I can smile and wave. But he doesn't. And then he's gone.

It was dark by the time we got to the woman's house. She was waiting for us at the door with her arms folded across her chest. She didn't say hello, just looked me up and down and turned to Tarik.

'You took your time.'

Tarik shrugged and walked past her into the house. I stood there, wondering whether to follow him in. Then she said to me, 'Have you got anything else to wear?'

I peered down at my jeans and yellow t-shirt. 'No,' I said. 'Granny told me— '

She cut me off. 'Never mind. We'll find something more suitable in the morning.' She turned and led me into the house, up a set of dark stairs and into a bedroom. There were five mattresses on the floor and a dirty blanket tacked across the window as a curtain. A girl – older than me, wearing cut-off jeans and lots of makeup – was sitting cross-legged on one of them. She was picking off some skin from around her nails and looked up as we came in.

'This is Gentijana,' the woman said, nodding her head towards the girl. Then she pushed me into the room and closed the door.

The lipstick woman claps her hands again, looking pleased, and turns to where I'm standing. She gestures for me to come to her. I walk onto the stage. The wetness between my legs makes me feel like I've peed myself. My pants are soaked. I keep my head down, trying to ignore the ache in my belly. About ten rows of seats are facing the stage, but most of them are empty. Glancing up through my fringe, I can see about eight people sitting there. A man and a woman in the front row; three rows behind them is a man in a straw hat; two men standing at the back of the hall; and a few other men scattered around. The hall is big, bigger than the gymnasium at school, although the ceiling is a bit lower. I think there might have been a party here not too long ago, because there are crêpe-paper streamers hanging all over the place. The lipstick woman takes my hand in hers and swings my arm up and down, as though we were mother and daughter out on a walk together. Then she lets go and tells me to spin around. She's using a voice that's put on – really warm and friendly but as fake as her smile. She says something in that foreign language, a joke, I think, but only the man in the straw hat laughs. Probably to be polite.

'Do you know yet what foster parents you're going to stay with?' I asked Gentijana in the dark, as I lay down on my mattress.

She let out a laugh that didn't sound funny at all. 'Is that what they told you?'

The door opened and we both squinted at the sudden brightness spilling in from the light on the landing. It was a boy, wearing a towel around his waist. His hair was wet and he was shivering. The woman came in behind him and tossed some clothes on the floor.

'Wear these tomorrow,' she said to him. 'I'll have to burn the others.'

She left and closed the door behind her. There was a clicking sound as she locked it. The boy slid down onto a mattress and closed his eyes.

'I'm Mila,' I whispered into the darkness.

There was no response. After a long time, when I had almost fallen asleep, he whispered back, 'I'm Besnik.'

I don't know what they're saying, but I think it's between the man in the straw hat and the couple on the left, now. The lipstick woman's voice is slightly higher-pitched than before. She sounds excited. The man in the straw hat raises his hand and calls out – fünf; the couple lean in to one another and whisper, the woman pulls the corners of her mouth down and shakes her head. The lipstick woman claps her hands.

When I woke up in the morning, I felt a gnawing in my lower belly. A sparkly pink dress lay at the foot of my mattress.

The man in the straw hat smiles and gets to his feet. On his way towards the stage, he pushes the chairs aside. Their legs scrape the floor noisily. My wings shiver, sending a tingling though my chest and down my arms into my fingertips. The man shakes the lipstick woman's hand and smiles down at me. He has fleshy lips and grey teeth and I know that Gentijana is right, he won't be taking me to my new foster

parents in Germany or Holland. The blood is trickling down the inside of my thighs now. It's hot and syrupy, not like pee at all. I clamp my legs together but I can't stop the flow. The man strokes my hair, lets his hand travel across my cheek. My wings shiver again and I can feel the wire beneath my skin. But it doesn't hurt anymore. I move my shoulders back and forth and realise that by doing this, I can make the wings move.

The man reaches into his jacket pocket, but the woman shakes her head and points to Tarik, who has just come down from the stage. The man counts out several notes and hands them to him. My heart is beating very quickly now because I know that if I try hard enough, I can get the wings to move faster. Then suddenly, the man in the straw hat lets out a grunt and points at my legs. The woman follows his gaze and gasps. She turns back to him and speaks very quickly. The man tries to take the bank notes back off Tarik, but he snatches them away. The man shouts something at the lipstick woman. He is angry.

I concentrate, my heartbeat is in my mouth, my arms, my legs; with every beat my body releases a little more blood, until my feet are covered in red, then I move my shoulders faster, faster, and my wings are flapping, beating together in a whisper, and I'm raised onto my bloodied tiptoes, my feet leave the floor and I fly upwards, the blood flowing now from between my legs, gushing, a waterfall of sweet, brilliant red that begins to cover the ground beneath me, inch by inch, until the entire hall is a pool of my blood, and the lipstick woman is screaming, and the river of blood rises higher and higher, until they are all swimming in it, and I fly up to the ceiling to the streamers and find that I can twist and turn and dance in the air among the streamers and it is glorious, and beneath me, they struggle to stay at the surface but my blood is thick and hot and dark, and I wave goodbye to Tarik before he goes under and see the fleshy lips of the man with the straw hat take one last desperate breath before he, too, drowns.

Tarik makes me sit on a plastic bag. He doesn't

want me to stain the seat of his car. I keep quiet during the drive, and Tarik doesn't say much either. It's only when we drive past the rocks that I peed behind that I stop feeling scared. About five kilometres from my village, Tarik stops the car. I open the door and get out. Tarik looks at me and I think he's going to say something, but then he just makes a U-turn on the dusty road and drives off. At least he let me keep the dress.

Edwardian Postcard, Dunoon
Marion McCready

The punk-black Firth.
A single ketch cruising,
mizzen mast abaft the main mast.
Then the Waverley, punching its steam,
punctuating the air with smoke signals.
The wrath of clothes, the colour of bladder wrack,
loitering on the pier's timber planks
beside the red-tiled, plumed pavilion.
And Mary, standing back,
bronze Fury of the Firth,
her unaltered gaze blazing,
beacon for a distant lover.

Flitting
Rob A Mackenzie

From Tynecastle to Easter Road –
a small step for a Glaswegian.

Shibboleth

Irene Hossack

Glasgow's splendour is cloaked
in the remnants of her industrial age;
a yellow pea-souper rising
as her people criss-cross the ancient cores
of Kelvin, Clyde and Molendinar.
The indefinite road ahead,
the lurking invisible threats,
are faced with stoic solidarity.

Being here is to be
in the condition of shadows,
bound by complex boundaries,
where close-to intimacy,
transparency and undeclared equality,
are discerned by the glottal stop
and distinct intonations of voice.

TLC, Leith

Kevin Williamson

In the bins behind the Chinese supermarket
two teenage girls kick a man to death.
The day has hardly begun.
If the Old Town is our Manhattan
then Leith Walk is Broadway.
Speedway Al, Depressing Davie, Mental
Mikey with eyes like toffee apples on stalks.
Except it wasn't to death. He got up.
Brushed himself down. Staggered on
board a 22 bus and jerked himself off,
at the back, all the way to the shore.
Stubbled morning drunks gather in the doorway
to Alhambra, an ocean pearl set in emerald green.
Each has a fast horse, last night's boast,
a beach scene from here to eternity
tattooed on his scratched knuckles.
'I says to the wife the boay wiz lucky.'
A silent consensus is reached.
Spraypaint Sam is the local purveyor of art.
He drinks alone, slumped in a snug bar,
cornered by a midget with a meat knife.
'Ye wanting any o these sausages?'
'Half the price o Tescos ya fuck.'
The syntax, the rhythm, the metre of speech.
Each craftsman is a world champion of Leith.
Except for the tight lipped cunts.
The tight lipped cunts have clammed up.
The tight lipped cunts sit on bar stools
nursing their grievance.
The tight lipped cunts won't open up to anyone.
I love the tight lipped cunts.
I love their resilience, their sense of community.
I place a Leith kiss on their baldy heids.

It's Easter and my woman
Martin Donnelly

It's Easter and my woman
puts rabbits on every surface:
she would like to be pregnant

One day a sunburned nose
Martin Donnelly

One day a sunburned nose
will appear
out of nowhere
and make you wish
you had been kinder
to the catholics of Scotland

At Polmont Prison
Nikki Magennis

i)
Under slabs of grey cloud
rubble crushes the life out of you.
Endless layers of want, and days
thin as fingernails.
Eight hundred boys mark time on the bars.

Four hundred feet below,
ghosts dig the shale bare handed
swim forever in a river of grit
forgetting which way is up
they curl into tunnels
stuffed thick with blackdamp
and whisper promises into their hands,
their words as dark and dense as coal.

Halfway between the surface
and the empty, hollowed out tunnel
the rescue-men's brass bell
lies intact.

ii)
In Number 23 pit lies a piece tin
where someone left a note - *Dear Wife* -
and the last scrap of sweet tobacco.

In the Gutter Hole,
honeycombed with old workings
and unstable as a Friday night drunk,
a seam of good, clean air waits for
the miner, rich with soot tattoos,
whose trapped dreams still beat
on the walls, visions of burying himself
in his warm and willing woman.

iii)
even now, the boys laugh. Their voices
leap and dodge, hidden and
fierce as underground rivers.

HMYOI Polmont is the UK's largest Young Offenders' Institute. It is built above coal mine shafts at the scene of the Redding Pit Disaster, where, in 1923, forty men died.

Learning Scouse off Ian McCulloch
A P Pullan

I'd given him a lift.
Anything with a 'k' he said. Try
Nick Nack Paddy Wack, Big Mac Macca?
Also it's Lennon doing that Jabberwocky.
      There are purple crocuses in the verge.
      Two lambs stand on top of a pallet.
Mister geeza fella, mind if I light up for humanity?
No probs. I let the window down half an inch. Now try
Formby, Crosby, Kirkby, hurdy-gurdy at number thirty
or big boobied Beryl from Bootle. He laughs at that one.
      Buzzard.
Zing-zang Mister Blister's sweet sister mind if I lap
at the feet of the gods? Aye knock yourself out and he fetches
the bourbon from the glove compartment. Glove compartment?
Very bourgeoisie. Cava? Merci. I shrug my shoulders. He can tell
I'm hurt.
      I need to ring my parents tonight.
Listen he says, ever had it pumping through you,
million miles an hour – eyes wide as a chippy pan – heart knocking
on heaven's door our kid? Don't do drugs Ian.
No sweet Jesus – love, ever done love? Yeah, I think so.
Fucks sake and he stares out at the woods near where we stay
and I think of my wife awaiting our arrival, perhaps
putting on too much foundation.

Two Extracts from *Ghost Moon*

Ron Butlin

EXTRACT 1

SUNDAY

THE BLIZZARD WAS full-on – three hours instead of one with freezing fog, black ice and snow-snow-snow all the way. Broughton, the Devil's Beef Tub, then tailgating the same Argos lorry over the Moffat Hills, snailing it behind Mr and Mrs Cautious down the M74.

A one-man avalanche from Edinburgh – you've made it. You're here. That's what counts.

And so...

Time to get psyched up, get focused.

But first things first—

Log on. You've been driving forever, so there's bound to be something. So many messages, so many puffs of oxygen to keep you breathing. It's not just you, of course – you can see it in people's faces when their mobiles ring, the relief that somebody wants them.

C U @ 8 lol J x

The lovely Janice. You text her, confirming... and that's you back on solid ground. Another Sunday, another visit, then a Seventies' download and the body-contour leather to carry you safely home. Second shave, second shower and into the second-best suit – for Janice, plus all the trimmings.

Takes care of the day, takes care of you.

Your phone snapped shut, you breathe easy once more.

Life's good.

Well, isn't it?

Zap-lock the car.

Her path'll need shovelled clear and salted.

A good six inches' worth – if only you'd thought to bring your magic wand! But no probs. Fifteen minutes tops will see it—

No.

No. No.

The front door's locked and her key's still in the mortice, inside. Jesus. How often have you told her about that key, about not leaving it in the lock? Maybe she's not been out all weekend? Maybe she's fallen? Can't get herself out of the bath?

Which'll mean breaking down the door.

Not again.

A good loud knock first, loud enough to wake the—

No. Don't even think of it.

Thumping your fist big time. The snow's running ice-wet under your collar, the wind's razor-cutting your face. *Stamp-stamp-stamping* your feet on the front step to stop them turning into blocks of ice. You spoke on the phone only a few hours ago. She sounded fine, looking forward to seeing you.

You're freezing. *Stamp-stamp-stamp. Thump-thump-thump....*

Ninety years lying crumpled in a heap on the living room floor like she's—

Don't even think—

Thank God.

The time it's taking her to turn the key in the lock...

'Yes?' Her tone of voice, like she's never met you before. Not opening the door enough to let you in.

'Mum? It's Sunday. I've come to—'

'Your *mother*? Are you sure you've got the

right house?'

'Let me in, Mum. I'm freezing out here. It's me. Tom.'

'Tom? You know Tom?' Her face suddenly all smiles. Opening the door a little more. 'You've some news of him?''

'News? It's *me*, I'm telling you.'

'But you do *know* Tom?'

'Of course I know—'

'Then you'd better come in.'

At last. Into the cottage, into her sitting room – and a coal fire blazing in the grate. That's more like it.

'Well then, and how *is* Tom?' She sits down.

'But, Mum, can't you see it's me?'

'I was told he'd be well looked after, so I hope he's fine. Mrs Saunders was most reassuring.'

'Mrs Saunders? Who's Mrs—?'

'Tom won't remember her, of course. He was far too young. Between you and me, it's best he never hears her name. Best for everyone.'

What the hell's she on about? The melted snow's dripping into your eyes, down your neck, your back. You want a towel. You want a seat. You want to get warmed up.

'Don't you recognise me, Mum? Today's Sunday, I've driven down same as always to see you—'

Noticing you've glanced across at the tea trolley beside her, laid out with the usual straggled columns of playing cards—

'Learned to play patience during the war, and still keep it up,' she tells you. Like you didn't know already. 'Learned how to cheat then, too. The way you cheated turned into new rules so the game could go on. It had to, so you'd survive.'

Like she's talking to a complete stranger.

'Played it while waiting for the bombs to fall, sitting there in the black-out, waiting and waiting. Hearing the planes, the anti-aircraft guns in Leith...'

Best to move things along. 'I'll make us some tea.'

Through to the kitchen. Water. Kettle. A towel for the hair.

Tea in the pot. Mugs, milk jug, plate of biscuits. Finish off the drying, set up the tray. Then through to get the afternoon back on course.

'Here we are, Mum. I found a packet of HobNobs.'

Getting everything back to a normal Sunday. Some tea, some talk. Fix what she needs fixed. See to her path, then hit the road in time to begin the arctic crawl that'll take—

But... her photos? What's she done with the signed publicity shot of you as Mr Magic? It should be on the mantelpiece. And the lace curtains? What's she taken them down for? Might make the room seem brighter, but—

'... if the game worked out. We got bombed anyway. I was the only one in the family to survive. Nowhere to stay till the laird in the big house took pity. Lived here ever since. Sixty years and more, would you believe?'

Talking like you'd never lived here yourself, weren't brought up here. Like she's never seen you before. Doesn't even *know* you.

Can it happen that sudden?

She's half-rising from her chair as if to greet you for the first time. Such a warm, warm smile – you've not seen the like for months. So unexpected, so different from how she usually—

'You needn't worry, I'm really pleased to see you. I really am. I always knew you'd come.' She's almost in tears. Happy tears.

'But I always do, Mum! I come every Sunday, don't I? When we spoke this morning I—'

'I *knew* you'd come.' She's taken your hand and begun drawing it slowly down her face so your fingertips rest briefly on her eyes, her cheeks. Her lips.

What the hell's all this?

'I'm so very, very happy.'

Next thing, she's led you across to the window where you stand side by side gazing out at her garden and the countryside beyond, a complete white-out of fields, woods and sky as far as you can see. Now the snow's easing off there's a few patches of faint blue, a last handful of tumbling flakes.

Gripping your arm: '*That's* how I knew.'

➡➡

Pointing to what at first looks like a smudged fingerprint on the glass, the daytime moon: 'Everything'll be fine now, won't it, now you're here?'

And next moment she's touching *your* face, *your* eyes, cheeks, lips. She smiles again, 'And you *are* here, aren't you?' She's so happy, happier than you've seen her in a very long time.

Quite unexpectedly, she steps up close and kisses you on the mouth.

'Mum?'

At the same moment she's put her arms round you, pressing herself against you: 'I'm so pleased, so—'

'Stop, Mum! What're you doing?' You pull away from her. 'No. No. You can't—'

'Michael! Michael, please—'

Michael? Your father? She thinks that you're—?

You take a step back. As gently as possible, holding her at arms' length.

'It's me, Mum. Tom. It's Sunday, same as always, and I've come to you see you.' Does she understand what you're saying? 'Mum? Don't you know who I...?'

The utter desperation in her face now, the wretchedness.

Then her anger, sudden and out of nowhere: 'Yes, I know who *you* are. I know all about you.'

Her anger, then utter fury.

'Get out of my house!' Screaming now, almost losing her balance as she staggers a couple of steps. 'Get out! Get out!' Her arm waving wildly towards the door. 'OUT!'

You can see what's going to happen next. About to fall, she's clutched at the trolley...

The trolley tips over, scattering playing cards everywhere...

You rush over and manage to catch her just in time.

Saving the day.

Nice one. That's you – a safe pair of hands. *Mr Magic*, right enough. Forget the no-kids and marriage number three flushed down the pan with no regrets, *you're* all she's got. She knows it, too. Deep down. She must do. She loves you.

And it's only a moment later, when you're helping your mother back to her seat, your arm holding her and keeping her steady – that she turns and spits in your face.

EXTRACT 2

ONCE OUT OF Stornoway, the Portnaguran bus rattled and bumped along the single track road sounding its horn every few minutes to warn slow-moving horse and carts to pull into the nearest passing place. It stopped to let off passengers at small villages, at road ends and junctions, at single houses even. When it crossed the open stretch of causeway the bus seemed to fill with light and, on either side, there was a glitter of sun-splashed waters and endless sky. The peninsula itself was flat moorland, utterly treeless. Maggie began keeping watch for road signs announcing the next huddle of cottages and an occasional black house with its turf roof – the village of Knock... then Melbost... Garrabost...

The photograph showed a stone-built house set well back from the road. The Callanders were distant family. Maggie had never met them, but for as long as she could remember there'd been an exchange of Christmas cards between the two households. On taking over their croft a year or so before, they'd written to her parents inviting them to visit any time, adding that their daughter, if she was still living at home, might fancy coming over for a longer stay. She could help around the croft and with the peat-cutting, they'd suggested – and there were more than enough local men back from the war who were still looking for a wife! 'Maybe you'd have better luck in the Hebrides than in these awful dance halls,' her mother remarked as she'd propped up the photograph on the mantelpiece, next to some postcards. '*John and Isobèl – Ceud Mìle fàilte*' was scribbled on the back, 'a hundred thousand welcomes'.

Maggie peered once more at the photograph, holding it up close to the window to see better the weathered-looking building with its storm windows set deep in the wall, the cement path with vegetable patch on one side, drying green on the other, and the moorland stretching beyond the fence. Not a tree in sight and hardly a bush even, nothing to break up the emptiness of the landscape. While pacing the ship's deck she'd gone up that front path a score of times at least, trying to decide how she'd introduce herself – and she'd still no idea.

Mr and Mrs Callander, John and his wife Isobel, had done their best to take up a happy-family pose on the front step of their new property – arms round each other, the promise of kindness showing in their faces, and Callander squinting into the sun's glare with a hand raised to shield his eyes. Maggie tilted the photo to catch the best light.

'SHULISHADER!' The driver had to call out several times before she realized she'd come to her stop – she'd been far too engrossed in what she could make out of Mr Callander's face and in the cheerful smile his wife was giving to the camera.

The bus drove off leaving her in the middle of nowhere. There was a scattering of cottages, the peat-bog, and a clear-sounding *peewit, peewit* from high up in the sky – no bird to be seen, however. Ahead lay the dazzling sheen of sunlight caught by the sea. Like the landscape in the black-and-white photograph but friendlier-looking, and with the pleasing warmth of the sun on her skin.

To her left an unpaved road led down towards a bay. There were no street signs, but this had to be the right direction. She began walking. The houses on either side stood a good fifty feet apart, each on its own patch of ground. She made her way down the street inspecting them as she passed. It was hot now, but with a chill undercurrent blowing in from the sea. At the last house on the right, she stopped. Yes, here was the place she knew so well from the photograph. Someone had made a start on pebble-dashing the front wall and small stones lay heaped nearby. Maybe she could offer to help them finish? A life-sized jigsaw where all the pieces were the same – easy! The wreck of a dark-blue car, wheel-less, with its axles up on blocks and one of the side doors missing, squatted over by the fence. Its bumper trailed in the uncut grass.

Pushing the gate so that it swung open to admit her... Waiting for it to close with a dull *thwack* of wood against wood...

Forcing herself the three, four, five, six steps up the path.

The door turned out to be varnished a dark brown. There was no bell. She put down her suitcase.

A deep breath. Her hand lifted ready to knock—

Her last chance to turn back.

Her firm rap on the wood panel echoed inside the house. Such a dull hollowness was nothing like the cheerful tongue-and-clapper jingle made by a city tenement doorbell swinging on its wire to announce that she'd arrived at a friend's and was waiting downstairs, eager to be let in. Back home, in a decade that had seen parts of Edinburgh and Glasgow turned to rubble, the purely physical summons of bare knuckles battering on someone's door would have suggested urgency and alarm, a warning that something terrible was happening or had already taken place – a house bombed, the danger of fire, escaped gas or the building's imminent collapse. Here on the Outer Hebrides, however, her knock would hold no such threat. It was a friendly tap on a door, nothing more. This was how things were done here and always had been, she told herself, a commonplace gesture of neighbourliness. Having knocked once, she lifted her hand away... and took a step back.

No need to repeat the knock. Maggie could hear someone coming, calling ahead in a rush of Gaelic as they made their way from the back of the house. In time, she thought to herself, she'd probably have to learn the language.

The door swung open. A man stood in the half-darkness of the interior. John Callander, it had to be. Red hair, red face. Smaller than in the photograph, dressed in a collarless shirt and waistcoat. Slippers. What had probably been intended as words of welcome were broken off in mid-phrase.

Now they were face-to-face, was he about to greet her, to smile and shake her hand?

To step aside, perhaps, ready to throw the door wide open?

➡➡

Was he about to take charge of her suitcase, and invite her in?

Was he hell.

John Callander stared at her and said nothing. There was a movement in the dimly lit hallway behind him, a suggestion of sweeping yellow hair and pale-coloured jersey. This would be Mrs Callander. Leaning against the inside of the door, she, too, seemed in no hurry to do anything.

Maggie looked from one to the other and back again. Red man. Yellow woman. John and wife Isobel. Their combined silence blocking her entry.

She cleared her throat. 'Hello, I'm Maggie Davies. I've come from Edinburgh and—'

'Yes, we know who *you* are...'

The contempt in his voice, the disgust.

As if a charge of electricity had found a hateful circuitry already in place inside her, she felt her body seize, her every muscle lock tight. She couldn't breathe even, the next few seconds swelling up in her chest, her throat – a solid, choking mass.

'... and we know *all* about you.' Callander took a step back into his house. And slammed the door in her face.

Stumbling over to the derelict car to slump against its rusted bonnet, tears running down her face. Not even the strength to wipe them away.

The partly pebble-dashed stonework, the vegetables planted in their rows, the trackless moorland, the very sky itself – everything around her suddenly reduced to a meaningless slapdash.

She'd come to where the world stops.

She stayed there.

It was not until later, when she heard the sound of a vehicle going past on the main road, that she glanced up to see a van crossing the featureless landscape – she watched it getting smaller and smaller, its windscreen catching the sun's glare for a moment as the road curved. Finally it vanished. At one point a teenage boy wearing an oversized army coat came out of the cottage opposite. He took his bicycle from where it leant against the wall and wheeled it across the garden before mounting. A last wave to someone at the window before he set off across the peat bog, his too-long coat tails flapping with each pedal thrust. Like the car earlier, he too grew smaller and smaller as he headed further into the flat, empty landscape. Finally he too vanished.

The Callanders remained indoors all this time. What did they do while waiting for her to leave? Did they flick through the newspaper? Listen to the radio? Read their bibles? Did they glance at each other every few minutes: *Has she gone yet?* Or did they sit completely at their ease, secure in their faith, confident that sooner or later they'd hear her footsteps retreat back down the path, followed by the afterwards *thwack* of their wooden gate as she took herself and the disgrace of her unwanted pregnancy out of their lives – helter-skeltering herself straight back to Hell where she belonged?

When Maggie eventually managed to haul herself to her feet and stumble out onto the unpaved road, she was aware of being grimly observed from behind the tight little window – no doubt they were making sure she hadn't left her suitcase behind.

With only the unseen *peewit* for company, she dragged herself and her suitcase all the way up to the main road. Four hours later, a bus appeared. She stared out the window all the way back to Stornoway, seeing nothing.

Waiting for Nightfall
Regi Claire

'HOT BATHS WAS what I gave him. The hotter the better. Get the idea? Might speed things up a little, I thought. Why the hell can't he die faster, I told him and—

'Oh, sorry, formalities first. Well, call me Angie – nice name, great song. No real names or details is what it says on your website, right?

'No, never saw an advert; no personal recommendation either. Found you through Google. I don't want my friends to hear about this, or my family – don't want anyone round here to know, ever. And you seem perfect: based halfway round the world, just a face to talk to. Ageless, beautiful, distant even when you smile, like now. A bottomless well I can throw pebbles in and any muck I like, and afterwards the surface simply smooths over. No ripples, no nothing.

'Are we all set now?

'Okay, then. Those baths... no, wait, not the baths, they came later...

'After the hospital discharged him – washed their hands of him, more like – he wasn't much more than a piece of meat. Paralysed down the right side, unable to speak, read or write – that part of the brain was fucked, pardon my French. The doctor said his days were numbered, so we called a priest.

'Not my father, no. My previous husband. His parents cried buckets over him, their only son. A stroke at thirty, imagine, a bad one. As well we didn't have kids.

'But he just wouldn't die. Refused to, stubborn-like. I waited. And waited. Cleaned him, fed him, shaved him. Wiped the snot off his nose, the vomit off his face, the shit off his bum like he was a baby – sorry, but that's what it was, a shitty business. I waited and waited. And waited. Began to clear out his shoes and clothes. Then all the stuff from when he was a gangmaster, because he wouldn't be doing that again, near-vegetable himself now. Ironic really.

'A gangbanger? God no, nothing like that. I wouldn't have married him, would I? No, he used to be in charge of farm labourers. Hire out their services. Heavy lifting, that sort of thing. Potatoes, turnips, carrots, onions. Lots of root vegetables in this part of the world, so there's always a demand for muscle. I mean real muscle. Biceps. He made good money, too. Had a fleet of vans, a big gang of men.

'Anyway, I filled more than a dozen bin bags. Took them to a charity shop – Chest, Heart and Stroke place, as it happens – for someone else to step into his shoes. There's always people to fill the gap, isn't there. And I had more room in the wardrobe and cupboards.

'Didn't I love him? Of course I did – before the stroke. He was my husband, after all. But then he became a mere husk. A zombie...

'So what? I'm a realist. In the end, we all get our ticket punched, some earlier, some later. Think probabilities, the bell-shaped curve.

'Believe me, the waiting wore me out, and all that nursing and nannying. Because, quite frankly, we'd both become zombies, not just him. We'd been caught in a twilight world where he couldn't die and I couldn't live.

'I'd been taking time off my work at the bank and the branch manager was beginning

➡

to breathe down my neck; kept phoning and asking when would I be back. What could I do? I knew that Matt, let's call him Matt, wouldn't last, the doctor had made that crystal clear. Nothing short of a miracle can save him now, he'd said.

'And we both know about the likelihood of miracles, don't we?

'So, instead of praying until I was blue in the face, I revved up the thermostat. The bathwater was steaming; radiators almost glowed in the dark. And he couldn't complain, could he – couldn't even speak.

'Cruel? Unkind? Kind? They're just words. There comes a point when no amount of sweet-talking, hand-holding or brow-mopping can cut it anymore.

'Yes, those hot baths *were* terrible. Terrible and terrifying. For us both. Don't think *I* didn't suffer. I only ever wanted to help things along. If I'd had a syringe and... Trust me, you can't imagine... Hell doesn't even begin to—

'What do you mean? You're supposed to listen, not criticise. Of course I'm sorry for what I did, but—

'Don't shake your head. I am sorry, I swear it. See: cross my heart and hope to die.

'How could I ever forget? The jungle heat of that bathroom...his skin like boiled lobster... the splashing, hopeless-feeble... the snuffling, his lips all blubbery and flecked with spit, opening and closing, opening and closing... and then his eyes... That was the worst. I tried not to look at them. Tried hard. So pleading and dumb, the dumb pleading of a beast.

'But he didn't snuff it. Just wouldn't, spiteful-like. And I didn't have the nerve to up the ante. Who'd want to go to prison for killing a cripple?

'I'm so glad now. Thank my lucky stars.

'There was only one way to finish things: I withdrew my share of the money and told his parents I couldn't hack it any longer, I'd be moving out next day – he was all theirs, he could go and die on *them*.

'Best decision I ever made, and no mistake. Because ever since, things have looked up. Until last week, that is.

'Anyway, I had a complete makeover. Said goodbye to my snaggle teeth, became a blonde and got my face done: nose, eyes, lips, jaws, the works. Maintenance jags aside, it felt like a new me. Like I was starting over again.

'Within months I got promoted to personal banking. I am a financial advisor now, have been for several years. And I'm next in line for branch manager. I bought myself a pair of fake glasses for that professional look – helps deal with certain customers. That's how I met my new man, Charles. He came into the bank one day and the following spring we were married. Registry office, low-key. Charles is a gentleman, a few years older than me and fit for his age (got him to have a health check before we tied the knot, just in case). A divorcee – but then, aren't we all?

'Oh? Welcome to the club. And here I thought you were perfect: some sort of super-woman with a halo.

'Sorry, that was out of order. I apologise.

'Back to Charles. He's got three grown-up kids, so step-mothering is easy. We lead a happy life. Couldn't be happier. Not a cloud in the sky, you might say. Not until last week. Friday to be precise.

'That was when this new customer was shown into my office: middle-aged, shaven-headed, black leather jacket, Ray-Bans. He had a long, meaty-looking dog in tow, some breed of hound with short legs, droopy eyes and mop ears.

'"Would he like some water?" I asked.

'The guy kind of stiffened in his chair and shouted, "No. No water." Then he apologised, saying Zak wasn't allowed anything from strangers.

'It was only once he took off the Ray-Bans that I recognised him: Matt, my ex. Alive and bloody kicking... I let my hair fall over my face and pretended to type stuff on the computer. He hadn't made me, I was sure. But still... After a while I adjusted my glasses, flashed him a business smile that showed off my new teeth and the heart-shaped new chin. "Okay," I said, doing my posh accent, "let's get cracking."

'And we did. He wanted to invest in bonds. Gave me his passport and a utility bill for proof of identity and abode.

'"Classy address," I said.

'He grinned, pleased as Punch. "Yeah, I'm lucky."

'Turned out his parents had left him some money, lots more than he'd expected apparently, and he'd bought himself the lower half of a townhouse. "Zak hates stairs and so do I. I'm a bit disabled."

'"Sorry to hear that," I said, trying to sound sympathetic.

'No, honestly, I felt no love or affection – not even a twinge at the heartstrings. A lot of water flows under the bridge in twelve years...

'But I did feel uneasy. Guilty, I suppose.

'All I wanted was to get him out of there. I rush-talked him through the forms (I knew he couldn't read them), told him about cards and PIN numbers, got him to scrawl his signature and handed him the Welcome Pack.

'"Goodbye, Zak," I said as I pushed back my chair.

'And that was that. I heaved a sigh of relief when the door closed behind the pair of them. He'd walked without a limp, the bastard. Off to the pub, he'd said, to meet some mates. Like he was normal, a man about town. Place of his own. No mortgage. Pedigree dog. How the hell had he managed to recover? How dared he behave so confidently, as if nothing had happened? As if I'd never washed and cleaned him. Fed him. Run his bloody baths. And the bugger didn't even recognise me!

'No, you're right, of course I didn't want him to. Why would I? It just got to me, him not limping, and looking so happy and all. Made me feel sick. Like I'd been punched in the guts. Like I'd been cheated of something. Had to lock myself in the toilet. I retched and retched, but nothing came.

'Afterwards I stood in front of the full-length mirror by the door. Stared at myself long and hard, critical-like. So this is you, I said to myself. The new you: Angie R. You've just passed through your baptism of fire. Relax. Accept you've changed. You're a different woman now, with a different name. Ange T belongs to the past.

'You're nodding. You know what's coming, don't you? Because, yes, there was a nasty little voice, buried inside me, saying, No, you're wrong. Deep down, you're still Ange T. A snake's a snake, whatever the colour of its skin.

'That voice got so loud it was shrieking inside me. Had to hug myself with both arms to hold it in. Holding myself together, more like. Then suddenly it was all around me, bouncing off the floor, the ceiling, the walls, the door, the mirror...

'And what will Ange T do now, when she goes home to her not-so-new-anymore husband? Her growing-old husband? Will she tell him who she saw today? Will she confess? Or will she simply bide her time, wait until he too has a stroke? She can already see the redness in his face as he over-exerts himself at night, can't she?

'I felt pretty bad. Bloody awful, if you must know. Which wasn't helped by the fact I was needed at the counter. Pre-Christmas they come out like mice from their holes or squirrels down the trees, all the little old ladies with their grey, whiskery faces and furry hair – their liver-spotted hands gripping bank cards to draw out dosh for kids and grandkids, then stuffing it into their handbags like nuts.

'Sure, I'm bitter. Bitter and twisted, if you prefer. Angry, too. And no fucking wonder. Because Matt hasn't left me in peace since that afternoon at the bank. He's started haunting me, the bastard.

'No, he isn't stalking me – not in any real sense. I guess it would be easier if that was all there was to it: a man following me around like a dog. I could handle that.

'Instead, he's forced himself into my dreams. Turned them into nightmares. I see him staring up at me from steaming bathtubs. Only now the hot water doesn't seem to bother him. Because when I tell him to hurry up and die or get the hell out of my life, he just laughs and starts splashing me, almost teasingly. Splashes me with scalding arcs that make me cry out in my sleep, waking Charles.

'And every time I stand there like I'm paralysed. Let myself get splashed and laughed at all over again. He laughs right into my face. Giggles his head off the way he used to after a

➤➤

meal of magic mushrooms with his gang. But it's not a happy giggle anymore. Not the giggle that had us running round the house naked, playing hide and seek and—

'Scalding, yes. Here, let me show you. See? *Real* blisters.'

'Hi again, it's Angie. No smile for me this time? Did I shock you so much last week?

'No? Good. Your bread and butter, I guess. But, pardon me, you do look ghostly today.

'Not ghastly. *Ghoſtly*. Otherworldly. You know: grainy image, a little fuzzy and wavery. Your voice, too: full of echoes, broken up. Just goes to show that nothing's ever quite as nice and straightforward as it seems, doesn't it.

'Get to the point?

'Coming over loud and clear now. All right then. Go on, ask me. I know you're dying to. Ask why am I wearing this bandage here. And why do I have a split lip.

'Yes, I've been sleeping in the spare room. Better for Charles. When the nightmare returned, I remained silent. Simply stood looking at Matt as he stared up at me from the bath. And it was curious. I could have sworn that he *wanted* me to say it. Wanted me to tell him to hurry up and die – I could see it in his eyes. In the end he whacked his arm down into the water, hard, to soak me. I never cried out. The water was tepid.

'I woke, wet with sweat, and it was the middle of the night.

'The following evening I took a sleeping pill.

'The next time the nightmare tried to suck me in, I was ready to slam the door on it. But something, some kind of force, stopped me. I couldn't step outside. Couldn't shut that damn bathroom door. I stood and looked at Matt, and he stared back at me. And then I thought, Fuck it. Fuckitfuckitfuckit. And then I heard myself blurt out, "I'm sorry." Just that. And then I woke, no blisters, no sweat, and I had a drink of water.

'When I fell asleep again, there he was once more. In the bloody tub. Still staring up at me. Glaring almost. Angry. Why the hell is he angry now? I kept thinking. Why now? I've told him I'm sorry. What the fuck else does he want?

'I woke. And I knew. Knew in that sudden flash sort of way. I put on my clothes, some lipstick, packed a few necessities and left. It was three-thirty in the morning.

'I drove across town, through the empty streets, in that deadly, pre-dawn quiet. Hardly any cars about and only a few people, drunks mostly and short-skirted fireflies, some druggies. As I got closer to my destination, my foot kept slipping off the accelerator. The steering wheel felt clammy.

'When I reached the side street with its overhanging trees and bushes and old townhouses, I turned off the lights and it was like cruising down a tunnel. Dark and hushed, expectant.

'I decided to park at the bottom. Speeded up again. Moments later a shadow ran out in front of the car. A dog? But the tail was too bushy. I braked. Skidded on a wad of wet leaves. Banged my head on the steering wheel... The fox – of course it had to be a fox – got away. I used the raw steak I'd brought to tempt Zak as a cold compress. Then drove home in the undamaged car. A lucky escape, you might say. That was yesterday.

'Airbags? What about them? Don't you believe me?

'Well, that's your problem.

'Yes. Really. I've said all there is to say. I'm sorry, but I'd rather lie down now. Head's starting to hurt again. Shame I threw that steak away. Chucked it into some shrubbery for the fox. I knew he would go back. They always do, don't they? If they don't get what they want, they go back and try again.

'Well, they need to eat, too. We'd be the same if we had to hunt and forage for everything. Just picture yourself: stuck in a hole under a tree. Hungry. Desperate. Nothing but the smell of dirt and roots in your nostrils. A dead stillness in your eyes as you wait and wait for nightfall...

'Anyway, I'm off to bed. Have to be fit for whatever happens next. I owe myself that much, don't you think?'

Meeting Mr Sand

Andrew Crumey

INTRODUCTIONS ARE USUALLY self-conscious affairs and I knew that when Richard Sand arrived for our interview things might be a bit stiff at first. We'd agreed to meet at the recently re-designated Cafe Mozart – formerly known as The Dolphin until it got a complete make-over and the waitresses took to wearing what appear to be imitation eighteenth-century smocks. I wondered if this really was the best place for us to discuss his book, which I leafed through after nervously ordering my Mozart Mocha.

Richard Sand should enjoy this place though, given that imitation is one of his major themes and provides the title of his essay collection. He calls imitation the most fundamental human impulse, but regrets that where once it was seen as essential in any artist's training, now it's acceptable only in places like Cafe Mozart.

Elsewhere he comments on introductions: self-conscious affairs, he says, citing Nabokov's forewords to his own novels as an example. Pride, ambition, doubt; these are characteristics made particularly obvious in those awkward opening moments when the right effect is being sought; and this is why I resolve that when Richard Sand appears at the glass door of Cafe Mozart, looking just like the photograph on the back of *Imitations: Essays on Style and Substance*, I shall try and imagine that really he's a waiter come to take my order, not someone I need to impress.

Walter Scott by contrast, Richard Sand says (sitting down casually and looking at a menu) is an author whose prefaces are frequently better than the novels that follow. Richard Sand regards Scott's foreword to *Guy Mannering* as his masterpiece, and orders an ice cream.

When Richard Sand comes to the door, therefore, I'll aim for an introduction in the manner of Scott, rather than one in the Nabokov style. I won't, for example, say that the conversation we're about to have will be one of my more "attractive" ones, explaining for him the delicate pleasure I took in choosing our meeting place, arranging the time; nor shall I say I could supply additional information about rejected alternative venues "if I took myself more seriously" (Foreword to *The Luzhin Defense*).

No, I shall tell Richard Sand that three weeks ago I was walking along the street on my way to pick up a programme from the local art house cinema (because their website is hopeless) when I saw on the other side of the road that The Dolphin had had a make-over. 'That'd be a good place to conduct an interview,' I decided. I'd just split with Fi.

But Richard Sand will care for none of this. 'Häagen-Dazs,' he says, examining the tub he's been brought. 'Where do you suppose that name comes from?'

I toy with Norwegian, Danish; he shakes his head. Still teased by the conjunction of double-A with umlaut I suggest Finnish, then Turkish. Richard Sand smiles and says nothing. I resort to the Ural-Altaic complex, possibly one of the less obvious dialects of Samoyed, though the suggestion is admittedly made in desperation. Richard Sand says calmly, 'Some

➤➤

marketing people in America made the whole thing up. Everybody knows that.'

The ice cream was created in an instant, like the universe itself, and meant to suggest a past that wasn't there; spurious influences, a false history. Apparently everyone knew about it except me. It's like the British soldier, killed in action, whose body was used in a piece of wartime counter-intelligence, discussed at some length by Richard Sand.

The allied invasion had been booked for Normandy, the beaches had been carefully studied. It was necessary to make the Germans think the attack was to come from elsewhere, unexpected as a sudden waitress.

'Mozart Mocha,' she declares. I make sure the cup stays well clear of *Imitations: Essays on Style and Substance*, in which Richard Sand explains that a dead soldier was given an invented identity, clothed in a uniform he never wore in life, supplied with false papers. As a final touching detail, a love letter from a non-existent girl was written out, folded carefully, and carried in someone's pocket for days until it looked authentic. Then it was put inside the dead man's clothes and he was fired from the torpedo tube of a submarine to be washed up on a beach. His real name was never disclosed; his heroic action remained as hidden from his relatives as it was from himself. The Germans were fooled, they looked the wrong way while Normandy was invaded, etc, etc. I told Fi all about it, but she already knew.

What if some maniac were to walk into Cafe Mozart while I'm talking to Richard Sand? What if Richard Sand is just about to speak of Borges and Conrad when a guy pushes his way through the glass door, brings out a machine gun and sprays bullets everywhere in the room? Holes and gashes appear in the recently repainted walls, the marbling effect is quite spoiled, the Gaggia machine becomes punctured and sprays a jet of hissing steam during the otherwise silent moment of terrible calm that follows, when ten or twenty people, some with iPhones still in their hands, lie motionless on the tiled floor?

That'd really show Fi.

But Richard Sand is a busy man, and every now and then he glances at his watch. Richard Sand considers Borges the most perfect writer since all his best works seem like introductions and also imitations. Richard Sand cites Kafka's 'The Great Wall Of China' and Conrad's introduction to *Nostromo* as the source of most of what we call "Borgesian", in the same way that a few brown smocks and the name Mozart can evoke, for the average coffee drinker, eighteenth-century Vienna; or Häagen-Dazs can equal in transatlantic minds and wallets a continent as unreal and vivid as the misruled world of Don José Avellanos.

By now I was wishing that a crazed madman would come in and kill us all (except me). Just to show her.

I was walking along the street three weeks ago, on my way to pick up a cinema programme. I've been to see lots of films since we split. It's good to have the freedom.

'We live in an information age,' Richard Sand continues. 'In a world of ideas, language becomes the wholly dominant medium of human discourse.'

This hardly seems a radical innovation, but it needn't interfere with the cooling of my Mozart Mocha.

'Ultimately it's not what we say that counts, but the difference between what we actually say and what we could have said otherwise. This idea is made explicit in modern algorithms for transferring video signals, in which changes of image alone are conveyed, as a way of saving bandwidth.'

All this is in *Imitations*. I was reading it while breaking up with Fi.

'It's precisely because we live in the Age of Imitation,' says Richard Sand, 'that imitation is what we most fear and despise. We describe everything in terms of its similarity or difference compared to something else; a new movie is a cross between *Pirates of the Caribbean* and *Lord Of The Rings*, a new book is *Cloud Atlas* meets *Fifty Shades Of Grey*. We reduce the world to erroneous etymologies of our own invention.'

Toying with the ice cream tub he ordered, whose remaining contents liquefy before our view, he then takes my hand.

'Philip,' he says, 'Forget Fi. She wasn't worth it. Believe me, I'm an expert in everything, and I know.'

Richard Sand has had many affairs but says the best are those that never happened, those which exist only as suggestive prefaces. All our affairs are prefigured in ones that have already been done far better by other people before us. This ought to comfort me, but right now it doesn't.

Three weeks ago I phoned my friend James in London and he said the easiest way to get yourself in print is to interview somebody interesting. Now *that's* what I call advice.

'Think of Fi as being somewhat like Flaubert's *Temptation of Saint Antony*; a necessary mistake,' Richard Sand provokes. Right now I want him to piss off. Fi gave me *Imitations* for my birthday; by the time I got to the end we'd split up. So thanks a bloody lot, Richard Sand.

The day after my conversation with James I was walking along the street on my way to get a cinema programme when I saw the gleaming new Cafe Mozart, formerly called The Dolphin. 'That'd be a good place to interview somebody and get myself in print,' I thought.

There the matter might have rested, but for the chance conjunction two days later of a piece of dog shit and a shower of rain. The dog shit passed under my shoe while I was walking in the direction of Topman, having decided that a change of wardrobe would suit my new state of freedom. I had resolved to become a "top man". Perhaps I'd even buy one of those bizarre jackets with no collar and fifteen buttons like the ones footballers wear at press conferences after their first major transfer deal. I was scraping the turd from my shoe on the kerb when I noticed that the rain had started. I could furnish further details about this incident "if I took myself more seriously", but shall say only that I decided to shelter in Waterstones, the bookshop where Fi had bought me *Imitations: Essays on Style and Substance*. The fact that she left the receipt inside the book before giving it to me was a sign, I now realise, that already by then her mind was on someone else.

I hoped I didn't smell of dog shit. Being suddenly and unexpectedly single can make you feel strangely self-conscious, I've noticed; perhaps because every encounter becomes a potential introduction. In the bookshop I saw a poster advertising a forthcoming reading and talk (with complimentary glass of wine) by Richard Sand.

The man who'll soon appear at the door of Cafe Mozart, invited here by me.

The man whose thoughts I already know (I've read his book after all), and which I'll describe in an article the local paper has more or less promised to run.

The man who represents my first step on the ladder. Though he isn't here yet.

'Forget her,' Richard Sand insists. 'Forget me, forget everything. Forgetting is the sweetest thing. When Odysseus went on his voyage he forgot all about Penelope. Nostalgia isn't a Greek idea, it's a German one. They simply gave it a Greek name to make it sound more classy. A bit like Häagen-Dazs.'

Once my article gets published, Fi will come across it in the local paper. She'll have left her lover asleep in bed, gone to the newsagent on a lazy Saturday morning, and when she returns and sits at the breakfast bar in her kitchen, sipping orange juice while her risen lover blandly inserts the slender nozzle of a miniature cappuccino machine into a jug of milk (a jug that I bloody well bought her, incidentally), she'll suddenly say:

'Christ! *Interview with Richard Sand. By...*'

She nearly chokes on her croissant. In fact I hope she does choke, Richard, I tell him.

'Forget her,' Richard Sand repeats, placing his hand upon my knee. 'You're constructing a false etymology of your own life. Free yourself of her influence. Learn to imitate yourself once more.'

Borges imitated Conrad and Conrad imitated Flaubert, says Richard Sand. I told Fi about it, and she yawned and asked if we could switch off the bedside light now please. I told her about Häagen-Dazs, the allied invasion of Normandy, and she said she already knew.

'How come you know so much?' I challenged. I was sure she was bluffing.

➻

'I know lots of things. A lot more than you realise.'

What she was really telling me was that for the last two months she'd been in love with someone called Martin. He's in management consultancy, for fuck's sake.

'It doesn't matter,' says Richard Sand, stroking my knee soothingly. 'You and me, that's what counts. We could make a great team.'

The waitress comes and asks if I'd like anything else.

'Do you have any chocolate ice cream?' I gamble.

'We've got Midnight Rhapsody, Chocolate Chip, and Belgian White Chocolate.' She says it with her arms folded. Like it's some kind of snub.

'What's Midnight Rhapsody?' I ask.

'It's basically just chocolate.'

'I'll have that then, please.' She writes something down and walks away. Will I be equally sheepish with Richard Sand when he arrives? My freedom from Fi, for all its advantages, has also left me with an occasional sense of inadequacy during social interactions.

'Do you ever suffer from a sense of inadequacy?' I ask Richard Sand, preparing to write down his response. Since I don't yet know if I'll be able to write quickly enough I've also brought with me a digital voice recorder purchased in John Lewis.

I didn't buy it for the interview. It was a month ago, and I had finally begun to suspect Fi. I'd been alerted by one of the essays in *Imitations*, I explain to Richard Sand, in which he describes the correspondences between Flaubert's *"Un Coeur Simple"* and the death of Bergotte in *À la Recherche du Temps Perdu*. To be honest I wasn't really following the essay; it just happened to be what I was reading at the time.

'A sense of inadequacy is something I've never suffered from,' says Richard Sand. 'Unreality, yes; inadequacy never.'

Richard Sand's essay also went on about Nietzsche and Wittgenstein and God knows what else, asserting that literature only becomes possible when we learn how to say one thing while thinking about something else entirely. And as I read, my eyes would skip briefly over the top of the page every so often, like a soldier's in a trench, and I'd watch Fi gathering up items for the laundry.

It became clear to me from Richard Sand's essay that during times when I was out she was meeting someone else in our flat. A digital voice recorder, subsequently obtained at a reasonable price from John Lewis, seemed like a good way to settle the issue.

I quickly encountered technical problems, however. The manufacturer's claim that the device's single AA battery could give ten hours of continuous use proved to be an exaggeration. I was out for six, but only the first four had been preserved when I got back. The sound beneath the bed during all that time had been nothing but a low, distant rumble of traffic, increased in pitch but not in content when I ran it through on fast forward.

So I went back to John Lewis and bought an AC adapter with built-in timer. This handy device enables any low-voltage household appliance to be automatically switched on or off for up to four separate periods in a twenty-four hour cycle.

'What on earth did you buy this for?' Fi asked, poking her nose into the carrier bag I'd rashly left unattended next to our stained-pine CD rack.

I told her it'd come in handy if we went on holiday and wanted it to look as though we were still at home. We could set lights to come on every evening.

'But what about the curtains?' says Richard Sand.

I agree with him that my excuse had certain inconsistencies that must have aroused Fi's suspicions.

Then the waitress brought me my Midnight Rhapsody. 'Enjoy,' she said curtly as though it were a command.

Richard Sand can guess the rest. The digital voice recorder, playing itself back to me in secrecy one evening when Fi had gone out with friends, created its own kind of nocturnal rhapsody; one made not of frozen milk, eggs and sugar, but rather of grunts, moans, and a reminder to be careful.

'So that's why I'm here,' I tell Richard Sand. 'I've now explained to you all the tiny accidents and absurdities that have conspired to bring about this conversation. My introduction is complete.'

'If you don't mind,' says Richard Sand, 'I'll go and take a piss.'

He stands up and walks confidently towards the far side of the room. He doesn't have to ask the way or look around with a 'please tell me where the toilets are' expression. Christ, how I wish that I was Richard Sand.

He's left his jacket hanging over his steel-framed chair. I lift the jacket and put it on. There's a wallet in the inside pocket containing driving licence, credit card and other identifying material of Richard Sand. I'm wearing his entire existence; it fits perfectly. In another pocket there's even a handwritten letter, scented and neatly folded. I open it and discover, though without any sense of surprise, that it's from Fi. *I love you, Richard Sand*, she writes.

Suddenly he arrives at last. The crazed gunman.

Wearing a face-mask and dressed in combat gear he bursts through the glass door of Cafe Mozart and raises his weapon to unleash a blazing volley that quickly rips to shreds all the work that's been done on this place, tearing away the fake Mozartian elements, shattering the mirrors to reveal little bits of Dolphin decor underneath. Screams everywhere, panic, the sort of thing you don't expect on an ordinary day in an unremarkable town that nobody would otherwise have heard of, but which will briefly become an item of morbid curiosity to anyone glancing at the world news while flicking through a hundred channels on a remote control. At least I'll get myself in print now. In the following day's newspaper, my face is shown alongside an account of the tragedy, explaining that I was found dead beside some melted ice cream and a copy of *Imitations*, wearing the bloodstained Marks and Spencer linen jacket by which I was mistakenly identified. And Fi, silently swallowing her croissant while tears gather in her eyes, finally understands the heroic nature of my sacrifice, when for a single glorious moment I truly became Richard Sand, serving as the selfless decoy whom his would-be assassin killed in error.

An hour later and still no sign of the fucker. The waitress hands me the bill.

The Tenth Muse

Andy Jackson

Does it matter what it was
that brought him to the boil
like that? I heard a knuckle crack,
felt the quiet room recoil

watched him as he calmly tugged
the ripcord of his mouth, letting out
those trammelled imprecations.
At no point did he shout

but rather let the swearing do
its grisly work. I didn't know
what half his curses meant,
inventive portmanteaux

and reference to body parts
I'd never seen, each new profanity
a drawing back of shutters
on a charnel house, till all could see

the pulsing foulness. I admired,
despite myself, his slashing fluency,
wondered if he'd worked for years
to purify his caustic obloquy,

preparing for the moment when
object and subject coalesced.
They say a spectre comes to them at night,
carving wild inventions on their breast,

Malakas, the outcast Muse,
floating like a grawlix in the space
above their head, seducing then
polluting them with noxious grace.

My own minced oaths are signs
that I exist within myself, my neck
wound in, condemned eternally
to burn, alone, in the flames of heck.

 A grawlix is a string of typographical symbols, used (especially in comic strips) to represent an obscenity or swearword.

Fertility amulets (Roman)

Judith Taylor

Whose   dicks are you?
– trotting so perkily
with bells on   and your tails up
your blunt bronze noses up
questing towards their goal.

           How were you used?
Did someone offer you
at the right shrine?   Did she polish you
or hang you up above her bed for luck?
And how do I know   with so much certainty

that she's a *she*?   You amuse me
but to her you could be
life or death.   A contract
is a contract: there are penalties
for those who don't deliver.

           Did she buy you
in the temple or the market?
Was she given you   by the husband
or the mother-in-law?

I see by your jaunty angle
you're as big   natural optimists
as the real thing:
is that the way   you worked it?

Did you nuzzle
into the hollow of her hand
and give her courage? And
           did you do it for her
dicks, when push   came to shove?
Did you give her something to smile at?

Into the Dark
Jim Ferguson

absolutely
love impossible
here or anywhere

empty street
full of lonely
graffiti –

dancing before you
impossible writing
in a language

from a different planet –
what does it mean
strange streetlife

from the heart
of the addict –
slip quietly

into a nightclub
which once was a church
now somehow detached

from its own nature –
a soul destroyed
cast into the desert

without boots or clothes
and naked
behind a mirror

sits the essence
of beauty –
watch for the humans

they're rough and ready
a jumble of good
and a rag-tag of bad –

see them all bankrupt
in night's endless sands –
walk into the dark

Let It All Go
Jim Ferguson

sleep
why don't you –
don't walk around

on
long sad platforms
without any trains –

find a place
to lie down
take off your boots

don't mind
the looks
on the faces

of stranded
companions –
swing

from the girders
on a flying trapeze
without any net

get to land safely
on the head
of a snowman –

socks soaking wet
but
no complaints

there's no where
to walk –
no destination

and nobody waiting
with arms open wide –
keep your eyes open

dissolve in the mirror –
sleep
why don't you   let it all go

The Headaches Are Back

Mark Russell

They are like that couple we used to know
when we lived near Great Yarmouth,
the ones who borrowed the steam stripper
and wore those matching blue berets.

If I recall correctly the husband
was named Les and his wife was Billy
though it could have been the other way round:
they were the perfect interchangeable couple.

She made flat and tasteless madeleines –
I think it was the absence of almond –
and Les laid carpets all over the village
even at the bus stop and on the church roof.

I can hear their voices over the white noise,
through the steam, and they never return the stripper.

Rite of Hole

Graham Fulton

at the junction of
this road and another road
three men wearing testosterone boots
and core-of-the-earth-yellow jackets
are making a hole
or filling in
a hole
or making a hole then filling
the hole in again immediately
for several days
for a steady pay
with their mythological picks
forged by titans
slamming down on the tarmac
outside the nursery
and their knee-trembling spades
scraping
and clacking
and raising all the lumps up
from the very ground we walk on
and dumping it lovingly at the edge
of the pavement
next to their masculine white van
where a fourth man shovels it up
and puts it back in the hole again
like he's filling in a grave
with everyone laughing and whistling
and there's
a charged Stravinsky rhythm
and shape and meaning
to the whole procedure
as the men dance and croon
and display the cracks of their arses
to young women when they bend over

Try
Larry Butler

lying down
doing nothing
not sleeping
but not trying
not to sleep
not thinking
but not trying
not to think
not dreaming
but not trying
not to dream
not reading
but not trying
not to read
this – try this
just lie down
and do nothing
and don't try
to be somebody
but not not being
somebody or nobody
but simply resting
drifting while testing
the hypothesis
when trying stops
everything gets done.

It's the touch that's dangerous
Samuel Tongue

It's not about sex, you frightened religious,
with your high fences around gardens
and thick walls to guard the holy places
(even though it's here you must remove
your sandals and uncover your feet).
It's the touch that's dangerous,
religion at skin level.
The eye sees distance.
The touch closes distance.
Even in love, a man can be touched
inside his thick warm thigh and left
limping as the sun comes up.

Just Boys, They Were
Carol McKay

ANDY REMEMBERED WHEN the boy was born: the smell of sweat from his parka jacket; the glare of bright lights; the stick and release of soles on squeaky clean floors. And then the boy himself: perfection ripped from a burst wound, skin plump and moist, and smeared with blood.

Now he was coming for the weekend while his father went to a work's training session. He wouldn't be a problem. He'd bring some device to keep him occupied and there were cartoons on cable. He'd stay two nights until his father came back for him. His mother was long gone. Of course it wouldn't be a problem.

Andy stripped his bed and spread it with fresh sheets. He folded an extra blanket at the bottom in case the boy was cold, being used, as he was, to central heating. Both pillows were stained with dribble and they smelled, but there wasn't time to wash them, so Andy pulled two slips on each of them. The boy wouldn't notice. When had he ever noticed when he was that age? He and the boy's father slept in the double bed in the end room together, back in the old house, despite the age difference. Moving the empty bottles from the side of the bed, Andy remembered his brother's loosely curling hair, sandy brown, the soft down on his cheeks and smell of grass that hung about him even by the time Andy got to bed.

He hadn't expected the boy to bring his hamster. When the doorbell rang, Andy inhaled to compose himself. 'Alright?' he said to Frank and the boy, seeing them like that, together on his landing, Frank with one hand on the boy's shoulder and holding up the animal's cage in the other. The boy was grinning.

'Hope you don't mind babysitting Sprocket,' Frank said. 'He'd have been okay on his own but... somebody says he'd miss him.' He gestured towards the boy.

Standing in the hall with one hand still propping the door open, Andy said, 'No – no bother. Come in!'

'Thanks, Uncle Andy!' The boy ducked under his arm with his schoolbag. He flumped down on Andy's couch and started scanning through the TV channels with the remote control. His father stood in the doorway.

'Coming in?'

'Aye – five minutes. Fill you in on the picture.' He lifted the cage up higher as he stepped in. 'Where do you want me to install this?'

Andy closed the front door. 'Anywhere you can find a space.' They cleared newspapers and the ashtray off the coffee table and sat the cage on it. The hamster was scraping about in the sawdust.

Frank didn't sit down. He nodded to the boy's bag. 'He's got his pyjamas and his toothbrush. And a change of clothes just in case, but he shouldn't need them.' He looked Andy up and down. 'You sure you're okay about this?' After a pause he added, 'I meant it when I said about no drink.'

Andy squinted. 'It's a bit late to back out now if you don't trust me.'

Frank nodded. 'I guess. Right – you've got my number if you need me.' He grinned, one cheek dimpling despite the leanness of his adult face. 'You take care of Sprocket, then, son. Okay? Don't leave it to your Uncle Andy. Promise?'

'Promise, Dad. Bring me back something?'

Frank stood with his knuckles on his hips, the fingers of one hand jingling his car keys. 'Aye – a dad in a better mood for having a weekend away from you!'

The boy stuck his tongue out. As they walked back to the door, Frank said, 'Mind, if you need me, get in touch, but I don't expect he'll give you any trouble.'

Andy patted his shoulder. 'No worries. Enjoy yourself.'

Andy closed the door and stood for a moment. He could hear his brother's feet trot down the tenement stairs and behind him, in the flat, the cartoon chaos the boy was watching. He forced his breath to slow then went into the living room. 'Alright, pal?'

The boy looked up then back to the television, eyes absorbed behind his glasses. 'Fine, Uncle Andy.'

'Good.' He sat on the couch beside him. No point pushing to do anything for now if the boy was happy. The hamster was gnawing the bars of the cage, his pink front paws gripping like hands. 'Does he always do that?'

'Sprocket? Yeah. Or on his wheel. Sometimes I let him out.'

After the programme ended, while Andy was boiling the kettle, the boy brought the hamster through to the kitchen. It had soft-looking short brown fur on its back and a creamy white underside. All four paws were pink with long clear claws. Its eyes were black beads. Its whiskers twitched incessantly while it explored the boy's hands as if sniffing for an exit.

'Why did you call it Sprocket?' Andy asked as he poured the tea.

'Just fancied it. My dad suggested it.' The boy's face was smooth and still quite tanned after an October break abroad with his father. He had his dad's hazel eyes and that single dimple that was only visible when he smiled.

'Do you know what a sprocket is?'

'No.' He pushed his glasses up on the bridge of his nose. 'What is it?'

The beast kept trying to drop off the boy's hands, clinging on to the upper hand with the claws of its back foot, only for the boy to put his free hand underneath to catch him. It was in constant motion.

'It's a kind of wheel. A notched one, with cogs on it. You've got a bike, yeah?' The boy nodded. 'It's the wheel the chain fits on. And you get them in tank tracks.'

'Cool. Did you learn that in the army?'

Andy blinked. 'Probably. Tea?'

That night, after the boy was in bed, Andy lay on the couch in the sleeping bag and watched the hamster gnaw the bars. Now and then it dodged past its bed and food dish to spin on its wheel, its four feet running while its eyes stared ahead into the cage wall. Then it ran out to the front bars again as if expecting to find itself in a different landscape. On and on it went, during the night. Andy drifted off, but woke up whenever the animal changed its routine. Each time he woke, he thought about Frank in some four star hotel. He wondered if there was a free bar. Wondered if the weather was rough there, as it seemed to be turning here, with wind rattling the slates and huffing against the brickwork, and whistling in where the rubber seal round the window glass had perished.

When the grey light of morning came in through the gap at the curtain rail, Andy woke, his shoulder aching from lying cramped in one position too long. He leaned up on his elbow. The beast had gone to bed and Andy watched it pull the tufts of bedding around itself then wash and tuck its head in ready for sleep. Andy reached for the remote control, turned the TV on quietly and fell back to sleep with it playing in the background.

He wasn't going to let the boy waste time on his gadgets for the whole weekend. First, he took him to the supermarket for a good breakfast. Then, they'd hire a canoe at the water sports centre in the park. As they walked down the hill out of the small town towards the green space, clouds were looming. Andy and the boy arrived at the artificial lake to see wind lifting its normally flat surface. The man

➻➻

in the kiosk told them he was locking up the boats for the day. Andy held his hand over his ear to block the vicious wind.

'What will we do instead?' the boy asked.

Andy pulled his collar up. It was only eleven o'clock and there was the whole of Saturday to fill. 'Brisk walk round the lake?'

The wind penetrated his jacket, despite the warming of the fry-up. The boy's face looked cold, too. There was no trace of the dimple. His cheeks were white and his lips were a red gash which his tongue kept licking. They walked along the path that skirted the lake, sometimes turning their backs to the wind to keep it off their faces.

Even the dogs were scampering to get home to the fire, dragging their owners with them. 'What are we going to do, Uncle Andy?'

'What do you want to do?'

The boy sniffed. 'I don't know.'

'Football? Bowling alley?'

A gust blasted them. There was no rain in it but the threat of it, icy with hail. They'd walked half way round the lake, now. 'I know. Ice skating.'

'Ice skating?' It would still be cold but they'd be out of the wind.

They trudged round the rest of the lake, following the path, heads down and hands in their pockets till they reached the mouth of the tunnel under the motorway. Inside its walls, they let their voices echo, the boy's bright and sunlit and Andy's brown and bass. The walls were daubed in blue and green graffiti.

Inside the building which housed the rink, the air was warm and damp, condensing on the boy's glasses. It was lively with pulsing music. Competing with that, what sounded like sea-gull calls shrieked out. Skaters spiralled anti-clockwise, the insides of the loop travelling faster than the outside like some kind of wheeling, multi-coloured bird flock. Huge flat screens pieced together a wall of music clips. Andy and the boy exchanged their shoes for skates, the long red laces trailing down from the heavy blue boots as they carried them.

'Have you skated before?' Andy asked him.

'Yeah, Dad takes me.'

Andy watched the boy push his feet into the boots and followed suit. The blade was a curved scythe, looking lethal. 'These are safe?' Andy grinned, glancing from the eager boy to the crowds spinning round the rink.

It took a while to get the hang of it. He edged round the outside of the rink trying to keep up with the boy, who was bent low – one of a dozen who wove at speed between groups of more sedate or cautious skaters. Andy watched him over the heads of the crowd, thinking he'd never be able to let go of the side. Then a new tune came on. The pack pushed out in time to it, right skate then left skate.

'Come on, Uncle Andy!' the boy said, surging past and away from him.

And there was that rhythm. Right foot then left foot. Andy loosened his grip of the rail – right foot, slide left foot. Round and round they went – right foot then left foot – and Andy grew confident: a part of something bigger. Right foot and left foot. Right foot and left foot.

Then he was down. His weak shoulder took the brunt of it: the cold, hard impact with the ice. What speed had he been doing? He sat up, holding his arm, conscious of the way the crowd split and flowed on either side of him. His shoulder was stinging.

Ice sprayed in an arc. 'Are you alright?'

'I'm fine,' he said, biting the ache down. The boy and the steward helped him to the edge. Still wearing his skates, he walked on the rubber-clad floor like a man on metal limbs.

'It was a bad bump – I'll check your shoulder,' the steward said. 'And that's a bad cut.'

His hand had been sliced. How had that happened? Lips of skin peeled away from each other in the hollow of his palm. Bright red blood dribbled down the line it made.

'Was this your idea?' he said to the boy as he sat down beside him. It was the wrong thing to say. The boy's eyes teared up behind his glasses. 'Hey, cheer up! It was me it happened to, not you!' Andy raised his arm to wrap it round him, but pain seared through his shoulder.

'You'll need to get that checked.'

They were five hours at Casualty. Each time the outside door opened another blast of cold air blew in, bringing crisp wrappers and a few sheets of newspaper with it. And when they were shown into the cubicle for treatment, there was that all too familiar enveloping smell.

'Are you coming in to keep your dad company?' the nurse asked as she pulled the curtain across behind them.

'He's not my dad!' the boy said, the emphasis on the first word. 'He's my uncle. I'm on a sleepover with him for the weekend while my dad's away.'

'Oh, yeah,' she said, peeling open the sterile dressing for Andy's hand. 'I bet he's loving that.' She met Andy's eyes conspiratorially. He refused to wince as she cleaned the cut.

Swivelling on his stool, the boy prattled on. 'Is this the hospital I was born in?'

'Aye,' Andy said, meeting the nurse's eyes again, 'but in a different part.' Perfection ripped from a burst wound, skin plump and moist, and smeared with blood.

By the time they got home, Andy with one arm in a sling and that dressing on his hand, it was dark and they were starving. The boy opened the door with Andy's keys. Straight away they heard the hamster.

'Sprocket's awake!'

The flat was freezing. Andy plugged in the electric fire then heated soup while the boy squatted to put out grains and seeds for the animal.

Sitting on the couch in front of the fire, still with his jacket half on, Andy fought the craving. Just one drink would have done it – taken the edge off the throb in his shoulder and the sting each time he uncurled his palm – but he'd promised the boy's father. Besides, he didn't have any. Had made sure he'd finished it before the boy got there. Safer that way. Now he ate his soup. Oxtail with bread and cheese sandwiches. The boy fed bread through the bars to the hamster. Cheese, too. The hamster sat on its back feet and stuffed it in its cheeks then banked it in a corner to scoff in privacy later. That's what Andy should have done: pushed a bottle down the side of the couch for when the boy was in bed.

After soup, they watched the lottery and the boy went to the ice cream van for crisps and cola. Andy watched him from the window, handing over the ten pound note he'd given

him and then reaching up for the bottle and cradling it in the crook of his arm like a baby.

Andy swallowed down painkillers with the cola but they didn't take the pain away, not even when the boy was in bed in the other room with his 3DS. It was a different kind of bottle he needed.

Andy put the light out and eased himself into the sleeping bag. It was hard to do up the zip with his arm in a sling and his other hand bandaged. Cars went by in the dark, their headlights sliding over his ceiling while the hamster turned on its wheel. Andy listened to it. The wheel stopped and the animal scampered in the sawdust. It went quiet for a minute then the gnawing started again. Enamel on metal. On and on like a knife scraping bone. Andy's bone in his shoulder. The old injury. He heaved over on to his side, facing the back of the couch, and kicked the swaddling bag out with his feet. He needed a drink. All the sinews in his body pulled in towards his belly and the churning drew them tighter, twisting in a slow circle.

Right foot then left foot. Right foot then left foot. Freezing rain wet their faces but they kept going. Shoulders ached from bracing their packs. Right foot then left over rocks and peat bog. Their feet slipped inside their boots, causing more skids than the snow on the ground. Wind burned the rims of their ears, and their pulse beat with the trudge of boots on shale. But they kept going: right foot then left in a steady rhythm.

A blast threw them. Andy's shoulder hit shale. Men streamed towards them.

The cutting and gyrating of a helicopter. The all too familiar enveloping smell.

Andy woke with a start. He rose to sitting, blinking in the dark. Just boys, they were: perfection ripped in burst wounds, skin warm and moist, and smeared with blood. He rubbed his shoulder. The door handle creaked.

'Uncle Andy?' The hamster gnawed the bars then skittered over the sawdust as if towards the boy's voice. 'I heard somebody shouting.'

➠

Andy patted the space on the couch beside him and the boy dropped down. They sat with their feet on the coffee table while the hamster dashed from wheel to bars, its four feet running, constantly running.

'Are you alright, Uncle Andy?' The boy's face was bare without his glasses.

'I'm fine, son.'

The boy bit his bottom lip. His top teeth were out of proportion – not yet grown into. 'It's just that Dad says...'

'Dad says what?'

The boy wriggled his shoulders. 'Sprocket's noisy during the night-time, isn't he?'

It was one weekend. It wasn't going to torture him for a lifetime. Andy put his good arm round the boy's shoulders and pulled him in beside him. Frank would be here after lunchtime. He remembered his brother's loosely curling hair, sandy brown, the soft down on his cheeks and smell of grass that hung about him, even by the time Andy got to bed, that summer he was on sick leave after the Falklands.

He ruffled the boy's hair. 'Do you know, son? Sprocket's just fine.'

A Wee Minding

Mary Paulson-Ellis

UP IN THE graveyard, up on the hill, there's a wee minding buried in the grass if only you can see. The wind blows and creatures watch me from beyond the broken wall. The scrub is gone all grey in the moonlight, but I know where to find her. I know she's here.

I list them – all the things that connect me still to her. Jam, wool, petticoats, Mrs Sheppie's tablecloth, Mr Sheppie's rag. Also the million rivers running through my veins.

Up here I listen to the beach, to the sea sucking at the cliffs far below. Up here the wind tugs at the buttons on my frock, fingering my breastbone. Up here I'm a mermaid ploughing the grass, dipping beneath the waterline then rising again to take a gasp of air. Up here I listen for the schroosh, schroosh, schroosh of the pebbles as they walk her along the beach once more, coffin hoisted on Mr Sheppie's shoulder, Mrs Sheppie carrying me behind.

My mother lies where she has always been these fourteen years – laid out beneath the ground, head pointing back towards the village, feet pointing out towards the sea. I curl next to her and stretch my arm across her stone. My wrist is pale in the moonlight. A slender thing, nothing but the newest branch of a tree. Easy to slice off if you know where to hold the blade.

Beneath my skin I feel it. The beat beat inside, like the beat beat that flowed out of her. My fingertips carve out all she left behind.

MOTHER

They never bothered to put anything else. Not even her name.

'Fell out of her like water from a jug.' Mrs Sheppie sits in her armchair, wool the colour of a cardinal's cap spooling from a basket at her feet. She is making hats for the babies of Chernobyl, even though Chernobyl is much older than me. 'Stood up, so she did. Went, Oh. Went, That's not right, is it. Touched her hand to the edge of my tablecloth. Then she fell down.'

My mother is one of the stories of this place now. The girl who lived and died without ever leaving these ochre cliffs. She belonged to our congregation, with Mr and Mrs Sheppie and Mr and Mrs Kennoway and Old James Ross and his niece Evelyn May. When she sang her voice rose like a skylark surfing the air. The congregation was seven then. Now it is only three. Mr and Mrs Sheppie. And me.

I sit on the sofa, bare legs rubbing against draylon, and imagine my mother lying on Mrs Sheppie's kitchen lino in the midst of a dark, spreading pool. 'I held the tea-towel to it, so I did. I held the dishcloth to it. I held my slip to it – no bloody good, 'scuse my language. Rubbish man-made stuff.' Mrs Sheppie swears sometimes when Mr Sheppie isn't in to hear. 'I even held my tablecloth to it. Never did get that clean again.'

Mrs Sheppie still wears a slip though her waist is wider now than it must have been then. It dips beneath her skirt as she stands at the cooker getting Mr Sheppie's dinner ready. I lay the table like I've always done. One fork on the left. One knife on the right. Salt and pepper shakers shaped like the Eiffel tower.

'White she was.' Mrs Sheppie mashes potato in a pan. 'Like a dead thing dragged up in one of Mr Sheppie's nets.' Mr Sheppie goes to work at night when everyone else goes to bed. Out in the darkness he rides over the waves, trawling for things that will never see the light of morning. When the sky turns, he comes home.

'I said to her, Don't you worry, stay where you are. Then I ran to the airing cupboard. Or maybe the scullery.' Mrs Sheppie has a way with stories. She works at them, like those little baby hats – the same pattern, but different details year after year. 'I held a towel to it. I held a sheet to it. Didn't make no difference. She still bled out all over my linoleum floor.'

Just like my mother I am a story in this village now too. I slithered out into a dark pool and was wrapped in Mrs Sheppie's petticoat because there wasn't anything else that would do. 'Such a wee thing. Crumpled.' That's what Mrs Sheppie says. 'Came too soon.' She dribbles thick mince over a pale mound of potato and I wonder who I might have been if my mother had kept her legs together for just a bit more time. 'Said to leave you, so they did.' Mrs Sheppie hands me the plates to lay on the table. 'But we're all God's creatures, aren't we. Every one.'

We live in a small place, but it might as well be the whole world as far as everyone who lives here is concerned. There is oil for the lucky ones in the big houses on the hill. B&B and fishing for the rest. There's a bakery with a trail of flour that runs across the high street from the oven to the shop. Also fourteen different congregations one way or another, all of them singing on a Sunday, all of them competing for anyone they can lure in.

Just like them we sing every Sunday too, to the memory of those that have gone before – Mr and Mrs Kennoway, Old James Ross, his niece Evelyn May. Also the hope that soon we will be seven again, or maybe fifteen. It is our duty, Mr Sheppie says, to strengthen our congregation whatever way we can. So once a week we call up the glory and more members for our church, standing in the front room because we can't afford the chapel hall any more. Mr Sheppie beats out the tempo on the arm of the best chair, like the beat beat inside

me. Then he lifts his voice. And Mrs Sheppie lifts her voice. And I lift my voice too – a small lark surfing the air. When we get to the end, we start over. 'Repetition,' Mrs Sheppie says. 'Helps get it into the brain.'

After dinner when Mr Sheppie has gone out to plough the waves, Mrs Sheppie crouches before a bird cage, tiny seed pinched between her lips. She holds her mouth up close to the bars and makes a chirruping sound in her throat. In the furthest corner a bird huddles, feathers cloudy green like the Bitter Lemon Mrs Sheppie takes every evening instead of something hard. 'Got to keep the spirits up,' she says putting away her latest baby hat and opening one of her small bottles with a fizz. 'Or who knows what might happen.'

Sometimes, when Mr Sheppie is out of an evening and Mrs Sheppie has taken her drink, she opens the cage door and lets the bird fly free. It flutters up towards the ceiling where neither of us can follow and perches on the curtain. There are small white messes along the whole of the rail. 'Dirty,' Mr Sheppie calls them. 'God's creature,' Mrs Sheppie replies.

Before bedtime I sit at the kitchen table and eat a piece of thick bread spread with jam made from berries scavenged in the graveyard. Big black things, saturated with salty air. I make sure my feet don't touch the floor. It is late, but Mrs Sheppie is down on her knees scrubbing at an invisible pool. 'I've wanted to change this linoleum these fourteen years.' She wipes at her forehead with the back of a yellow rubber glove. 'But he always says no.'

Mrs Sheppie cleans the linoleum every night before she goes to bed. Takes her bucket and fills it with water steaming from the kitchen tap, frothed up with bubbles. Then she scrubs, from one end of the kitchen to the other, to mark the end of her day. Scrush, scrush, scrush over and over, while I chew on my piece. 'Waste of money, that's what he calls it.' Mrs Sheppie leans in with her yellow gloves towards her glimmering floor. 'Dirty, that's what I say.'

Mr Sheppie likes his linoleum dirty. I've seen him when the light in the sky is just rising and Mrs Sheppie is still in bed. Upstairs she lies on her back, little puff puff puffs escaping one by one from the side of her mouth. Downstairs a girl stands on the back doorstep before an ocean of polished lino, school bag in her hand.

The girl's skin is as pale as a creature that lives in the deep. Her wrists are still slender. Her dress is still buttoned to her chin. I stand on the landing and watch Mr Sheppie bring the bird cage through from the parlour. He is still wearing his fisherman's clothes.

In the kitchen the girl's chest flutters, just like the bird's. She makes a noise like a laugh in her throat. Mr Sheppie unhooks the metal door of the cage and loops his hand inside. His wrist is thick, like the bread I eat for my suppers. He is making a cooing sound in his throat too. The bird huddles in the corner, but Mr Sheppie has long arms.

All that I can see in Mr Sheppie's fist is a tiny, green head. The girl touches the head with the tip of her finger. The bird is silent. The girl makes that sound again. Mr Sheppie smiles and makes his sound again too. He lowers his fist towards where the girl's dress spreads out from her knees. Then he opens his fingers wide.

Round and round the bird flies, round and round again, caught beneath billowing cotton. The girl dances and beats with her hands. She is making a different sound now. Mr Sheppie laughs. Behind the door I press a hand to my mouth. The bird beats the same path once more. The girl is crying. 'Get it out! Get it out!' Mrs Sheppie will wake up soon.

Mr Sheppie puts his hand on the girl's shoulder as though to hold her down. 'All right, hen,' he says. 'I'll sort you.' And puts his fist beneath the girl's skirt again. The bird flies out and perches on Mrs Sheppie's saucepans. The girl makes another kind of noise before Mr Sheppie takes his hand away.

Afterwards, Mr Sheppie wipes his fingers on a rag taken from his pocket. The rag used to be the colour of Mrs Sheppie's wool, but it is covered in stains now. There was a stain on the girl's thigh too before she left, like a smear from the ochre cliffs. But she hasn't been anywhere near the cliffs today. Mr Sheppie watches me through the crack in the kitchen door as he wipes at his palms. Neither of us says anything. Then he beckons me in.

'Like two peas in a pod.' That's what Mrs Sheppie calls us as she makes breakfast. Mr Sheppie and I sit on either side of the kitchen table and wait to be served. 'My wee mindin'.' That's what Mrs Sheppie calls me as she leans back of an evening to survey the gleam of her red linoleum floor. I grin at her through a mouthful of bread and mashed up berries. I've always had two mothers. But I've only ever had one father, as far as I can tell.

Up in the graveyard, up on the hill, the bird lies silent in my fist now. The wind blows and the grass is grey. I stroke the bird's little belly and sing to it. 'Rise up, rise up and Praise Him.' The only song I've ever known. The bird trembles in my hand, the beat beat beneath its feathers as swift as the beat beat under my wrist. I won't let it go. Releasing it into the night would be cruel. A seagull might have it. A mink, all gleaming and brown. Instead I touch the bird to my cheek. Then I stick the scissors in.

Up on the cliff in the moonlight I can hear it. The schroosh, schroosh, schroosh of the pebbles. The chip, chip, chip of the stone. The scrush, scrush, scrush of Mrs Sheppie's brush. The sound of my mother as she falls. I list all the things that connect me still to her. Jam from the berries. Wool the colour of a cardinal's cap. Mrs Sheppie's tablecloth held between her legs. And in my mouth, Mr Sheppie's rag too. All doing our bit for the future of the congregation until the Lord comes down.

Up in the graveyard, up on the hill there's a wee minding buried in the grass if only you can see. The wind blows and creatures watch me from beyond the broken wall. The scrub is gone all grey in the moonlight. And so have the million tiny rivers spilling over the grass now. I dip my fingers in one of those rivers. It is warm, like a home ought to be. Then I write.

BELOVED

My wee minding to her.

Sandhills

Gillian Philip

SPIKE HAD A theory, the way Spike often did. Those people, they were actually still around, said Spike. There were pockets of air under the dunes and that was why you could hear them, if you pressed your ear to the sand in a particular spot. It wasn't that they couldn't get out; it was just that they'd never tried. Otherwise, said Spike, you'd hear them screaming. And all you could ever hear was the murmuring voices.

So Spike said. I could nestle my head against the dune till fine sand filled every cranny of my ear and my hair was thick with it, but I heard nothing. That did not disappoint me.

When we were boys Spike was my best friend, and not just because of the limited edition Icarus Ripstik that was only the latest of his mother's sacrificial offerings. The Ripstik was not usable on the sandhills; for those Spike had his beautiful copper-coloured hardtail mountain bike. That was his present for Easter, instead of an egg. *Easter*.

It took too much effort to pedal further on the yielding sand, so we stopped that day, panting, on the crest that overlooked the estuary, where the pines thinned out and the land sloped steeply to the mudflats. Spike threw the bike down against a scraggy wall of landslip and stood very still. He narrowed his eyes and I saw his jaw tighten.

'Don't start that again,' I told him.

Spike didn't answer. I'd have preferred him to shout at me or storm off, but he said nothing, just lifted a finger to his lips and closed his eyes. His lashes flickered, as if he was in a trance and his eyeballs were spinning below the lids. Whenever Spike was silent, a coldness chattered from the nape of my neck and all the way through my bones.

'Just don't,' I said. 'Stop it.'

'Sh,' said Spike. 'They're moving. In the village.'

The forest that anchored the dunes was crusted with silver-green lichen, patched with sunlight. A bird chittered in the undergrowth, a butterfly dipped and jerked like a puppet; far away on the motionless air we could hear the shrieking laughter of much smaller kids and a yipping dog. They could have been miles away, or just over the next wind-scoured ridge.

Spike's mountain bike lay abandoned, one wheel idly spinning. I wished I had the nerve to ask Spike to give it to me. Already the paintwork was scarred and dented, and one spoke was bent like a cheap fork. The bike was his mother's adoration, and Spike was testing it to destruction.

A breeze whispered through stiff marram grasses. A broken pine-twig bowled past us, bounding towards the wide beach, and eddies of sand stirred on the dune-tops.

'One day,' said Spike, 'the wind will rise and blow all the sand away, and the village will be right there, like Pompeii.'

'It'll have to blow a lot of sand,' I said.

'It did that before,' said Spike with a shrug. 'And now we can't even find the church spire. Nobody can.'

'Anyway,' I said, 'that's what the trees are for. They planted them so the dunes don't move any more.'

'They still move on the edges.'

'Listen, your stupid village is gone and they're all dead and they have been for hundreds of years and if we don't go back now the shop'll be shut and we won't get ice cream.'

'How can they be dead?' said Spike. 'You can still hear them talking.'

The woman who ran the Spar in town said the spire had been found once. Two girls found it, back maybe in the nineteen-thirties or forties. But how would that woman know anything? She'd only just moved up from Birmingham.

The grassed-over dunes didn't move, not now that all those pines stitched them together with thick ropes of root. Once someone had found the chimney of the manor house, and once the topmost branches of an orchard, but they were all gone now, dead and properly buried. Somewhere in a thousand acres of trees you were still supposed to be able to find the tip of the church's slated pinnacle with its rusted iron cross, so all the kids hunted for it until we were bored, except for Spike, who never got bored. Not of combing the dunes and the forest, not of listening for the murmurs of the dead.

The only thing that bored Spike was his mother's love. He spent his days peeling off its clinging tendrils, bolting for my house and for freedom. Spike wanted away from his mother but he hated to be alone, and I hated to be without Spike, so it was a perfect partnership. He'd swerve his bike into our drive in a rattling spray of gravel and we'd escape to the football pitch or the waste ground behind the fish gutting sheds or – more often – the dunes that had smothered a village. His mother must have thought, as mothers do, that the sand could still rise up and drown you, just out of badness. She did not like us loitering in that man-made forest.

'Just be careful, boys,' she'd wail when we returned hours later, all sunburnt and gritty and itching with salt. She'd twist her hair, and then she'd squeeze her hands together to stop herself grabbing him. 'Don't go down there when it's that windy.'

And Spike, who would be hungry by that time, would condescend to lean into her and bestow a hug, all while he winked back at me and mouthed *Tomorrows. Same. Time.*

'She's paranoid,' he told me as we jabbed twigs at the darting fish in a leftover ribbon of tide. 'It's all my dad's fault for buggering off.'

'Why's she paranoid? It's not like you can leave,' I pointed out, rolling back on my heels.

'Quite,' he said, 'but she's all how it was all-her-fault and he left because of her. It's all in her subconscious but she's as mad as a fruit bat, my mum.'

'She must be mad,' I told him. 'She buys you that much stuff.'

'There is that,' said Spike. Standing up, he chucked his twig into the stream and we watched it drift in the sluggish current. He sighed and frowned and blinked. His lashes were the same colour as his hair, and his hair was the exact same colour as the sand.

'Imagine,' he said, 'there's a whole little world still under that forest.'

'No, there isn't,' I said. I kicked the wheel of his copper-painted hardtail bike.

'Fine,' he said. 'Whatever. Let's go up the Gut and look for the church again.'

The Gut was where the river used to be, before the sand made new mountains at the estuary three hundred years ago and sent the flow north. Now it was a sheltered sand-walled gully, a long straight sloping track to the mudflats where a bike could pick up dangerous speed. Going back up was harder, but it did take you to a pond that was thick with wild iris and dragonflies.

'You know what they say?' said Spike. 'There were smugglers who buried their stuff in the dunes and they never found it again.'

'That would be more use than a buried church,' I said.

'That's how fast the dunes move,' said Spike, turning in a circle and staring through the ranks of pines. 'It's just as well there's the voices, or we'd never know where to look.'

I got angry with him, then. 'You should stop making up that shit,' I said.

'The wind rose that fast,' he said, 'they never had a chance in that village. They went

➥

to sleep and in the morning the sand had buried everything. The houses and the farms and the big manor house and the trees and everything.'

'Like you'd know that. Maybe they all got away.'

'No, they didn't.' Spike made boogie-woogie eyes at me. 'That's how come they're still talking down there.'

I climbed back on my second-hand bike and pelted off on it, fed up with him. I stood up on the pedals to pump harder, wobbling crazily as I rattled it down the Gut. Of course it only meant I had to struggle back up a second time, when I got my breath and my temper back. When I reached the pond again, Spike was standing with his head tilted, his hair scuffed up by the breeze, making like he never even knew I'd gone.

'Those screaming kids finally shut up,' he said.

I propped myself against a tree while I got my breath back. The air was all salt and sun-dried wildflowers and the tang of pine. Way above us, the highest tree-tops thrashed in the rising gusts, even though it was muggy at our level, and the midges were rising to dance in the evening. It could be that the wind had blown the children's yells away. Or it could be that they'd gone. Them and their parents and their dogs and their cars, everything that connected the forest to the world. The sky between the treetops was dark and golden and heavy with threat.

Hairs prickled on my bare arms. 'We should maybe go.'

'Do you not hear the voices *now?*' And Spike turned abruptly and folded his arms and stared at me.

Not me. I did not hear a thing. I did not hear anything but the high-up wind soughing in the pines, and the murmur of the sea and the whisper of waves licking the shore, and the distant mourning of gulls. I swear I could even hear the pitter of bird-feet on the mudflats. I did not hear human footsteps, though the grass shifted on the lip of the Gut, and grit and tiny pebbles came bouncing and skittering down the sandbank.

I yanked my bike up by the handlebars.

'Your mum's going to kill us if we're late.'

I didn't wait for Spike. I pedalled hard up the sandy forest track, and hoped that the crunch and hiss and the soft exhalation was Spike behind me on his copper-coloured hardtail bike, following so close his breath was on my neck.

She didn't kill either of us; she was too frantic. She was out in her garden in the last slanting hazy sun, pretending to dig, and she flung down the muddy fork and hurried to the gate when she saw us turn into the street.

She swallowed and dusted her hands and pretended to be all unconcerned, but she never took her eyes off Spike till he was inside the gate. She clashed it shut on me, and almost grabbed him. Spike winced, mortified.

'Did you not see the forecast, Spike?' she scolded.

He rolled his eyes. 'It's going to be windy.'

'People get hurt in the wind,' she said. Obviously she couldn't bring herself to say *People get smashed to death by falling trees.*

'And people get lost in the woods, I told you.'

'Oh,' said Spike. 'I get it. I forgot it was your anniversary.'

It was a clattering rain of gravel against my window that woke me, though the branches of the laburnum had scratched against the pane all night and the glass had rattled and the gale had made the house shake. When I shoved the window open against the blast and peered down at Spike, I saw him standing in a litter of leaves and branches and broken slates. Bins were tumbled across the road and next door's trampoline was upturned on a shattered plastic bird bath. The wind was still high and it blustered Spike's hair over his forehead.

'Have you seen this?' he called up.

'I have now.' I shut the window and got dressed and crept downstairs with my trainers in my hand to join him.

The world outside was soaked in thin tea-coloured light. Somewhere there was a sunrise, but even the rampaging gale couldn't dispel the misty gold dust that veiled the sky and the horizon. When we rode out onto the main road, the source of the atmospheric stain became obvious: sand piled so thickly on the roads and fields, we had to get off the bikes and wheel them across its quaggy surface.

'Sandstorms,' I said in awe. 'We had a sandstorm.'

'We're still having one,' said Spike. 'There hasn't been one like this in a century. They said so on TV.' As he shoved his bike up another new dune that was yesterday a corner of a B road, he stared off towards a coast curtained in airborne sand.

'Your mum,' I said, 'she'll murder you if she catches you going to the woods again. Did you get in trouble?'

'Nah. She just cried and went to bed. It was two years ago yesterday he left.'

'I forgot,' I said.

'Me too.' Spike shrugged.

Perhaps if his dad hadn't gone without a word, Spike's mum wouldn't have lost it in quite the same way. His parents had a furious row, said Spike, and he woke up next morning and his dad was already gone. But he wasn't that bothered, said Spike. It was more peaceful now. His mum might have gone off her head, but not Spike. Spike was practical and had no neuroses. Spike usually knew what to do for the best, and the best in this case was to shut up and get on with it. Anyway, his dad had said he might go some day. Frankly Spike was surprised his mum hadn't kicked him out sooner. His father was like a parental guidance DVD, he said, and what he meant by that was: some gambling references and occasional mild violence.

'Ow,' I said, tweaking grit from my eyes. My bike wobbled. 'Sodding wind.'

'It'll be better in the trees,' said Spike.

I opened my mouth to argue. I did not want to turn down the track beyond the car park and head into the woods, not at six in the morning when the place was empty of cyclists and cars and shrieking children and yelping dogs. Daylight was not quite daylight yet, and perhaps, today, it never would be. The golden air thickened the closer we got to the coast, and all sounds died in it except the hiss of the wind.

On the other hand, my tongue felt stormblasted and my teeth crunched on fine grains of sand, and my eyes watered and stung. Spike might be right. Maybe it was better in the trees.

Sure enough, when the forest enveloped us and the branches knitted overhead, the air grew more peaceful around us and the sand settled. In the stillness there was nothing but the crunch of our wheels, and small tornadoes of dust on the track, and the wind reduced to a gusting breath on the nape of my neck.

'This is great,' said Spike. 'We've got the place to ourselves.'

It felt to me like the other way round; like the place had us to itself. Somewhere a gull sobbed, but I could see none in the sky.

At the crest of a low rise, I put my feet on the ground to stop my bike with a jolt. 'This is crap,' I shouted into the eddying breeze. 'I'm going back.'

Ahead of me Spike skidded to a sideways halt and contemplated me.

'Don't be stupid. You can't leave me on my own.'

'No,' I began, but Spike had already turned and pedalled furiously down the hill. He was over the next incline and out of sight before I'd formed the next word, and a gritty warm wind rattled on the back of my neck. I shivered and shouted his name and cycled after him.

The tracks webbed the whole vast forest; from the viewpoint of a coasting gull it must have been like a well-planned grid, but at the level of a human eye it was easy to lose your sense of direction. I'd lost Spike, for what felt that day like forever. It took a while to occur to me to follow the pattern of his wheels in the fresh dusting of sand, but when I did, it seemed stupidly obvious where he was heading. All that about the shelter of the trees and he was making for the fringe of dunes above the mudflats. I hated him.

I hated him more when I saw him on all fours on the ridge of the Gut, staring down. He wasn't even looking for me, had trusted I wouldn't turn back, didn't even turn as I chucked down my bike and scrambled up the slope beside him. I hated his faith and I hated him for not turning. I hated the wind that hurled sand in our faces now, scouring every bit of exposed skin.

'What is it?' I dropped to all fours beside him, trying to shield my eyes. The storm had moved the sandhill, had scooped out a new hollow: no grass, no scrub, just pleated sand.

'I knew it was here,' he said. 'I knew it was somewhere here. I knew the dune would shift again.'

'You're feckin' deluded,' I said, and the gale made my voice shake. 'I want to go home now.'

I saw no spire. I wasn't expecting the whole church, of course, but nothing jutted from the floor of the new hollow except a tangle of bleached wood. Not the church at all; just a last vestige of the orchard, the topmost tip of a dead tree that would never stir in the wind again.

'I want to go home!' I shouted, louder; and then again, louder still, because I wanted not to hear the muttering voices. They were nothing more than lonely birds on the mudflats and the rustle of pine needles on swaying trees.

'There was sand on her spade,' Spike said. 'In the morning, see.'

He staggered to his feet and slip-slid down the slope into the hollow, and I went after him. There wasn't much to see down there and the wind must have shifted again, because the walls of the dune seemed to block out the storm, and the silence closed in suddenly, heavy and horrible. Right in the lowest point of the bowl the white twigs jutted from the ground, bare and smooth and weather-bleached and circled by a tarnished wristwatch.

'I'm not going to tell her I found him,' said Spike. 'I just wanted to know.'

'Right,' I said.

'And neither are you.' He glanced at me. 'Going to say anything, I mean. Are you?'

I shook my head. I drew another circle in the sand with a twig. An actual twig.

'I had a funny feeling,' said Spike.

He wasn't the only one. Our backs were to the hollow and we sat on its edge, watching the golden sky bleed into a coppery sea. I did not want to sit like that, my back to the hollow and what was in it, but I didn't want to turn and

face it, either.

'I heard them fighting,' he said. 'And then it stopped.'

Spike snapped off a blade of grass and chewed it, so I did the same. After a bit, we stood up and dusted ourselves down.

'I did think he'd just left,' he said, and peered down into the hollow. 'But I sort of knew he hadn't. Hang on.'

I still didn't want to turn. I didn't watch Spike slither-slide down there again, but I heard the scuffing of a trainer and the patter of kicked sand, and I heard him breathing harder with effort. When he clambered back up the slope and appeared at my side, he dusted his hands and stared at his copper-coloured hardtail bike with its scratched paint and its dented spoke.

'That wheel's really knackered, isn't it? He raised his head and sniffed the air, and lifted a finger to check the wind direction.

'I'll have that bike,' I said. 'If you're getting a new one. Can we go home now?'

'Yeah,' he said. 'There's more wind forecast anyway. I won't be a bit surprised if the dunes shift again.'

Scavenger
Stephanie Brown

DEE SLAMS HER foot on the accelerator, eyes in the rear view mirror as she plasters on the slap.

'Look, mum! Look!' I shout gleefully as Barbie dangles out the window by one leg.

Cars stream past like rides at the fairground, shot like stars through the night sky. I like it like this, just the two of us. Suddenly an angry trombone tears past; I snatch Barbie inside on time but Dee is already screaming;

'Jesus, did you just stick your arm out the window?'

'No...'

'For FUCK sake.' Barbie looks frazzled; Dee has an angry red line across her face. I giggle but this time it's not funny: sharp nails like claws take a swipe at my face and miss. I slide down in my seat and stroke Barbie's hair. Then, too soon, we're in the car park and Dee's climbing out of the car like a tangled daddy long-legs, precarious in those killer high heels.

John or Joe or Dan or Bob stands waiting, sucking on a fag with narrowed eyes, leaning on the wall like they do in the films. Looking at my mother once up, once down. She trots over like Bambi and I shuffle behind, staring up at the neon stars of the Showcase and the real stars beyond. Not looking where I'm going, I trip, and Dan or Bob or Joe or John snorts out something like a laugh. I frown at him so Dee frowns at me. I stick my tongue out impulsively and drag my feet on purpose through the revolving doors once, twice, three times like a merry go round as fast as I can, and propel myself out and across the sticky blue carpet.

In the cinema, someone throws popcorn at my head. I scuff my legs on the floor and Dee tells me to ssshhh, turns back to whatshisname and they move together strangely in the darkness. I blow bubbles in my coke and chomp through a fizzy loveheart, which he got me just so I'd shut up. The disgusting creaking of his leather jacket is all I can hear, as he writhes around, enveloping my mother like a slug. They aren't even watching the film. Another piece of popcorn lands on my lap and I pull Dee's sleeve urgently. She ignores me so I go into her bag instead and take out her lipstick and compact mirror, and look down into my own blowfish face, splashed with the light of the big screen as car crashes and explosions happen. I give myself a big red clown mouth then kiss the mirror and put it away daintily. Then I crawl underneath the seats away from the stink of sugar and sweat and perfume, people grunting and complaining all the way till I reach the aisle and pad across the expanse of patterned carpet to the exit sign.

Out in the corridor I lean against the wall for a while, popping the bubble gum sweet I'd been chewing and waving Barbie around by her hair. Then I get bored and wander over to watch the popcorn swirling. 'You want something, hun?' a smiley lady says to me. I shake my head 'no' and wander off towards the spinning doors. Once, twice, three times as fast as I can, and a family is frowning at me, trying to get in. I walk out along the pavement, as if I have somewhere to go, along the side of the building into the shadows, where the car park meets wasteland,

➤

nothingness. Everything is quiet now, with everyone already inside: nothing but the buzz of the big lights and the breath of the motorway across, some laughter from McDonalds, some way away. Then a part of the darkness gathers itself up and lopes towards me. I pop my bubble gum and the creature stops dead, one paw in the air, looking straight at me. With blithe unconcern he turns away, revealing a long snout and little snub nose. Imagining his rows of jagged teeth, I follow him as he slides like a shadow between the cars, stopping to sniff at the ground every so often.

I've seen a cartoon about foxes, so I know he must have a little fox wife somewhere and fox babies that he's trying to feed. I pick a half-eaten burger off the ground and trot after him, half-hoping to feed the baby foxes.

'His babies must be starving by now,' says Barbie as she twirls acrobatically on the end of my right hand.

'Maybe the farmer has already buried his babies,' I say, because this is what happened in the cartoon, except that the farmer's dog managed to save them.

'Why do farmers do that?' Barbie asks, her hair like a wild halo round her head.

'Ugh, Barbie, you don't know anything. Because farmers are mean. They drown kittens in bags too.' Barbie's arms stick out straight in shock. Meanwhile I have followed Mr Fox to the dank mouth of the motorway underpass. Because it looks like it smells, I hold my breath all the way through. On the other side, Mr Fox trots up to the bins beside a drive-through Burger King. Following him doggedly, still holding my sodden burger and dancing girl, I suddenly see something I've looked for on every road, every day for as long as I can remember: Davy's truck.

Davy was the only one of all of them who was ever nice to me. He used to whisk me up on his shoulders and pretend he was going to drop me. He took me to the shows and bought me ice cream; he called me 'his lassie.' His truck was big and orange and blue; I'd seen it around a few times. Each time I'd look back as it flew past, trying to catch a glimpse of him at the steering wheel. Dee would glare at me for doing this,

she hated Davy for being a lying cunt. I was just happy to know he was out there, and secretly, I'd always known I would find him again.

It was then I realised that Mr Fox had been leading me here the whole time, like lassie when she's trying to tell people things, because Dee's new men were always evil, and Davy would save me from their weird leather jackets and too-sharp teeth. I nearly burst into Burger King in joy to see him again, but then Barbie gave me a good idea.

'Let's surprise him!' she said, bobbing up and down excitedly. First, I carefully placed the half-eaten burger on the ground near Mr Fox. That was his reward. Then I sneaked up to Davy's truck and hauled myself up onto its high step with all my might. By reaching up as high as I could, I managed to touch the handle. Luckily, the door was open, so I crawled in and wrenched it closed after me. Then I hid myself in the deep space under the dashboard of the passenger side. Davy's truck was the best truck because it said: *Irn-Bru*. I couldn't wait to see his face. We would go on a great adventure together, me and him. I would live in his truck with him. I was never going home, ever again.

The Drone Goes to a Multi-Disciplinary Art Exhibition about Drones
Harry Giles

Shiiiiit, here are her crosshairs re-represented
as a satire in crochet. Here is her silhouette

chalked on an Istanbul street corner in crime scene
pastiche. Here is the Light of God, and here,

a children's choir singing "She'll be coming round the mountain
when she. When she." She examines herself in lino-cuts

and Snapchat screengrabs. Each installation
is wholly unable to neatly describe her

technical infrastructure and makes of its failure
a rasping howl. She walks through the gallery

as though it were crossfire. She gets the bus home
and sits on the sofa and tries, very hard, to rust.

The Drone Gets a Cat

Harry Giles

The cat patrols the top floor flat with clandestine style.
She was bought in to be a comfort in anxious hours.

Low maintenance, unlike the drone, she (the cat) requests
only two full bowls and a length of string to be more than

at ease. She (the cat) lies warm on the drone's whirring stomach
each morning and offers a meatier purr. She (the cat) could never

be operated from a solar-powered military base in the desert:
she (the cat) has only a tiny, breakable skull and its insides.

She (the cat) is a predator. She (the cat) requests only to sleep
nineteen hours each cycle to be more than content.

The drone looks into her (the cat's) vertical-slit eyes,
so like her (the drone's) own, and imputes satisfaction, and only

sometimes does she (the drone) begin to worry
what it might mean when she (the cat) sits poised

on the windowsill and makes a low, uninterpretable sound
at each seagull that passes. Only sometimes does she (the drone,

of course, the drone) stand with her cat
and, under her breath, ask if the hunt went well.

The Drone at Play
Harry Giles

Her line manager does boxing Fridays.
Gloved and all, but still: teeth, bruises.

Her pilot takes his steak very rare
indeed. That awkward date, the rusty ooze

had her swallowing hard. Their team leader
red-rings the Glorious Twelfth on each motivational

break-room calendar. At the next desk,
her least favourite colleague has bought

a spittoon, used with smug regularity.
Most of the staff, she imagines, have sex

as often as they can manage,
or more. But the drone, oh no –

not for her the damp slap of meat
on meat. She keenly separates work

and play. At home, she keeps an Atari
7800, a Master System, a Commodore.

She commits nightly alien genocide.
Pixel limbs are heaped around her.

The Drone Learns of the Death of Margaret Thatcher via Twitter

Harry Giles

A ticker tape of vindicated joy – see!
it can be killed! – and occasional bursts

of aberrant grief. The drone is at work
plotting flight paths. To be precise

she is slacking off and now slack-jawed,
watching the news spread like venereal

disease: careless, gleeful, murderous.
The drone, as usual, feels nothing. Not

the parade, nor the well-planned scramble
for beatification, nor the nonplussed

mourning of fellow Americans remembering
an iron hand at their backs. None of this.

It is more as if she is standing in line
to view the embalmed corpse of a well-known

revolutionary hero-dictator, a face painted
so much on tourist matryoshka, seen so often

in stamp collections, a face so t-shirted
the corpse's glass case has the slick unreality

of reality TV. Which is to say: this is not
a caricature. This is not a rehearsal.

This is a pair of unblinking blue eyes.
She closes the window and gets back to work.

The Drone Has Lunch with an Old Friend from University Not Seen in Seven Years

Harry Giles

In Feb '03 they bussed to march against war.
She still enjoys samba as though it were drumming euphoric

aesthetics of failure, so this is the soundtrack she wears.
He's sporting a waistcoat and camouflage trousers. They try

to negotiate hugging. They order and talk about work/life
balance and nuclear policy. She sees he's avoiding

big questions and messily bites into her seitan.
He laughs away tension, the way, in films, she'd pour

vodka onto a chainsaw wound. It kills
his desire to make her an object of study.

They touch at the station. She pictures him in bed
at 4:15, waking, realising he'd forgotten

that all through their lunch she was carrying warheads,
grabbing his phone and finding her number and passing

his thumb softly between the button marked call
and the menu option for delete.

Humanity

Night Boat
Alan Spence
Canongate, RRP £14.99

Alan Spence has written some of the best poetry and prose of the last 30 years so it's always exciting when something new appears. His latest novel, *Night Boat*, is subtitled 'A Zen Novel' and that is as good a description of what unfolds as I could ever come up with, not just in content but also in tone. *Night Boat* follows the life of Iwajiro, a young Japanese boy who enters the gates of hell at a frighteningly young age, and who becomes the celebrated Zen master Hakuin. From that arresting opening a complex and enlightening life unfolds, one which is far from perfect, and which doesn't pretend to be otherwise.

Even for those well versed in Japanese culture, the world in which the novel is set will be quite alien, and it is initially difficult to focus and adjust to what unfolds, but this is not to do with language, character or setting. In fact some of the language is wonderfully familiar. At one point a woman comments "What's for you will not go by you", a Scottish Zen aphorism if ever there was one. What is unusual is the pace of the novel. *Night Boat* is a book not to be rushed, and I believe it would be impossible to do so and fully engage with the challenges it presents. It is a novel of contemplation, not only for Hakuin and his followers, but also for the reader.

There are aphorisms and ideas that will have you thinking on your own life, and some that you will never contemplate again, because this is actually a more familiar and human story than it first appears. Or should I say 'stories', as *Night Boat* is structured as a set of short tales, each one an encounter which Hakuin has and which contains a lesson to learn, or a truth to discover. Hakuin never claims that he has all the answers, only more questions (which can infuriate those who seek his guidance, but not the reader as they get the bigger picture). Hakuin knows that what he teaches does not constitute an absolute truth.

Once you have adjusted to life in 18th century Japan you will want to spend more time there, learning at the master's feet, even when his own self doubt is painful. It is that which makes the story believable and recognisable. The array of characters who seek him out range from the superior samurai doing his master's bidding, a young women possessed, demons who hide in the shadows, and immortal monks, but there are also the more recognisable, everyday people such as disappointed parents, jealous co-workers and single mothers.

The unrelenting humanity that runs through *Night Boat* is something that can be found in all of Spence's work, as well as a black, and rather wicked, sense of humour. It is stated more than once that "Existence is suffering", but what comes across is that existence is absurd, with even those who spend their lives contemplating what it all means coming up with subjective answers and further questions.

Night Boat is a novel to immerse yourself in, one to return to and reflect upon. Although it is a very specific setting, its lessons, and the lives of its characters, could be applied to anyone at any time, reminding us that there is more that unites us than divides us. When you finish reading you'll find that while the world may remain the same, how you look at it will have changed. Isn't. That. So?

Kes

In Schrödinger's Box

The Secret Knowledge
Andrew Crumey
Dedalus Press, RRP £9.99, 234pp

Andrew Crumey writes big fiction about big ideas; his previous novels confidently discuss the work of real-life thinkers such as Schrödinger or Goethe, and his latest is no exception. *The Secret Knowledge* opens conventionally enough as an historical novel; in 1913 a young composer Pierre Klauer asks his sweetheart Yvette to marry him. After she agrees, he promptly disappears. Minutes later a gunshot is heard; Pierre has apparently committed suicide. Then we switch to modern day Manchester, a pianist happens upon Klauer's last work and wonders if this will help invigorate his flagging career. But as we continue to read, we realise that something richer and stranger is unfolding. The initially realistic setting quickly reasserts itself as a world or worlds in which characters and their histories change and dissolve before the reader's eyes.

Crumey used to be a theoretical physicist and it shows in his work, *Mobius Dick* uses the ideas of quantum physics to question our idea of reality; are we just characters in someone else's version of reality, and can events in our universe be influenced by those in another? Similarly, *The Secret Knowledge* explores the implications of this theory. As one of his characters suggests, we are living in the box alongside Schrödinger's cat, where all possibilities are available to us. So, as with this cat, the people in this book are both dead and alive, they can be both heroes and villains, and even Klauer's music itself may be both real and a forgery.

This degree of complexity could quickly become unravelled and incoherent in a lesser writer's work, but Crumey keeps every plate spinning, and ensures that we engage emotionally with at least some of the characters. He draws upon the biographies of real-life philosophers; Walter Benjamin's suicide in a Spanish border town during his flight from the Nazis in 1941 is a key plot point. This citing of Benjamin, as well as Theodore Adorno's and Hannah Arendt's work, is designed to make us think about the nature of morality. If we live in a multiverse where every possible outcome to each of our thoughts and actions is taking place at least somewhere in space-time, then how can we make meaningful choices about the way we should live our lives?

The physics ideas underpinning the novel are never made explicit, apart from a brief and teasing reference to Schrödinger's cat and the wave function used in quantum mechanics. And in this book Crumey has extended his earlier work to show that the implications of the multiverse are personal and political. In fact the theories of quantum physics were anticipated by political thinkers, the nineteenth century French revolutionary Blanqui (whom Crumey refers to) came up with the concept of the multiverse, and Adorno used it to criticise the endless 'now' of capitalism.

The blurb on the back cover describes the book as 'a multi-layered story that spans a century' and sets up a rather thriller-ish expectation that there is a shocking truth to be discovered; read on reader! This rather too conventional description is misleading and it's a shame that the publishers seem to not have the courage of their convictions after having decided to publish such a complex and carefully argued novel.

The thread linking the different sections together is a slight MacGuffin, the story of the secret and threatening Rosier organisation chasing Klauer's work is never entirely convincing, and we get the feeling that Crumey is more at ease exploring different characters and their points of view – as a literary symphony in this interconnected multiverse – than having to wrap up plot ends. But the book as a whole is an extraordinarily clever enterprise that repays close reading.

Bear of Little Brain

Icy Words

The Sea Change and Other Stories
Helen Grant
The Swan River Press, RRP £25.00, 144pp

Helen Grant is probably better known for her young adult novels such as her debut outing, *The Vanishing of Katharina Linden*, which was shortlisted for various prizes in the genre such as the CLIP Carnegie Medal. Here we have her first short story collection for adults brought together by a small independent press out of Dublin in a beautifully produced limited edition of four hundred copies. Also interesting to note that while her young adult novels are written in a female narrative voice, all the stories in this anthology are voiced from a male perspective.

There are seven stories in this collection, all previously published in various magazines of the supernatural genre such as *All Hallows* and *Supernatural Tales* dating back to 2005. Not surprising then that each of these stories contains some mysterious ghostlike figure, a person gone missing or a mystery unresolved. In Grant's first story, 'Grauer Hans', a child is tempted by a mysterious Saint Nicholas-type figure appearing nightly at her windowpane only to discover that this amiable visitor is a grotesque monster in disguise. In the eponymous 'The Sea Change', a deep-sea wreck diver is also seduced into remaining too long on the ocean bed with dire supernatural consequences. In 'Nathair Dhubh', a young climber goes missing, supposedly taken by the spirit of the mountain. In 'The Calvary at Banska Bystrica', a man fears that his brother has been physically consumed by a painting of The Last Judgement on the walls of an abandoned church in Slovakia.

By their very nature, the narrative structure of these stories becomes predictable. What sets them apart though is the context and the writing. Grant appears to be equally at home in describing the world of a deep-sea diver as she is the challenges of being a mountaineer. She is wonderfully assured in her descriptions of life in a 17th century French village as she is wandering around a small town in Eastern Europe. She is not heavy-handed either. Apart from the description of the leprous grey demon in 'Grauer Hans' with its evil little red eyes, a long triangular hole where its nose should be, its gleaming teeth like skinning knives, the menaces in Grant's stories are wraithlike or fleeting glimpses, sometimes hardly described at all. Often the reader is left undecided as to what has really happened, as if some spectre has passed its shadow over the pages of the book. The effect is chilling and unnerving, leaving a lingering sensation of unease long after the story has ended.

Her writing style is crisp and clean, each story polished until any rough edges have all but disappeared. It is for this reason that the occasional clumsy and trite line or two stands out awkwardly as in: "Thilo's revelation made me sick with horror. I think I went very pale, for he smiled maliciously. I wrapped my arms around myself, as though to keep myself safe. 'I don't believe you,' I said, tremblingly." But this kind of paragraph is something of an aberration, a slight nodule in a text that is normally so smooth, the reader's engagement glides easily across the icy words.

Altogether this is a highly accomplished and polished collection of short stories, very typical of the genre in terms of style but not too challenging with regard to structure or invention. This anthology comes beautifully packaged as well but it will take an avid fan of either Grant or the genre to justify the hefty price tag on this limited edition.

Tarka The Otter

The World Awaiting

What Long Miles
Kona Macphee
Bloodaxe, RRP £8.95, 64pp

Kona Macphee has a strong back-catalogue in *Tales* and *Perfect Blue*, which won the Geoffrey Faber Memorial Prize. In *What Long Miles,* we have poems that are careful to go beyond the simple subjective gaze out onto the world or into the self, that bane of less-assured lyric poets. For Macphee, there are difficult 'long miles' between language and self-representation, between self and world. This collection journeys across these distances without ever offering the easy comfort of a resting-place. In 'Prodigal', the protagonist 'wracks' her

> ...old life's webwork,
> feeling the snap as each drawn strand
> reaches some secret limit and lets go [...].

What seemed at first a break for freedom becomes a hard teaching; one's free will might not be one's own free will at all:

> Would you learn, at last, that any heart
> will shred to tatters when what hauls it on
> is some crazed engine hulking in the dark
> of what it can't unlearn and can't outrun?

Like the unfortunate pheasant that has been killed by a train and covered the long miles "in the undercarriage, / while flesh and mechanism reaffirmed / the compacts of their loveless marriage" ('Pheasant, Waverley Station'), flesh is fragile in the face of these greater 'mechanisms.'

Macphee is adept at mining a conceit for its hidden possibilities of juxtaposition, at telling stories aslant. In 'Singularity', a black hole's event-horizon furnishes the poet with a vocabulary to address a descent into dementia. The gap that opens up between husband and wife even when "any decent marriage / must partner stargazing with stoic

going-on" is poignant and perfectly pitched.

Different historical and fictional characters inhabit the collection, helping the poet negotiate varied styles, registers and forms. The 'long miles' take their toll on these characters' fleshly bodies. The indomitable Captain C E Reade who toured Scotland on a tricycle in 1882 is 'The Wheelman' in a poem that demonstrates Macphee's formal narrative skills, the metre and rhyme scheme keeping the poem "barrowing the load / of a mutilated body on a set of brand-new tyres". Napoleon Bonaparte is slowly poisoned by the wallpaper of the room in which he is confined ('Scheele's Green'). Macphee is also no stranger to popular culture and her 'Poem for Roy Batty' is both a lament for the replicant antagonist of the cult classic *Blade Runner* – his search for more life, for more than 'tears in rain' – and a recognition that his fictional death haunts the real "hurt leak of my pulse – / beat gone, beat gone, beat gone."

Sometimes, very rarely, Macphee's inventive explorations pass me by, failing to register in the ways that the majority of her poems achieve. 'Tense' scatters phrases without her usual satisfying correlative anchor and 'The secret life of numbers' moves away from the focus on fleshly fragility into an abstract world that is difficult to conjure. That this poem is immediately followed by a meditation on 'Three sketches of a mandible' ("This half-mouth quintessentially unkissable; / this stunned jaw dropping nowhere and forever") reasserts the poet's remarkably deep perception of the absences and gaps that animate what we think we know and can grasp, in body and mind. It would seem, however, that in the end, the long miles draw too wide; the final poem 'Paschal' leaves all in doubt: however we frame our ideals of forgiveness or redemption, "this much we will not know".
Moley

Mything about in Boats

Found at Sea
Andrew Greig
Polygon, RRP £8.99, 72pp

In the acknowledgments to this collection of poems, Andrew Greig nails his colours to the mast. He wants to "myth" a sailing trip he took from Stromness, Orkney, to the island of Cava with his friend Mark Shiner. They are men "in the middle of life... scunnered." They're at sea.

I was sometimes resistant to Greig's myth-making. I felt he tried to make the outing mean too much. Wasn't this just a jaunt? Sometimes I felt the metaphor of life as a "dark and gurly sea" was done too weightily. Weren't they simply messing about in boats? Look at them, I thought: they have a boat; I wish I had a boat. Statements seemed too often to be reaching for profundity, as with, "This was not the plan / but we are where we are." But Greig undercuts himself. "Wherever that is!" someone shouts. Snatches of conversation between the poet and skipper ('Crew' and 'Skip') bring levity and make the language more natural. Then someone shouts, "duck!", the boom swings across, and we're back in the moment, back in the boat. Greig's touch has lightness as well as weight.

It was the lightness and smallness that I enjoyed most. What first got me was a warm-hearted description of Orkney whalers and the loving, cooing assonance of "themselves harpooned / by memories of warmth, booze, home / – those barbs of love that don't pull loose." I enjoyed small, solid images I could hold. The boat's hull is a "squat wineglass". The boat propels like "wet soap / squeezed in the hand." I liked, too, the solid details. To build the sailboat's ballasts, parts were taken from the town hall's organ bellows. Descriptions like this made the boat personal, characterful and real. Greig loves the technical language of sailing. At times my ignorance meant talk of gunwhales, keels and lees lost me. But other times I could see the physical boat and the movements of the jib and mainsail. I liked the real boat more than the mything.

But when Greig reaches Cava the focus changes. Here, it's about the lives of Meg Peckham and Ida Woodham, two women who moved to live alone together on the island, its "sole inhabitants... for near-on thirty years." Now the poet and his friend pick around the ruins of their house, finding vivid objects like "yellowed sheet music". Meg and Ida's daily lives were modest, and Greig's descriptions are rich because of their simplicity, specificity and smallness:

> Ida rode her motorbike for peats.
> Meg rowed for paraffin, calor gas,
>   batteries and tea,
> Picked up mail and library books.

The women are a mystery to Greig, as they were to people at the time. But as the Ida and Meg poems continue, a handful of details create an enigmatic, moving story of dedication and companionship. Greig creates, in the end, a very human myth. When Ida and Meg first set out for the island, they are pulling a tea chest on pram wheels, with a cat in a carrier. Again, with a few precise objects, the moment is solidly and mythically drawn. For me, Greig's collection is at its most lovely here, at its most sparing and simple:

> They packed everything that mattered
>   (it was very little)
>   (it was essential)

WOL

Reasons to Run

The Most Distant Way
Ewan Gault
Hólland House, RRP £7.99

The UK has long fostered a rich tradition of hosting divisive public spectacles, but none can rightfully claim to have been quite so intrusive as London 2012. Even the most committed hermits could never have hoped to out-run the daily waves of scandal and incompetence – the overzealous brand protection, the empty seats, and, during the build-up, a terrifying glimpse at the privatised future, courtesy of G4S and thirty unpaid workers made to sleep under London Bridge. It was easy (and in some cases wholly correct) to get caught up in all that anger, but it did drag the spotlight off one group of individuals who had some pretty pressing concerns of their own. They're called athletes, and many of them had to sacrifice what could be termed an even vaguely normal lifestyle to reach the stage they did.

It's these incredible stories so forced onto the periphery that Ewan Gault tackles in his debut novel *The Most Distant Way*. Set some years before the games themselves, the book follows Kirsten and Mike, two young long-distance runners in training with hopes of being selected for Team GB. Kirsten's father, who works as Mike's coach, has sent the pair to Kenya to train at one of the high-altitude facilities that allegedly help to produce the likes of David Rudisha, Geoffrey Mutai, and numerous other world record holders. The pair are approaching the end of their stay, with a few more days left at the facility before a gruelling trip back to Glasgow, via Mombassa and Nairobi. The upcoming election has upped tensions in the country, with mobs already roaming the suburbs, and the police all but happy to violently suppress anything that could be conceived as a threat. On top of that, Mike and Kirsten are clearly both experiencing growing pains – pains that have exacerbated themselves overtime,

having been so rudely forced out of the regular teenage routine.

The resulting novel deconstructs the hygienic myths that characterise the games, and the fantasy of sheer, undeterred, superhuman endeavour. The first-person narrative switches between the two with each chapter, and it's not long before we realise how delightfully flawed both characters are. That said, one of Gault's major achievements here is the creation of narratives delivered in such a naturalised fashion that we as readers initially think nothing of Kirsten and Mike's often-unhinged behaviour – whether it's Kirsten getting debilitatingly stoned in the middle of hyena country, or Mike taking an ice bath in a wheelie bin stolen from his neighbour.

The contrast between the two creates a fascinating tension. Kirsten is traumatised both by the violence that surrounds her in Kenya, and the violence of her past, which includes a father ruthless enough to bully his own daughter if it takes her any closer to the podium. Mike meanwhile struggles to relate anything outside the experience of running, despite an obvious desire for Kirsten's affections. He runs to affirm his own existence. Kirsten runs in an attempt to obliterate herself.

Ultimately, Gault's work is an unflinching, painful study of the lives of young people striving for greatness, and an unveiling of the brutality that often lies beneath the surface, and its devastating consequences. *The Most Distant Way* is an effective exploration of the individual's inability to reconcile their personal struggles with any kind of wider situation, be it their home-life, or the politics of a nation on the verge of collapse. The result is a powerful, unsettling comment on something that is not so far from home as it may first appear.

Conqueror Worm

The Joke

Naw Much of A Talker
Pedro Lenz
Translated by Donal McLaughlin
Freight Books, RRP £8.99, 240pp

The Goalie is a storyteller, a 'patter-merchant', born with the gift of the gab, never happy unless he is entertaining everyone with his stories, "whit ah needed wisnae a woman, but an audience". The Goalie is a pain in the arse who won't shut up, "conspicuously verbally aggressive" according to his psychiatrist, the drunk in the bar who will always be in your face. Which one is true? It just depends on who is telling the story and who is listening.

The Goalie is the hero of Pedro Lenz's debut novel, *Naw Much of A Talker*. A recovering drug addict and borderline alcoholic, he has just returned from a year in 'The Joke' serving a sentence for selling drugs, a charge he denies. The novel follows The Goalie as he tries to get his life back together, to find his old friendships, to convince Regula, a local barmaid, of his love, and ultimately, almost accidentally, uncover what actually happened to land him in jail.

Along the way, Goalie tells us stories, about his past, about friends and family, and about his world. Told in turn with humour and humility, anger and apathy, his storytelling opens him up to the reader. He is at once angry with and philosophical about the world around him. He is naive yet at the same time knowledgeable. He is perceptive of those around him but lacks self-awareness. He is searching for a truth but doesn't trust honesty and continues to hide in a world of stories, lost meanings and ambiguities. It is no accident that the town he lives in is called The Fog, as he cannot see what is in front of his face.

Lenz's characters are reminiscent of other contemporary novelists, like Niccolo Ammaniti, Willy Vlautin and Allan Wilson. White, male, urban, working class, disenfranchised, disillusioned dreamers, angry with the world and those around them, blaming everyone but themselves, where the next big scheme will be the one that changes everything. In reality, they blow it all – cash, relationships and life – happier to hide in booze and drugs than deal with reality. But in amongst this, Goalie shows great humanity, he entertains the reader with humour, wit and wisdom. And Lenz captures a world on the edge of society, painting a picture of the washed up and the washed out.

This novel is a remarkable feat of translation by Donal McLaughlin. Originally written in Swiss dialect and published in German, it was shortlisted for the Swiss Book Prize and won the Berne Literary Award. It has now been translated into the English language, but not in standard prose but a Glaswegian dialect that wouldn't be out of place on the pages of Kelman. It reminded me of discovering the Rebel Inc Classics in the 90s, like Knut Hamsun and Alexander Trocchi, where protagonists are armed with existential awareness but handicapped with the inability to escape their inevitable decline.

Created through a unique literary exchange between Glasgow and Berne, McLaughlin is almost a co-author rather than translator. Lenz himself is an acclaimed spoken word artist and the Scottish vernacular gives his text the life, energy and authenticity required. There is one story but two voices telling it – the original Swiss voice which is there, silent in the background and this new voice retelling the story. This creates a fascinating dynamic which shows that a story isn't static but is always changing: "Stories urnae like teeth, they don't grow in twice then that's it... There's an infinite supply of them".

Houyhnhnm

Humour and Pathos

The Good News
Rob A. Mackenzie
&
The North End of the Possible
Andrew Philip

Salt, RRP £12.99 each, 80pp

Salt's recent announcement that it will no longer be commissioning new single author collections but instead will concentrate on publishing anthologies of poetry adds a certain gravitas to reading these two handsome, hardback books.

Andrew Philip's *The North End of the Possible* asks how we are shaped by isolation, belonging and landscape. Writing in both Scots and English, Philip's poems are filled with an earthy musicality. A narrative runs through the collection in the shape of MacAdam, an enigmatic, Red Bull drinking, moon recycling character resurrected from Philip's first collection, *The Ambulance Box*. "Trauchled by the paraphernalia / of a life spent tinkering" MacAdam sets about "cobbling light apart" in 'A Child's Garden of Physics (1)' and "...like a cirque-du-freak performer, / he falls bedlong into the geography/of the tethered body" in the beautiful 'Skate and Samphire'. Elsewhere a newsreader mutates into Scots in 'Look North (and North Again)' and a piper is told "ye cannae play" in 'Tae a Lousy Piper'. '10x10' is a tender sequence celebrating a decade of marriage while 'Bereavement fir Dummies' jolts with the opening lines "Bonnie, unkent boy; bracken bairn: / deid pixel at the centre o ma screen". More curious are 'Oh, Jubilant Jute Lid!' and 'Cheer Friend of Both' written in a form Philip has developed – the abnominal – using only the letters of the dedicatee's name. Philip writes with daring and playfulness. As he tells us in 'MacAdam Essays the Truth of Each Dichotomy' – "...So many/choices, MacAdam, / and none without a smack of risk".

Rob A. Mackenzie delves into the subject of happiness in *The Good News* and all that accompanies the struggle to find it. The first of the book's three sections, 'The Lingua Franca Happy Hour', reflects Scotland at a pivotal point in its history in 'An Angry Queen Tours the Royal Mile', 'Tippexed Speeches on Scottish Independence', and a cento, 'A Scottish Cent(o)ury', constructed from lines by a hundred Scottish poets (Philip's collection features a cento consisting of lines and phrases taken from Mackenzie's first collection *The Opposite of Cabbage*). Mackenzie draws us close in the middle section 'Autistic Variations', a moving but unsentimental look at a family affected by autism against an Italian backdrop of displaced domesticity. Particularly poignant is 'The Trouble', reminiscent of Edwin Morgan's 'A View on Things' – "The trouble with me is the fog that enters the picture. / The trouble with the picture is that no one is able to draw it". Fragility and perseverance are explored in 'Consequential Egg' which, by way of an overheard conversation, imagines an egg being built from ten thousand egg shell pieces "until an egg the size of a bus wobbles on a tiny cup. / How does it end?" The third section 'Human Manoeuvre' takes us on journeys through faith and the human condition. No small subjects but Mackenzie handles them with delicate ease. Peppered with references to popular culture, poems like 'The Boxer' and 'Soundings' lead us to the bare bones of life's discomforts in 'Horizontal', a reminder that "We try to occupy each space and tame/utilities as if contentment were a right".

With crossovers aplenty these two collections are a pleasure to read together. Both assured and brimming with humour, pathos and linguistic surprises they lend themselves to be being read and reread and, while it is understandable that Salt couldn't sustain their rate of poetry publication in the current climate, it is heartening to read such ambitious collections that made Salt's list while the going was good.

Fiver

Chance Objects

Snake Road
Sue Peebles
Chatto & Windus, RRP £14.99, 320pp

Snake Road by Sue Peebles is an understated, lyrical exploration of an intergenerational family and the different ways in which they are affected by loss. Aggie, the narrator, drifting along in a faltering marriage and unmoored by a recent, personal loss, seeks to anchor herself in her grandmother's past. This exploration of her family history is given urgency by her grandmother's deteriorating memory, and Aggie becomes fixated on the idea of recovering the past and using it as a tool to make sense of her present situation.

Much of the action takes place in North, the family home; a tall narrow house with an orchard garden. Peggy, the grandmother, inhabits the top storey of the house, only emerging at night, when everyone else is in bed, to leave slippers in the oven, wash the kitchen floor with oats; her deepening confusion signified through the domestic. The middle floors are the domain of Aggie's mother, Mary: a place of warmth and comfort, where by day she restores the nocturnal disorder caused by Peggy. The basement is Aggie's retreat, the childhood bedroom to which she returns, in flight from her failing marriage. The three women move between the layers of the house, excavating the past through quiet conversations that take place around everyday acts; mixing a cake, hanging out washing, brushing hair. Peebles creates a strong sense of place as a shared past, mapping the house and the orchard through Aggie's memories and childhood stories, just as Aggie attempts to map her grandmother's life through chance objects and throwaway comments.

The writing is restrained and nuanced, carefully evoking the complex relationships that the characters have with each other, and the past. Peebles' description of dementia is a careful balance of dreamy realism and heartbreaking poignancy. There are moments of elegiac beauty in Peggy's night time wanderings and snippets of memory, which are described in almost magical prose and set against the painful realities of caring for an aged person, the clashes of will and the indignities of dependence. Fittingly, given her fixation with narrative, Aggie seems less aware of the day-to-day challenges of caring for a dementia sufferer – it is Mary who fights with Peggy to wash, to eat, to change her clothes. Mary's moments of frustration highlight how her mother's illness has affected her. Aggie is determined to record her grandmother's history as a testament, but it's Mary who takes care of her on a physical level; two different expressions of love and grief.

The male characters of the novel inform the narrative but we see much less of them than the female characters. Aggie's father hovers on the outskirts of the story – he doesn't seem as much part of the family as her mother and grandmother, most often to be found in the orchard, pruning the trees. Aggie's relationship with her husband is central to the novel, yet he, too, is a curiously peripheral character, more of an absence than a presence, which makes it difficult for us to understand their connection or why they care about saving their marriage. Even Kenneth, the friend Aggie meets at a local group, seems to act only as a foil to Aggie's feelings and struggles, and, perhaps because of this, their friendship and attraction fails to convince. However the heart of the story is the relationship between mother and daughter, grandmother and granddaughter and *Snake Road* is a subtle and poetic exploration of these complicated ideas of family and motherhood, loyalty and history.
Richard Parker

Persia, Profit & Politics

The Trade Secret
Robert Newman
Cargo Publishing, RRP £14.99, 384pp

Rob Newman, the author of *The Trade Secrêt*, is best know for his partnership with David Baddiel in the Mary Whitehouse Experience, a topical comedy show that aired on BBC radio and television in the early nineties. Since then Newman has written and toured extensively on such disparate subjects as the history of oil, climate change and theories of evolution. His previous novel, *The Fountain at the Centre of the World*, set in Mexico and Seattle, concerns a man searching for his brother in the hope of getting a bone marrow transplant. Newman is clearly someone with a wide range of interests.

The Trade Secrêt, which begins in late sixteenth century Persia before moving through Europe and then to England, was conceived of when Newman stumbled upon the history of two Elizabethans brothers, the Sherleys, while carrying out research in the British library. It is primarily the story of one of their servants, Nat Bramble, and his friend Darius Nourendini, a market trader. Bramble is entrusted by Anthony Sherley to trade some money. Perceiving quickly how he can make a profit, Bramble gets ambitious, at first earning money then just as quickly losing it. This means that he cannot go back to his post and instead he sets off with Darius to find oil, risking both their lives. As there is a fuel shortage they are able to sell the oil to the highest bidder on their return.

However soon afterwards, Anthony Sherley robs Bramble of his share. Bramble then becomes part of Sherley's entourage on their diplomatic mission to Italy to persuade them to join with England against the Turks. Bramble finally ends up in London where he is recruited to spy on another Sherley brother who is a pirate. Meanwhile Darius, who was badly burned when searching for oil, proceeds to try to win the heart of the wedding musician Gol.

The novel is both ambitious and confident and the careful research shows, from the author's knowledge of the diplomatic relationships at that time, to how wedding musicians are paid, right down to the typical colours of tiles in a bath. This detailed research is necessary to underpin such a complex novel but on occasions the level of detail and amount of description considerably slows down the progression of the plot. A lighter touch would have made for a more engaging novel and allowed more of the wit to come through.

Newman uses a floating narrative style and while Bramble is the main character we also get the perspectives of Darius, Gol, each of the Sherley brothers and other major and minor characters. This serves to give a multi-dimensional view of the story and is reminiscent of other novels, set in different time periods and political situations such as Rohinton Mistry's *A Fine Balance* and Hari Kunzru's *The Impressionîst* which themselves are Dickensian. On occasion the narrative style in *The Trade Secrêt* gets confusing but on the whole it is successful, for example when it allows us to see and understand why Gol is both attracted to and frustrated by Darius.

Newman is a master of his subject and with his knowledge of so many areas and the talent at his disposal I will be looking out with interest to see what he does next.
Aslan

Sitting Nicely

The Home Corner
Ruth Thomas
Faber, RRP £12.99, 277pp

There is something very attractive about simple stories. They can be hard to find, these days, so often obscured by fancy prose, intricate plots and excessive stylistic flourishes. But in *The Home Corner*, Ruth Thomas has told a simple story; it is down to earth, it is readable, and at times it is profound. It's a hard thing to do, to tell a simple story simply, to make characters both ordinary and extraordinary, to make an ending both surprising and inevitable. There are no stylised phrases or convoluted plot twists to hide behind. So when I say that *The Home Corner* was an effortlessly simple story, I do so with admiration and no small amount of envy.

The Home Corner is the corner of a classroom where children at St Luke's primary school can go for "Undirected Play." It has a little table and chairs, a sink, a washing machine, an ironing board, and is favoured by the girls. Luisa McKenzie, our bemused narrator and the school's newest classroom assistant, watches the children as they play and attempts to answer some of their more potent questions about God, death, wizards, the future, and why she has died her hair a particularly unfortunate shade of pink.

Luisa has just flunked her Highers, failed to get into university, been fired from her job in a local shop, and is already half way to being fired from this one. Underpinning this unravelling of "what her life was meant to be" is a trauma that is both commonplace and privately heartbreaking. She is lost, and *The Home Corner* is about how she finds herself again. It's also about family, about girls and boys, choices and mistakes, teachers and children; it is about growing up.

At only nineteen years old, Luisa unsurprisingly relates to the children more than she does to the teachers. The children themselves are wonderful creations, who say truthful but completely incorrect, hilarious but tragically devastating things in that direct way that only children can. Like when Emily Ellis announces to the class that she knows the Son of God, and that "His name is Edith." Or when Luisa catches a boy pushing plastic farmyard animals over a pretend cliff. She suggests that one of the cows might come back to life later, but he frowns at her and replies: "It's dead. It was meant to die. It's part of the game."

Part of the elegant construction of the book is that everyone matters. Each character is important and every interaction means something. I didn't notice while I was reading the book that pieces were being put into place, but they were, and they fitted quite expertly. I'm not going to tell you anything about how they all link up, and in fact I'm not going to tell you anything about the second half of the book because I don't want to give it away. Despite its simplicity and its inevitable neatness it surprised me; it jolted me into feeling emotions that in my cynicism I try to deny. And that's the thing about simplicity, I suppose. Sometimes it can knock you off your feet.

Golden Monkey

Small Press Poetry

Rider at the Crossing
Jim Carruth
Happenstance Press, RRP £4, 32pp

Lunar Poems for New Religions
Stephen Nelson
Knives Forks and Spoons Press, RRP £8, 87pp

The small press poetry scene remains as vibrant as ever. These two collections represent only a fraction of the excellent work published in the past six months. The interested reader is directed to www.scottish-pamphlet-poetry.com for further information.

As its title suggests, Jim Carruth's new collection represents a change of course for the rural poet, but maintains his acute ear for the universality of human experience. These poems continue his lyric exploration of life and death, nature and technology, peace and war. Although there remain the themes of landscape and nature that will resonate with those familiar with his previous collections, Carruth continues to innovate with subject matter ranging from Mikhail Kalashnikov (inventor of the infamous, eponymous rifle – on record as wishing he had invented a lawnmower) to the last player of the North African Biram harp. Endangerment and extinction are the crux of most of the poems in this pamphlet. At first glance, this is a straight story with humanity cast as the principal villain. But closer examination rewards the reader with subtle undertones of human frailty and the approach of middle age. 'Dead Horse' is metaphorically flogged to death in a knowing, circular play upon the old cliché. While, in 'Straight Flush', a po-faced Great Auk raises Man in a deadly game of bar-room poker.

It is in these poems and in his confident detours into Scots ('The Promise of Ice Cream' and 'Bethlem') that Carruth's language and wit are at their freshest. However the first four poems of the collection, while a continuation of his pastoral past, lack some of the vibrancy of earlier work. The language here is a little less engaging and occasionally verges on the over-used, but this is a minor quibble in what is another excellent collection from one of the most interesting poets writing today.

Such is the manic energy in Stephen Nelson's new collection *Lunar Poems for New Réligions* that it is easy to get swept away in the stream of consciousness. The book is in two sections, the first of which, 'The Moon from my Windowless Heart', includes the two-part epic 'Look Up!'. Part incantatory mantra, part wild-eyed, drug-induced rant, the narrator of this poem channels Ginsberg, Coleridge, Blake and every other mind-tripping versifier in history in a rage against the machine of mainstream culture. At least I think that's what is happening, as the jist of the poem mostly gets lost in the wild voice of the narrator. This is perhaps intentional, but if so it is not consistently applied: at times a lucid, authorial voice intrudes, "interestin how drugs ir used these days / tae reframe the fractured psyche". This is a shame, because the poem has flashes of genius. There is a debt here to writers like Jim Ferguson, Tom Leonard and Graeme Fulton, but what is missing is the concentrated anger and forensic humour of those poets' work. A pity, because it has such potential to communicate.

The second section of the book, 'Crescent', is more interesting and artistically sustained. It contains a long series of playful, alliterative, sound-rich meditations on the moon, the sea and religion, with wordplay that ebbs and flows then intensifies to a pleasing crescendo as the sequence progresses. These are interspersed with imperative-laden, oblique, mystical prose poems that invite the reader to find his or her own meaning. Overall, this is a promising and refreshing collection from a poet who is not afraid to experiment.
Moby-Dick

Still Lives
Mary Thomson

1
I know a painting of a table draped with a cloth,
its crisp folds, I imagine, put there by a woman
who had scrubbed and wrung the thick stuff,
lifted its weight on to a hedge or line,

folded it firmly under strong forearms and
placed it on a pile scented with sun and air.
On it the artist placed dishes of tin-grey pewter,
a blue and white plate with
four nacreous oysters
and a cut lemon oozing a drip of sharpness.

Next to the knife which rests on the linen's fold,
there are painted pendants of overripe grapes,
downy peaches and pair of polished apples;
before the day's end the feast will be eaten.

2
I know women who have shelves heavy
with tablecloths they have never used,
embroidered with flowers in featherstitch,
stiff damask linen patterned with shadows.

Those tired cloths, so long invisible,
once brought out on high days for high teas,
laid with bone china and tiered cake stands,
have become a burden,
acquired rust spots and
a sorrowful smell of airlessness and dust.

When the women who cannot let them go are gone,
their precious cloths will be found draped
on towel rails which pretend to be mahogany
on stalls purporting to sell antiques.

as if

Larry Butler

no one can respond nor ask how you are
where you've been how long you've been away
how long you shower, which soap you use
did you shampoo your hair — no one will ask
if you like smelling fox, smelling nail varnish,
smelling dope or why you vanished suddenly
when your name was loudly called a joke
because you drank a cup of cold cabbage juice
while dreaming by an open window wishing
you were elsewhere on a hill above loch lomond,
snow filling gaps in your head — no one need know
how pleasure grows when you relax long enough
when you slow down — so slow your blood gells
and clouds whisper of brain cells in your belly.

Everything is in 3D
Graham Fulton

these days   everything is in 3D.
and Abraham Lincoln's scraggy abolition beard
is coming straight at my face,
and his kind weary eyes are right against mine
and his stove pipe hat
is like some kind of giant 3D stove pipe hat
and I'm being smacked around the mouth
by the lip-quivering words of the Gettysburg Address,
and I can't believe there was anything
before 3D,
I have to have the latest things   I have to exist
in 3D.
or I don't exist.
and you've got to be in 3D   you've got to
have the special glasses   you've got to
keep up   or people
will laugh as you walk around
in two dimensions   alive and
dead.
and the World Trade Centre
is collapsing in *comin'-right-at-ya* mega 3D
with the smoke and the girders
and the running people
more real than reality.
and the Hiroshima bomb is falling in 3D,
and the Joker cinema massacre humans
are screaming in 3D,
and Martin Luther King
is being killed *Live!* on a motel balcony in true 3D,
and John F Kennedy is being pronounced deleted in 3D
with his brains uploading out of the screen
in between a message from our sponsors.
and the Universe is expanding in 3D getting further and
further as far away as possible until it's gone altogether in
beautiful 3D, and everyone is 3D   these days.
I have to be in 3D,
it's the only way to be.

Pins and Needles to You and Me

Roy Patience

Wool went web-like
from the windows
to the table legs. Piano keys depressed
in places by screws
twisted in at odd angles
from which other lines of yarn
dissected the room.

The property itself
could only comfortably be entered
with the aid
of sharp instruments
forbidden by the proprietor; the lines
connected each other
to the ticking contraption above
the door frame; several feet
of household craft materials
and an electric meter,
to you and me.

But this was serious.
As serious as the woman
you knew as a patient, sectioned because
convinced she carried triplets
past full term by seven years,
convinced they must be cut out
of her belly by her own hand.

I remember your compressed-lipped smile,
its perfect balance of
compassion and ignorance.
And think, without sense
or proportion, of the foot I miss,
that feels like another
reality (imprisoned in paraesthesia) and of
the doctor's response
to my enquiry
concerning his terms: 'pins and needles
to you and me'.

'Home is the hunter, home from the sea...'
Andrew F Giles

Spectres of comfort were the only ghosts
he knew, the division of egos bound
in the eggshell of his parents' lovemaking—

Indian driftwood, Derby coal & bone,
spliced from their bodies & gently cloned
under cloudlight; their first time

coupling with the phantom oracle
of history. Their son would be a miracle
to them always. Still, the veins in the boy's arms

stood raised like hackles, genes tacked to him
like wet silk on a dressmaker's dummy.
Their child wore an exoskeleton

of intention. He misunderstood, mostly,
the attention his body paid to the world—
thought the inscriptions on his skin ornamental;

acted intimately, his bible of techniques.
He paid court to what looked like comfort:
the commandments of avatars,

the safe electricity of his name in lights,
red-blooded danger,
the watery blot of the world

& its mistral of change that curled through him
under the cunning of hash,
weak fire of generosity,

blunt shackle of night...
Sinuous, this misunderstanding - looked like summer,
the beauty of anywhere lit by sun.

Aphrodite Hikes Up Her Skirt in April
Janette Ayachi

The wind lifts my hair like a dreamy lover
sipping coffee steam into her throat

the same way trees and tenements inhale
fog so to shift into a brighter afternoon.

I have never been so alone in my life
my wrecking ball suspended from stars

my heart defibrillated down a dotted-line
a collector of dolls but no puppet master

rows of silicon and pixel no strings attached
just sacred myrtle and diaphanous mirrors

the only women that matter are the ones
I have to chase, a consequence of the sea

the empty boxes in the calendar remind me
that I still have so much space to fill.

Oscar in Autumn
Fran Baillie

They creh'd yi sweetie-wife, shirt-lifter an ponce,
ain wha stravaiged aboot the boulevardes,
chessies rennin doon aa roonaboot an
yirsel, lichtsome as a pig in shite,
weel chufft ti be alev in gay Paree,
 yir jecket deckt oot wi a green carnation,
 thon badge the laddies wore wi pride.

Ti Pere Lachaise Eh come wi a wee sumthin fir yi,
sclaff through chessie mast underfit
tae pit russet tulips on yir fantoosh grave
cuvert in lipstick kisses.
On ivry haidstane a singl conker,
pit there beh Christ-only- kens-wha,
mibbee a seed-sign o hope fir an efterlife.

Eh see yiz aa there. Yves an Edith
jynin in a wee sang thegither,
baith hoastin wi ower muckle bevvy an fags,
bonnie Jim strummin yit, and yirsel an Moliere
sharin a wee blague, joshin in French parfait.
Yiz aa left ahent yi words wi canna forgit.
Yir wisps o sangs an poetrie'll
bide in the haid, dig in thir heels
an'll jist no laive.

Tent Revival in Ozone Park

Andy Jackson

'I've tóld you time and time again, Sal, that we're buddies, and we're in this thing togéther. There's just no two ways about it. The Doſtioffskis, the cops, the Lee Anns, all the evil skulls of this world, are out for our skin. It's up to us to see that nobody pulls any schemes on us. They've gót a lót more up their ſleeves beside a dirty arm. Remember that. You can't teach the óld maeſtro a new tune.'

Jack Kerouac, *On The Road*

They pulled some schemes on us, yes,
but here we are, inheritors of the kingdom,
writing our own catechisms, suitcase full
of marital aids, blank notebooks, old 78s.

There's tunes out there for all us, I guess,
blacktop ballads and diner dirges. Sing 'em
and you're tuned to angels, bum notes and all,
hang around for your cue and it's a long wait.

Treat every day like it's the last, and head west
if you like your oranges ripe. Keep your income
close to your outgoings, enter any shortfall
in the ledgers. Pay your taxes to the state.

We're always dogged by unbelievers, but flesh
is just a vestment of the soul, and not the sum
of what we are. Are you willing to testify? Call
His name, raise your hand. *Amen.* It ain't too late.

Disinhibition in Aisle 32

Mark Russell

You're never quite sure when they will come,
those moments, but you know they're abroad,
like sounds you once heard on winds and wires,
scrapings on doorsteps, the stinging sweats

on your forehead. You prepare for it
as best you can: reading some of the books,
watching the news, going to the movies
(it's all the rage, you hear, without irony),
and listening, above all listening.

But there is nothing in your homemade bag
of insights that provides a strategy
to cope when your father drops his drawers
in Oils and Dressings at Tesco and weeps
oh god, not another year of wanking.

Three Versions
Martin MacIntyre/ Màrtainn Mac an t-Saoir

EL CUENTO CORTO PODEROSO

Así en ti lo breve es lo grande
La gran sorpresa escondida en varios estuches
Así en ti se grita en los huequitos más callados
que el mundo entero no se entiende
tan débil
ni siquiera se pinta con colores bien usados
por mi cuenta o la de mi se ora.

Pero que ahí, allá, a poca,
siempre a larga distancia,
el sentido de
tus mensajes
surge;
mueven
despiertan
comprimen
lo mucho no escrito
y que además
existe
la posibilidad de que
el sospechoso obvio
de veras
lo hizo,
pero en otro cuento,
el de mi más querido vecino.

CUMHACHD NA SGEÒIL SGILEIL

Mar sin annadsa is mòr an goirid
an ulaidh aoibhneach falaicht' an ioma seòrsa cist'.
Agus annadsa bidhear a' glaodhaich sna h-oiseanan as tosdaich',
nach gabh an saoghal gu lèir tuigsinn
an seòl cho fann,
is cha mhotha thèid a tharraing le dathan claona caithte
air mo shàillibh-sa no air sgàth mo mhnatha.

Ach a-sin, thall, faisg,
daonnan air astar,
brùchdaidh
susbaint
nad bhriathran;
gluaisidh,
dùisgidh
dinnidh iad
am bàrrachd mòr nach deach a sgrìobhadh,
is leigear cuideachd
gum faod e a bhith
gur e dha-rìribh
an caractar a b' fhasa a thomhas
a rinn an gnìomh,
ach ann an sgeul eile,
tè leis an nàbaidh bu treas' dhan tug mi an gràdh.

THE WELL-CRAFTED STORY

Thus in you concision empowers,
the quite unexpected hidden in various little compartments.
And in you cries are heard in the quietest locations
that life cannot be understood
insipidly
or painted with hackneyed colours,
on my behalf or for my wife.

But that there, yonder,
near,
always at a distance,
the sentiments of your messages
surge;
they move
awaken
exact
the great unwritten,
and yet permit
the possibility
that the obvious suspect
really did do it,
but in another story,
one belonging to the dearest of friends.

Extract from *Time Laid Up In Store*
SMJ Cook

I CARRIED THE pavlova through to the dining room table and set it in front of Clare. She cut it into slices and lay each on its side on a dessert plate. A stripe of audacious red at the top, then a fat layer of creamy white, resting on a slice of purer white. A beautiful union. But I was shaken by my encounter with Vye in the kitchen and I no longer felt equal to the pavlova. I refused a slice, but picked a raspberry off Daisy's plate.

Across the table sat the men from the presbytery, or the morality men, as I had decided to call them. They slackened their jaws at the sight of the pavlova, all the better to fit the enormous slice of meringue. Wasn't there an animal that could unhinge its jaw to fit in its prey?

My eyelids began to get heavy. I wanted to hold onto that sleepiness and slip away. Too much had already happened that day. Or hadn't happened. I needed to be alone to organise and file each thing away inside my mind for easy reference later, then drift away into an afternoon sleep.

So I experimented with not saying goodbye; just going outside the back door, as if stepping out for some air, and instead of going back inside, I slipped away through the trees into the soft afternoon and the sanctuary of my caravan.

I opened a window to let the breeze play on my face, lay down under my blanket and replayed the morning in my mind: me watching Clare put the roast beef in the oven, which now seemed like days, not hours ago, Clare telling me to play something different on the organ,

Clare herself reading the pornographic parts of *Song of Songs*, resulting in me playing Leonard Cohen instead of Bach in the church, as well as Peter seeking me out behind the organ pipes after the service and him almost doing to me what I had been waiting for him to do, for a long, long time. Then Vye coming in and stealing our time away. Then Sunday lunch, marred by the presence of the morality men.

I lay there, with the lingering taste of that single raspberry on my tongue, and closed my eyes and felt myself sink away, to the fading sound of mourning doves in the pine trees.

Too soon, stealing my soft time, someone knocked on the door. I sat up and peeped out of the curtain. I could still pretend I wasn't there, if I didn't like the visitor. It was Donald Stewart, the gayer of the two morality men. I sat in the silence, waiting. I could ignore him and he would eventually go away but I would be left wondering what he was coming to tell me and I might end up helplessly going after him, or, I could let him come into my caravan and shut the door and he would be trapped in here with me, like a fly in a spider's web. I promised myself not to harm him or, at the very least, not scare him.

I stood up, checked in the mirror that my afternoon nap hadn't dishevelled me irreparably and opened the door. He had tiny hairs growing horizontally from his ears and a speck of meringue still attached to the corner of his mouth. He still wore his suit. Slim trousers, I wasn't sure whether they were unfashionably narrow or whether his suit was simply the same one he had had since the 1970s. I wondered whether he was taking in my Sunday afternoon uniform of very old cashmere jumper, baggy cords and bare feet. I was proud of my feet. I thought I had rather elegant toes and just the right amount of dark hair growing on the tops of them. I put one foot out towards him and pressed myself sideways against the narrow doorway and affected what I hoped was an elegantly yogic warrior pose, to allow him entry. He didn't say a word but squeezed past me. His face come shockingly close to mine. I caught his scent: something dark that I couldn't name.

I thought I understood then what he had come for but I found out later I was wrong.

I didn't speak. I wanted to let him explain what he wanted, or rather, let him provide a pretext for his visit. I stood and waited, only in half-warrior pose, now, or maybe only thirty-seven per cent.

—Do you mind if I sit? he said.

—Have at it.

He sat on top of my blanket, where my dozing head had been minutes earlier. He still didn't insert into the silence the nature of his mission. I didn't think he was there for spiritual intercourse or fellowship. I resisted helping him out.

I didn't want to offer him anything, but he left me no option.

—Some tea? I said.

He looked relieved and grateful.

—That would be lovely.

—Where's your friend?

—You mean Victor? In the minister's study with him. Having a chat.

—A chat about what?

He looked out of the caravan window towards the graveyard and the church, away from the manse, maybe to distract my attention from the manse.

—That, I can't say, he said.

—Because you have no idea, or you're not at liberty to divulge the topic of the 'chat'?

I felt off-balance. Things were going on around me over which I had no control: Peter closeted away in his study with another man only hours after closeting himself away behind the organ with me. This other man, who was

with Peter right now, 'Victor Rose,' as he called himself, could probably still smell me on Peter, although he wouldn't know what it was he could smell, unless he knew about the flowers of the Spanish chestnut. And had this man sitting here in my caravan been sent to interrogate me about Peter's activities, or come to sniff out what percentage of me was gay or simply keep me away from Peter for a while, long enough for him to be interrogated by 'Victor'?

I lit the gas burner, dumped the kettle on top and flung some throat clearing into the silence.

I wasn't the one with much to lose here. I could still carry on being gay at the same time as being a church organ restorer. Peter, on the other hand, could lose his marriage for this adultery and his church for being gay. I wondered about that word, adultery. Do you have to be an adult to do it? I went over to my dictionary and looked it up to fill in the time the kettle would take to boil.

Adulterate: to debase, falsify, by mixing with something inferior or spurious. Had one of us mixed with something inferior? If so, which one of us could be said to be inferior? I was probably inferior in the religious, or spiritual sense, but Peter, well Peter had, in my opinion, been leading an inferior life to me; inferior in the gay sense. I was far superior at being gay.

I made us Lapsang Souchong tea, hoping Donald wouldn't like it. I suspected his favourite would be over-stewed builders' tea, tasting of darkness. I put the biscuit tin on the table between us but didn't open it and didn't offer him one, although I really wanted one. A post-nap cup of tea was depressing and wet with nothing to dip in it.

He closed his eyes, held his mug with both hands and lowered his head to take a sip of the smoky tea. He winced and made no comment, probably taking pride in self-mortification, squashing his own appetites and passions.

—You see, I, or rather *we,* know all about you, he said.

This chilling comment was probably in retribution for giving him tea he found impossible to like. I pretended he wasn't scaring

→

me and rolled my eyes, opened the biscuit tin and took one for myself.

—You do, Donald? I don't even know all about *mysélf*. Do tell.

I dipped the chocolate digestive into my tea, waiting just long enough for the chocolate to melt then lift it out before it was soft enough to birth itself away into the tea. I timed it wrong. Half my biscuit collapsed humiliatingly and sank to the bottom of my mug. The man was watching, and this ruined everything.

I got up to put some music on and give myself time to recover from the biscuit incident. What would be least soothing to a religious man, out to uncover 'inconsistencies' in others? A complicated Bach? A fugue with multiple layers, incomprehensible to the untrained ear. Yes, Bach *Variations*, soothing only to me. I hoped it would smoke him out, like that infuriating sound that Vye had forced out of the organ this morning.

I sat back down and noticed that this man had bags under his eyes, of a tender purple colour. Had they been there before or had Bach put them there? I felt a little bad. Or maybe it was the task set before him that put those bags there; the task of getting me to reveal myself, when he had the same 'affliction' as I had. I decided to make it a little easier for him.

—So tell me, what is it that you know all about?

If he was going to tell me something unsavoury about myself I could tune it out with Bach's logical layers of harpsichord from another century. It was pure and puritanical, yet with flowery trills. Plain, yet enhanced. This was more Sunday morning music, not for the afternoon. Afternoon music would be something Chopin-ish; something looser, explorative, reaching into unexplored corners of the brain and other senses; more French, less German. More *Une Dimanche a la Campagne*.

I hoped he didn't know what I had been doing with Peter right before lunch. Or maybe I hoped he did. Maybe he would want to go up there with me behind the organ and do some of it too. And I could ask him to overlook whatever information he had come up here from Edinburgh to gather.

He pushed his tea, then the tin of biscuits out of the way so that the only thing between us was a bare and narrow expanse of red formica table. He clasped his hands on the table and leaned towards me over the divide, rubbing one thumb back and forth over the other. Maybe he was nervous, or trying to encourage some of his blocked body heat back into his extremities. I wondered at the nature of his secret sorrows; what had happened to him to throw him so much out of balance? I hoped I wasn't the cause of any of them.

—The thing is, I, *we* have a proposal for you. An interchange of transactions. A communion, as it were. What we need you to do is gather, um...I'm not sure how to say this...

—...gather up my things and leave?

—Oh no no no, quite the opposite. We need you to stay here and do something else. Gather intelligence. Report back to us from time to time.

—Gather intelligence on what? Not Peter.

He sat back and studied me.

—Well, if you don't feel up to it, we'll have to go ahead and split Peter away from this parish. On the other hand, if you agree to help us, I could put a moratorium on our activity; our looking into you and Peter, I mean.

The reverberations of this last comment hung about in the space between us. I found that I wanted him to expose his 'hand,' show what he had to offer me.

—When you say, 'interchange of transactions,' what do you mean, exactly?

—You don't remember me, do you? he said.

I had no idea what he meant. Remember him from where? From lunchtime? Of course I did. I had met him only two hours earlier.

He reached for a biscuit, broke off a small piece and put it on his tongue, closing his eyes, partaking in a private chocolatey communion. Then he drank the rest of his tea, still with both hands around his mug. The taste had grown on him. Or maybe he didn't dare stop pretending to like it.

—You haven't seen me for years. You don't remember, but I was at university with you and Peter. I followed you from a distance. I wanted to be part of your group but you never let me in. Hardly even knew I existed. But I did, you see. I did exist and I still do and here I am on the presbytery. *Ergo*, I have Peter's fate in the palm of my hands.

I didn't want Peter's fate to rest in the palms of those clammy hands. Nor in the hands of someone who took joy from peppering his everyday speech with Latin.

A vague memory came to me of a pudding-fed boy-man hanging about on the fringes, watching us, waiting for something from us. Had we been cruel, or simply not equal to the turgid stew of emotion we sensed simmering within him? I felt suddenly very cold.

—What do you want? I said.

—Other than a decent cup of tea?

—Other than that.

—You see, I am on the committee that is deciding whether a minister can be, shall we say, of the homo*secksy*oual persuasion in the church. Our committee has two years to reach our findings, then to conclude and recommend.

The Bach variations in the background kept on varying in their strict flowery way.

—And what would this entail, this, um... intelligence-gathering?

—Let us know if his, shall we say, *secksy*oual preferences get in the way of his ministering, what you think the implications are. Is it interrupting his duties, his faith, upsetting his parishioners? Give us the information and we will consider this when looking at the theological issues.

I hated it when people used the word, 'issues.' What the hell did that mean, anyway?

—The old women love him, as do younger men. It's the older men, who are distant. Being gay isn't catching, you know, I said.

—Oh, I know, but it's the older men who complained to us. They think being ministered to by someone they think of as less of a man than they are is unseemly. *Res ipsa loquitur*, as it were.

I was desperate for an escape from this man who was now using Latin phrases incorrectly. I found I couldn't summon whatever it would take to correct him.

I looked towards the manse through the trees, and saw Peter and Victor emerge through the front door and shake hands. Peter was nodding his head. Maybe Peter had consented to gather information about *me*. Another mutual exchange of satisfactions.

It came to me what this man inside my caravan smelled of. He smelled like a Catholic. Sandalwood. Frankincense. Had he come from another, higher church service early this morning? In this church, that would be worse than being gay.

I wanted this man to go away so that I could either be alone to relive my morning or be with Peter and redo the morning. Remake it into a Sunday afternoon with a lover.

I got up and held my hand out towards the door. I didn't have the energy to use words to ask him to leave. But he sat there and finished the tea he was trying to pretend to like, watching me over the top of his mug.

Then he put his mug down, not on the coaster I had given him, but straight onto the red formica table.

He walked out. Then turned around and said he would be hearing from me.

—This would have gone better for you if you had remembered me, he said.

I grasped his hand to stop him leaving. I wanted to say something that would vindicate Peter. I also wasn't sure how much damage this man could do. His hand was clammy and I couldn't feel bones; only flesh. I wanted to pretend that I had liked him, make him think that us ignoring him at university was a figment of his faulty memory, that in fact, we had all been friends. But I didn't know how to say any of that.

—Look, none of this is Peter's fault. And next time you want to talk to me, come and find me at work on the organ, in the church. Please don't come to my caravan.

He looked at the ground, listening, and changed his mind about the direction he was going. He turned away from the manse and walked up the hill towards the village. He squashed whatever might be underfoot into a pancake with every step. Vye's cottage was the first one he would come to. I wondered whether he would knock on her door for a casual chat

➼

and a mug of proper dark tea. Vye would be happily sorrowful to give him whatever he wanted about me, but not about Peter. She would only tell him good things about Peter.

I left the door open and put on some 16th century madrigals, turned up the volume and lit my one French cigarette of the day to scare away the sticky air he had left behind. I hoped he wasn't a madrigal man. Didn't seem like one.

The Ground Beneath My Feet

Iain Maloney

YET ANOTHER SUCCESSFUL evening. We've been doing this long enough, got it down pat, could do it in our sleep.

Six years hard at it, sailing around resort islands putting on a gourmet evening. Special alcohol, special dinner. Keep the guests interested, give the chef a night off, give the resort a flavour of elegance, elitism, whatever it is that's sought after. Every year we change the menu, change the culture. Last year was Turkish. The year before was... Peruvian, I think. Maybe that was the year before that.

This year is Japanese. Five types of very expensive saké each served with an accompanying dish which perfectly compliments the spirit. $100 a head, thank you very much.

She's settling up, cash, receipts. Money in the bank. Business is booming. Woopty-doo.

It was all supposed to be a bit of fun. A way of seeing the world, travel paying for itself.

I take my glass of Sauvignon Blanc and what's left of the bottle out onto the beach. Sand between my toes, crushed shell and coral beneath my feet. The yacht is anchored out beyond the Over The Sea bar. *Woodstock* she's called. Christened by the retired wannabe hippy we bought her off in Manila. Recently I've rechristened her *Blue Monday*. That feeling I get when I see her from the beach, when I climb back aboard, haul anchor and set sail: Monday morning. Back to work.

The island is quiet, near the end of the season, the weather unpredictable. At the height this beach is full of honeymooning couples, wealthy families, executives on enforced vacations, laptops and briefing memos next to cocktails with umbrellas. Now I can only see a Chinese family noisily arguing in the bar, a retired couple walking hand-in-hand towards their villa and the staff preparing everything for breakfast.

Sink down, making sure there are no crabs under me, push my heels into the colder, darker sand. Sip of wine. The thought of going back out there. The circuit down the eastern edge of the Indian Ocean, through the Singapore Strait up to Hong Kong via the Philippines, the new resorts in Vietnam, Cambodia, Thailand, back through to the Indian Ocean to start all over again. Laps of Asia, like a race car looping again and again. Burning fuel but getting nowhere, always back to the start.

I just want to stop. Enjoy the world again. Experience something. Six years ago I'd never have guessed this would turn into another rat race.

We met in Sumatra, staying at the same hostel. A one night thing, then travel buddies, then a couple, then partners. Always another step. We're both trained chefs, earned our pocket money cooking here and there, got to know the owners, built a reputation. Then the yacht was available at a reasonable price, a businessman we'd catered for put up the capital and that was us in business.

We went wherever we could get a booking. As we became more sought after structure crept in. Two bookings a week, then three, sometimes four if the islands are close enough. One day I realised it'd become a job. We aren't cooking in order to travel: We're travelling to

⇥

cook. Some days we're in and out like a special forces team. Like the Seals, the SAS armed with saké and condiments. We arrive, cook, chat, laugh, clean, collect our cash – in US dollars if you don't mind – and are off the island before the date has changed.

I want to stop. I yearn for a bed on dry land. Our idea was to live the slow life. Do enough work to survive, live and travel, be free and see the world. If all you see are jetties and kitchens, if all you do is plan menus and study charts, exactly how much of the world are you really seeing?

The wind is picking up, the palm trees moving more excitedly, *Blue Monday* a weather vein, pointing out to sea. The monsoon is coming, storms more frequent. We'll keep heading east, outrun it, get through the Strait, change seasons. She checks the weather every few hours, our bookings following the expected course of weather fronts. We came here in the wake of one. Turn, I find myself praying to the god of storms. Turn. Shut off our escape, dash our plans on this perfect white shore.

It's not unheard of. Anyone who still denies climate change should try spending a week sailing around the Indian Ocean. Predicting the weather was never much of an exact science but now the system's been knocked about so much you'd be better of with the entrails of a goat. Rainy seasons last longer; don't come at all. Storm fronts heading west will do an about-face and race off east.

Every time we make landfall, I pray for this the way kids pray for a snow-day. Just a few days off. Please.

By the law of averages, I have to get a winner one day.

I wake to clanging and swell. She's already up, cursing the weather feed.

'What is it?'

'It's turned.'

'Are we stuck here?'

'Shit. Looks like it.'

Roll away so she can't see the grin. Thank you, Storm God.

'I told you we should've left last night,' she says. 'If you hadn't got drunk we'd be halfway there and able to outrun it. But you had to open another bottle.'

No point arguing. Can't let her see how pleased I am.

'So what's the plan?' I say instead.

'Well, we've got two options, either we cancel tomorrow's booking and continue with the schedule or we shift everything forward a day or two. Ideally I'd do the latter, that way we don't lose any money, but the logistics are a nightmare and I don't suppose I'll get any help from you in calling all these resorts. Also if we move the entire schedule we'll piss off every resort whereas if we only cancel one then we only piss off one resort. I hate cancelling though. All that money lost. Damn this weather.'

'It's only money,' I say before I can stop myself.

'It is only money, I agree. It's only money we need to live on. Only money that pays for the fuel, the ingredients, our life, this yacht. Only money that keeps us literally afloat. But hey, let's just pack it in, sit on the beach and drink.'

Not a bad idea. 'Spending a few days here won't put us out of business. We won't go bankrupt taking a holiday.'

'A few days? It had better not be a few days or we'll never be able to cover the distance to catch up with ourselves.'

I don't care.

'Have you spoken to the boss?'

'Not yet,' she says.

'I'll go and tell him we need to lean on his hospitality for a few days.'

'For a day at the most.'

'Until the storm passes.'

I could call the water taxi but I want to get off her. Dive in and swim until it's shallow enough to stand, wash the alcohol out my mind. When I reach the shore I see the boss coming down to meet me.

'Morning Charlie,' I call.

'Morning Nick. I was just coming to see you both.'

'Saved you the trouble. It seems we might

need to stay a day or two.'

'That's no problem, Nick. We don't think the storm will reach us, but it is sitting right across your path.'

'Well, c'est la vie.'

'Will this be a big problem for you?'

'We'll miss one booking, maybe two, but what can you do? Weather is an occupational hazard in our job.'

'True.'

'And there are worse places to be stormbound than here.'

'Well, all the facilities are at your disposal, meals, the gym and everything.'

'That's very kind of you, Charlie. And if we can help out in any way, don't hesitate to ask.'

Nothing to do. Wonderful. I take a stroll along the beach as far as the wooden fence separating the resort from the staff's residential area then cut inland. What to do with my day? Tennis? Swimming? I could snorkel, float for hours, rising and falling with the waves watching the fish getting on with fishy things. I could lie by the pool drinking smoothies, maybe the odd cocktail. I don't have to do anything. No schedule, no charts, no prep. Nothing.

This island is tiny and I cross it in under ten minutes. Here the beach is a little narrower, less picture perfect. There are no villas on this side, just the spa and gym and beyond that the Korean barbecue restaurant, both raised over the water. On the sand beneath the spa a man in the loose white pyjamas all the staff wear is doing Tai Chi. His graceful movements and slow shapes remind me of a stork in a rice field, or kelp in a soft current. I sit and watch him go through his routine. I learned a bit of Tai Chi in Hong Kong but never had the discipline. Like all my attempts at fitness. I get an urge to go to the gym, do some weights, run a bit and that's me for a month or two. It looks good though.

There's a light breeze and apart from the grey clouds breaking up the horizon no one would believe a tropical storm was raging out at sea. I could stay here forever.

'Good morning.'

The Tai Chi guy comes over. He looks South East Asian. Malaysian maybe, Singapore.

Even in his casual uniform I can tell his body is taut, ripped. Tai Chi isn't the only martial art he knows.

'It is,' I say. 'Perfect morning for Tai Chi.'

'It is always a perfect morning with Tai Chi,' he says. 'We shouldn't start the day out of balance.'

I don't think I've ever started a day in balance.

'I am Goh Seng,' he says.

'Nick,' I say. 'Nick Johansson.'

'You are the chef, shipwrecked on our island.'

I like the sound of that. Shipwrecked. Robinson Crusoe.

'I am. What do you do here?'

'I am a fitness trainer and masseuse.'

'I could've guessed,' I say, nodding at his hard body.

'You wish to use the gym?'

'Maybe later.' I pat my paunch. 'Not much for working out, me.'

'You eat well.'

'I eat a lot, if that's what you mean.'

'No. Your complexion is clear. Your stomach is the result of alcohol, not food.'

'I suppose so. Not so much junk food at sea. No sail-thru McDonald's.'

'So you don't wish to use the gym?'

'Not just now, thanks. I'm happy just relaxing. To be honest I haven't had a day off in a while.'

'Stressed? How about a massage?'

Charlie said the facilities are at my disposal.

'You're not too busy?'

'No,' he says. 'There are few guests today.'

'Well, if it's no trouble, I think a massage would be just what I need.'

A magician. A wizard. Like that, all my stress is gone. I felt awkward at first, naked save for the tiny paper pants, but he put me at ease. The table stands over a porthole in the floor, so as Goh Seng took my cares away I watched the marine life on the coral. His hands, the aroma, the music. Utter bliss. I could stay here forever.

I want to do something to thank him. Not a tip: That's empty. An urge to make a

➡➡

meaningful gesture, a desire to splurge, to give. What can I do? Well, there's only one thing I can do well. Cook.

It's quickly agreed. Charlie has no problems with my idea. I'll use the Korean restaurant, which is closed tonight, to make dinner for the resort staff. Two sittings, so those on duty can partake but nothing interferes with the paying guests. He's a bit hesitant at first but when I assure him the whole thing is at my expense, he loses all objections.

With my new-found energy I swim back out to the yacht and pull myself up. She's there, doing an inventory, tidying, unfolding and refolding charts. Filling time.

'Morning,' I say.

'Has been for some time.'

'You should come ashore. No point staying cooped up here all day. We're stuck, might as well enjoy it.'

'You know I hate these resorts. Elitist playgrounds, parasites. You know on the mainland a young girl just got sent to prison because she was raped? A fourteen year old girl and instead of arresting the rapists – yes, there were more than one – they charge her with adultery and lock her up.'

'You made the booking,' I say. 'If you don't like them, don't do business with them.'

'That's different. Business is business. But I don't want to become buddies with them.'

'That just hypocrisy. It's like a vegetarian owning an abattoir. "Meat is murder but business is business." It's nonsense.'

'You can be friends with rapists?'

'These people didn't rape her. You're going to tar them with the same brush?'

'Don't you dare. Don't you dare imply racism. This is not prejudice, it's about principles. Something a selfish oaf like you would know nothing about.'

'Selfish? How am I selfish. I'll show you how selfish I am: I offered to cook dinner for all the staff tonight, at my expense.'

'You did what?'

'I offered...'

'At your expense. You mean at our expense. Our money. Our time. Our ingredients. And you're going to waste it all on the staff? Besides, we might not even be here tonight. As soon as the storm moves on we're off.'

'No, we're not.'

'Yes, we are.'

'Look, you can sulk out here all day, bitter and grumpy, or you can try and enjoy yourself. I'm not asking you to help me tonight, I'm perfectly happy to do all the work, I'm just asking you to relax. Whether you like it or not we've got a day off and I sure as hell don't plan on wasting it. Now. Are you coming for a swim?'

'You can go to hell.'

I fill a bag with spices and return to the island. Five minutes alone with her undid all Goh Seng's good work. I need another massage. I need a drink. I need a change.

In the back of the restaurant I go through the stores, see what we have, start putting together ingredients, ideas. Textures and tastes, compliments and juxtapositions. It's a treat to be working on a full meal. These tasting evenings we do are all very well but at the end of the day it's just finger food and drinks. Nibbles. Delicious and perfectly balanced though they may be, the difference between that and a meal with courses is the difference between a pop song and a symphony. Sure *Can't Buy Me Love* is as perfect a tune as you're going to hear but it doesn't satiate the way Beethoven's 9th does. A quickie is fine, but sometimes you want to make love.

By early afternoon I have a fish-based menu and start making a G&T to celebrate when Goh Seng comes in. I gesture with the glass, offer him one. He shakes his head.

'Don't drink?'

'I like wine with my dinner.'

'Me too.' I open the gin bottle but something about the way he said that stops me. Maybe it is a bit early. Rescrew the cap and pour us both a grapefruit juice instead. We go outside and sit on the steps, looking across the island.

'You worked here long?' I ask him.

'Two years,' he says. 'Before I worked in Thailand. Before that Singapore.'

'You're from Singapore?'

'Yes. You?'

'Christchurch, New Zealand. Have you been?'

'No.'

'How did you become a masseuse?'

'I did Tae Kwon Do. I was in the Seoul Olympics, but there aren't many jobs for retired Tae Kwon Do players. I became a fitness instructor, a masseuse, many odd jobs. You've always been a chef?'

'Yes. I didn't get many qualifications at school. Got a job in a restaurant washing dishes, went to catering college.'

'And now we both wander from job to job.'

'Island to island.'

'Yes.'

'You're coming for dinner tonight?'

'I thought maybe you would like some help in the kitchen. Or is three a crowd?'

'Three?'

'Your wife.'

'She isn't my wife.'

'Oh.'

'I don't think she'll be there tonight. She's... she's not so well.'

'So maybe you need a hand?'

'That would be handy.'

Goh Seng goes back to work. I return inside. That was weird. Where did that stupid pun come from? I wash the glasses, look around the kitchen. I'm all set. Nothing to do until it's time to light the grills. A drink? No, not the right mood. Then what? I feel like some exercise.

Back on the yacht I pack a bag for the gym and for tonight, fresh clothes, my toiletries. She's asleep. I leave her. Go for a run.

The dinner is a hit. It's awkward at first, the staff used to waiting on people, not being waited upon, but the food goes down well and soon everyone relaxes. A restaurant filled with laughter, the sounds of cutlery, people enjoying each other's company. I miss this. At the end everyone thanks me, pats on the back, happy faces, content stomachs.

'Thanks for that,' says Charlie. 'The staff loved it. Everyone works hard here, it's nice to give them something back.'

'No problem,' I say. 'I live for this. I'd do it every night if I could.'

'This? Can't imagine you'd swap what you've got for this? A different island every few days. A free spirit. No nine to five, no working week.'

'I don't know. I've been doing it a while. You know what they say, a change is as good as a rest.'

'Well, if you're serious, our head chef is leaving at the end of the season. I'd be happy to offer you and your wife jobs here.'

'She's not my wife.'

'Oh.'

'No, we're...it's just business. Are you serious about the job?'

'I don't want to get in the middle of anything. But yes, we need a new head chef. Have a think about it.'

Yachts aren't meant to be viewed from the back. They never look particularly impressive from that angle. The classic images of ships are never from the stern. The cruise liner majestically sliding passed crowds of admiring flag-wavers. Tall ships of wood and rope riding the waves on journeys of exploration. Aircraft carriers seen in a flyover, toy planes lined up on the deck. I guess the only time you see it stern-first is in movies like *Mutiny on the Bounty* where there's a shot from the perspective of those set adrift in the longboat, watching the *Bounty* sail away.

Sailing away.

The stern of *Blue Monday* really is ugly. I've never seen her from this angle before. I've always been onboard. Now she's up there by herself, charts and instruments and I'm here, no more at sea, watching the arse of that yacht waddle away like a fat woman in low-slung pants.

I turn away, pad barefoot along the jetty to where Goh Seng is waiting. His hands are clasped behind his back in placid readiness. On some people – on me, I guess – that pose makes them look pompous, like some aging major standing at the edge of a ballroom, but on Goh Seng it's dignified. Maybe it's the Tai

➤

Chi. Balanced mornings. He can teach me.

As we walk between the palm trees, hermit crabs fleeing our steps, he is silent. I can't get the image of her sailing away out of my mind. Did I make the right decision? To trade in the yacht, the island hopping for a job here. The same place for a couple of years. I've a lot of money sunk into that yacht. I wish he'd say something. His mild, calm voice might blow the storm away.

Tam and Linda

Frances Corr

THERE WAS A whoosh and a squawk as three big gulls came right up at the window fighting over a bit of toast.

Tam rarely took breakfast in the morning. Only the longtime habit of three rollies in quick succession as he came round amidst swirls of blue smoke, fixating occasionally on his mobile. Tea was the timekeeper. By the time two cups were drunk he was ready and would fold his baccy, papers inside, and do the dance of pocket slapping for keys, lighter, specs and dosh.

Linda wasn't pleased this morning as she didn't have the right colour of pants. You always get a naff colour in a batch, she noticed. Same in socks. Certainly they were a comfy pant, the grey. Comfier than some of the happier colours she'd chosen which, to her chagrin, proved to have little in the way of give. Selling themselves shamelessly, they took advantage of the enchanted in full knowledge that their binding was unyielding.

Strong pishing sounds came through the bathroom wall alongside the singing of a Johnny Cash number. Tam emerged from the bathroom pulling up his fly. Grabbing Linda, he bade her farewell and the day took him happily out the door. He had a tyre to see to. A fine morning for firing on a spare.

Linda contemplated the kitchen. At the back of the flat, it was the last room to receive decoration. The thought of it made her body feel like lead. The kitchen, impractically slim, did not feel like the engine of the house. If that was the engine then the vehicle was reluctant to start and was merely taking up a space. It could be clamped and removed. Different story then, she thought, as she saw herself animated, arms out and shouting obscenities through a gaping chasm into the close.

There were two holes where the microwave had been in a wall that Linda found hard to look at, as was the tube of quick drying filler which claimed ready to decorate in minutes. Aye, *it* might be, she responded and poked at the holes which were worse than she'd thought. Various blues, bits of filler and someone else's wallpaper. She left the tube on its side and wandered out with all the lazy bastard insults her mind could conjure, coming at her like gunfire.

She'd taken some cuttings from her Crown of Thorns, preparing a pot first each time so the brutal part would be over swift. Simple scissors had done the job. She'd been aware of her heart withheld as she performed the deed, but the plant gave little resistance, despite branch rather than stem. Inside it bled thin milk as she shoved the severed limb into the new pot, firming compost round it in the hope of comfort for it and her.

There were several babies she kept in a huddle for security close under the branches of their mother. She didn't want any of them to feel like she had done on her first day of school. There was little worry for the mother however – there was plenty of her. Whilst Linda felt repelled by the amputation sites there was so much new activity all around, triumphant, abundant and gloriously bendy green that she saw little point in feeling disgust.

It dawned on Linda that she was now

the mother. From here on it was herself who would provide the nourishment for these newly singular creatures, for they were no longer branches of the whole. Sustenance would no longer be provided to them via the stout arms of their biological mother. O God what have I done.

They were doing a job in a designer womenswear shop, laying in pipes and lowering a ceiling. As Tam arrived the early morning wisecracking had begun, set off by a notice advertising a colour co-ordination service. Jokes ricocheted around the walls about matching toolbags and vans, then, in a rare moment of frivolity the boss passed by with a pair of knickers on his head, priced at forty pounds, igniting uproar and hilarity amongst the workforce.

—Aye they pants are worth mair than ma tools.

—What're ye talkin about yir tools, they're worth mair than yir van ya cunt.

Outside the owner stepped from a two hundred and fifty grand car, his wife sporting a rock. On entering the shop Tam noticed an unexpected look of longing showing on the man's face as he absorbed the scene, eyes honing in on hands working tools, and tools working wood. Tam surmised it had been a long time since the man had held a screwdriver. His wife, chatting to the men, was unaware of their leg pulling as she offered them special deals on four hundred and fifty pound dresses for girlfriends. Knowing Linda's lack of time for the designer dress, Tam was amused at the idea and pulled one out.

—What about that one, he suggested to his workmates.

—Eh? What d'ye think?

—Aw aye that's lovely, they agreed. That's the one.

Meanwhile Linda sat in a combination of night and daywear near a form that was to be filled. Forms had a similar effect on her as the holes in the kitchen wall. She struck a deal with herself that she would at least pick it up and look at it. It asked all about her and what she did in the day and how many times a day she did it and

how many times in the week, and the month and whether she showered. Linda wished to hell that she could state the truth of the matter – that the sight of this form made her ill.

By the front window she dreamed of a realm where things undulated in a pleasing way and see-through characters gently bobbed with no malice. Creatures that could slither out from the grip of forms, dissolve in the face of such demands as name, address and national insurance number.

Beyond the window and street many sat in rows at computers for a living whilst buttercups and dandelions made their way through any crevice they could find.

That evening, a suggestion Tam had heard about how noodles could fool the belly was overruled by a weakness for burger and chips. Disappointment set in. In need of consolation he headed out, returning a short while later with a polystyrene helicopter.

So excited was he that he requested some time alone with it. Linda lay in the bath listening to the buzzing and the dunts through the wall as it hit the skirting. And his shouts of joy when it survived intact every time. Its light body caused no harm to itself or anything else. Tam's system ran with adrenaline as if this was it. Life's triumph at last.

Viewing herself horizontally, Linda remembered what it was like to have a baby in her belly and how special it was when the little person came out and looked at you. They had been you too but suddenly no longer when the cord was chopped. Almost like looking at yourself. Wrapped in tin foil from the neck down she'd watched a worn out nurse upturn her baby, and measure him heel to head in a ward whose days were numbered and whose sheets had run out.

There was a clattering in the corner. One awkward crash too many and the tail had acquired a twist. From then on the helicopter went in circles.

Outside, the pavements all chewing gum and moon sparkle, were quiet. A taxi passed in front of three sweepers in luminous jackets and a fairy seed curved in the other direction.

The next day as Tam was leaving, his heart opened when he remembered he was going to have two fried eggs on granary loaf for his dinner. Overwhelmed with amor he reached to clasp Linda. After he'd gone Linda got out the step ladders and put them in the kitchen beside the tin of paint, then put them all away again. The tube of quick drying filler had hardened. With a strange cocktail of regret and relief she pressed it a second time just to make sure.

Couldn't have put the top on right, she thought. Some air must've got in. Regret caused denial, and she put it back down as if another day it might be fine.

The phone rang. It was someone called Andrew who talked to her like he knew her and told her of a chance to win a kitchen in a prize draw. Only yesterday the recorded voice of a non-person asked if she was in the process of looking for a mortgage. Another day it was debt management. A great heat surged up in Linda's body as she put down the phone. It's not like you could even fit a kitchen in that kitchen, she muttered, passing the door to see what trash was shoved through her letterbox. From the kitchen cupboard she lifted out a packet of porridge oats. 'Easy open' it boasted. She took a knife to it and stabbed the fucker.

Linda sat at the front window with a pile of toast. Looking behind the thorns, she could see the newstarts line up in the school across the road. Hand in hand, their backpacks were bigger than their small backs. The sound of the bell still made Linda's insides shudder – she'd always felt cold in socks and oddly exposed in the school skirt. Now every morning she gave thanks that she no longer had to go to there. There was intermittent dashing in new bags and shoes, with much pink around the girls. It never failed to amaze her how young they seemed. Babies in schoolbags about to enter the world of queues and official shouting. Their parents nervous about the transition knowing their child's every mood and movement was now in someone else's hands, lost among all the others.

There was the sound of the key in the lock. It was Tam. A dod of muck from the sole of his steeleys was trailed about the house. His posture suggested anger.

—Well that was a complete waste o time, he ranted, waving and pointing. The boss's goin mental. He's doin a fuckin wardance outside the building. Fuckin painters. Got all the way doon there and the painters never showed up. Linda missed the odd syllable as she was still eating toast. Tam continued.

—They'll be for the high jump. They were given the keys cos they were supposed to be doin a shift this mornin.

—Oh, said Linda. She noticed that his jumper was on inside out. Ticket straight out the back of his neck.

—He's a grumpy bastard, he said of his boss. Growlin like a bear in the mornin. Ah know his back's fucked. Ye can see his spine's curved tae wan side. Workin like a bastard for the day he'll be aff the tools.

—There's loaf in there, suggested Linda, if ye want to make a piece. But Tam was on to next week. They would be putting a ceiling in a morgue.

—Ah'm no daein it if ah haf tae shift corpses, he protested, and disappeared again.

Out the window it was playtime. A girl fell. Quickly she was surrounded by others. They huddled round then marched off purposefully as one, to report, faces bent into that of the limper.

That night Tam slapped his belly and announced that he'd lost some weight so he was going to get some pakora. Perusing the viewing Linda came upon baked naked people grabbing each others bits like they were made of rubber and staring into the camera with worrying expressions. A telly channel uninvited.

—Cheeky bastards man, was Tam's response on his return, putting down his pakora for a minute. Linda sat by his moving jaw while together they ran through the menu on the screen in order to deal with the unwanted invasion.

—Piece o piss, said Tam.

—Piece o piss, agreed Linda.

Delete forever? asked the screen.

➻

—Too fuckin right, they said.

The following morning Linda performed the morning swivel and aimed her slippers in the direction of the kettle. Tam had already left. Today the only post a curry leaflet.

Over by the front window, flat planes of leaves worshipped the sky. Plants did not think twice about shooting aloft flowers in colours often vivid without a hint of self doubt. They had no need for *Télévision X*, but only stayed in heaven cheering positions. No plant looked at its watch nor had a care for the narrow concept of time that others held supreme.

Linda found herself hovering around the two holes in the kitchen. She stuffed newspaper into them. Then approached the tube of wood filler. Squeezing, she noticed it was mainly soft but nothing would come out no matter how hard she squashed it so she cut it in half with a pair of scissors. Inside there was plenty, stones of hard bits but plenty. Scooping nonchalantly with her finger she fired a dod into the paper filled holes, then proceeded to amble around the flat seeing holes and their stories she'd not noticed in ages. For a moment Linda could see herself as if from outside, and her arm moving, like this was a different Linda from the one that she knew.

It was early hometime for the newstarts. A flock of doos shifted excitedly from roof to roof. A swarm of adults and children filled the playground, then gone.

One day white paint was on the kitchen wall. The cuttings had sent out a cluster of leaves in all directions patterned with light and shade. Life had finally begun to move again through their traumatised limbs. The natural mother, on the whole looked pleased shooting out pairs of flowers that brought joy to Linda's sternum. Bent over, the weakest cutting had its two original leaves and two small new ones which seemed to be in sleep – still alive but not grown. There was a flower. Red and rubbery it echoed those of its mother.

Shoals of tiny fairy seeds hung in the air before flying off. The sky was full of beautiful sweeps and puffs.

That night Tam was speaking and at the same time eating a bun. It was a phenomenon. The sound of his voice seemed to actually travel through the bun at the front of his face, coming through the cream and then out in a strange distortion. He was trying to tell Linda that he'd had tatties instead of chips so he got himself a bun.

When he was finished he tapped a rhythm on the side of his plate.

—Underfloor heatin's come right down in price, he said, re-settling contentedly with the latest Screwfix catalogue.

—O aye, said Linda. What've ye got next week?

—Five hundred stair nosins, he replied.

That's good, said Linda, moving over to the window. She opened it, looked out to the night sky and breathed moon air.

On a midden 'mang the thristles
Andra McCallum

on a midden 'mang the thristles
on coals sleekit wi smirr
twa aungels dwall

ilk ither's wings they preen
ilk ither's een they kiss
waitin sowans nicht

naur by – a bonnie bairn
an naeb'dy can jalouse
wha's owreseein wham

the aungels wad haigle the wean
intil heiven's gairden ony time
buit god winna hae it

syne – the yuil comes an gaes

on a taigle o fochten tree an
haiselt orange huil –
twa aungels an a bairnie
wi a yuilsang in its nieve

The Soothmoother borrows a scythe
Colin Will

Let the blade's weight
do the work. If the edge is keen
the cut slices the sward,
folds it over into a flat parcel
of meadowgrass and herbs.
Keep whetstone and water
tied to your belt.

Grip the handles on the snath,
swipe low, twist from the waist,
keep arms locked and knees loose.
Skim, step forward, skim,
step forward, the rhythm
drives a flat swath
across the field. How it's done
creates a frame of forces, focused
on the cut line moving on,
and the sweet smell
of mown hay.

A Soothmoother is a Shetland term for an incomer

Tionndaidhean air Cuspairean le Kundera/ Variations on Themes by Kundera

Peter Mackay

AN LEUGHADAIR

Cha robh sgot againn
gun robh cuideigin
ann am preas caorainn
air cnoc Petrìn
a' spleuchdadh oirnn –

luchd-turais nar sìneadh
a' dàir san fheur,
a' brodadh a chèile, ag abaich
's a' spioladh leolaichinn –

gus an deach an spaistear seachad,
mar nach canadh e smid gu brath mu a leithid.
Cho fad 's as fiosrach leis
chum sinn oirnn gu dubh.

THE READER

We hadn't the faintest
there was someone
in a rowan bush on Petrìn
watching us –

tourists stretched out,
fucking on the grass,
fingering each other, ripening
and plucking at globe-flowers –

until he sauntered past,
looking as though he'd keep schtum
forever. For all he knew
we kept on till dusk.

An t-Ògmhios ann an Vác
Crisdean MacIlleBhàin

Mìos còisir mhòr nan eun aig ceithir uairean
sa mhadainn, mìos drùidheadh a-steach na grèin'
san fhlat, 's a gathan mar mheòirean, a' sireadh
àite pàirteachadh nan cùirtean, gus an tarraing
air falbh bho chèile, 's iad cho tan' a-cheana!

Mìos fosgladh gu farsaing gach uile uinneig, mìos
eadar-dhealachadh cudromach na teòthachd
eadar an taobh a-staigh 's an taobh a-muigh,
an aon sheòmar a tha againn a' fantainn
beagan nas fionnaire air fad an latha,

ach, mu fheasgar, a' tòiseachadh a' leigeil
na chruinnich e dhe theas a-mach don adhar.
Mìos cadal ciùin na margaid, 's meadhan-latha
a' dlùthachadh oirnn, gach mosgladh nach fheumail
ga sheachnadh, ach am fear a reiceas mìl

cumail fair' airson ceannaiche no dhà.
A' mhìos shubh-làireach, shiristeach, ach feumaidh
neach a' feitheamh ri làn-abaichead
nan apracot, no gus am bi gach peitseag
'na siansadh singilt', air a chur ri chèile

le ùghdar diofaraicht', na blasan uile
a' spreadhadh eadar mullach a' bheòil 's an teanga
cho luath, do-bhacaidh, is nach fhaighear cothrom
air an aithneachadh no ainmeachadh!
A' mhìos is ìomhaighean de chloich nan naomh

baroque tha rangaichte air cuilbh na plàigh'
air gach còmhdach geamhrachail a bh' aca
leigeil dhiubh. Gabhaidh deàrrsadh na grèin'
a mhealtainn fhathast leò cho fad 's nach fhàs i
loisgeach, garg mar a bhitheas anns an Iuchair.

Sa mhìos ud, bidh an teas a' cuimhneachadh
gach pian do-fhulang a thachradh air sràid
am martarachd 's an glanaidh. Ach a-nis
is stèidhicht', ciùin an còmhradh-san, an guthan
cha mhòr nach urrainn do chluais dhaonn' an cluinntinn.

A' mhìos, is sinn a' teàrnadh air an *gang*
gu ruig na h-aibhne maill, sam mothaichear
gu grad do dhraoidheachd làin an teile mhòir:
dh'fhàs a duilleagan nas duirch', is tha i
air a flùraichean a leigeil sìos,

a' dol 'na factaraidh dhe mhìl, 'na teampall
uain' is buidh' dhe chùbhraidheachd, nach lìon
monmhar nan cailleach dubh a tha ri ùrnaigh,
ach crònan mìltean sheilleanan ag obair.
Mìos an t-suidhe chofhurtail sa cheàrnaig,

aig cafaidh bheag nach eil fada bhon eaglais
is neul no dhà a' cruinneachadh mu chrìch
an lèirsinn, air cùl mullaichean nan taigh
a chaidh an togail san ochdamh linn deug,
mar actairean a' fantail gus a' mhòmaid

cheairt san fheudar nochdadh air àrd-ùrlair,
sa chamhanaich, an uair a thig stoirm bheag
le uisg' a dh'ùraicheas na càbhsairean.
Mìos nan coiseachd sèimh ri taobh an Duna
mun àm a thèid a' ghrian, 's i dearg, am falach

air cùl nam beanntan ròmach, uain' mu thuath,
far a bheil lùbadh mòr san aibhn', is crìoch
nan Slòbhagach. Nas fhaisge air a' bhaile,
cho luath 's a thèid a' phlanaid às an t-sealladh,
fàsaidh gnùis nan uisge deàlrach, bàn,

mar gum b' e teàrmann màirnealach an latha
a bh' innte, air neo teisteanas, no cuimhne
air an leus tha gèilleadh ris an oidhche.
A' mhìos 's na gobhlain-ghaoith' ag itealaich
air bhoile ann an ciaradh mall nan speur,

's a liuthad a mheanbh-chuileagan rim faighinn,
os cionn strì fhearachail na h-aiseige
an aghaidh 'n t-srutha, gus bruach chian a ruigheachd.
'Na dèidh cha shiubhlar gu àite sam bith,
oir cha bhi ceann-uidh' eil' ann ach an leabaidh.

June In Vác
Christopher Whyte

Translated by Niall O'Gallagher

Month of the great dawn chorus at four
in the morning, month when the sun bursts in
to the flat, its rays like fingers, seeking
the place where the curtains meet, to pull them
apart (though they are so thin already!)

Month for throwing each window open
wide, month of the vital differences
in temperature, between indoors
and out, our only room remaining
a little cooler throughout the day

but in the afternoon it begins to yield
the heat it gathered up out to the air.
Month of the sleepy market as midday
comes ever closer, where each unneeded
stirring is avoided, but the honey seller

keeps an eye out for a customer or two.
Strawberry month, cherry month, though we must
wait for the apricots to ripen
fully, until each peach becomes
a perfect symphony all of its own,

composed by different hands, all the tastes
bursting between the palette and the tongue
so quickly, unstoppably there's no time
to recognise or name them separately!
The month when baroque saints, cast in stone,

set out on the plague column have given
up the wintery covering each one wore.
They can still enjoy the shining sun
while it hasn't yet begun to burn
angrily as it does in July.

In that month, the heat reminds them of
each unbearable pain that happened on
their *via crucis*, where they were purified.
But for now their talk is quiet, fixed,
in voices human ears can almost hear.

The month in which we go down the *gang*,
towards the lazy river, where you
become aware of the great lime tree's
enchantment: its leaves have grown darker,
and it has shed its flowers, become

a honey factory, a green and
yellow temple of perfume, not filled
by the murmur of praying nuns, but by
bees in their thousands busy working.
Month of sitting at ease in the square,

at a little café not far from
the church, a cloud or two gathering
on the horizon, behind the roofs
of the eighteenth-century houses,
like a troupe of actors waiting in

the wings, for their cue to walk out on the stage,
in the twilight, when a brief storm comes
with water that renews the walkways.
Month of quiet walks beside the Danube
around the time when the red sun goes

to hide behind the green and awny mountains
to the north, where the great river changes
course, towards the Slovak border. Nearer
the town, as soon as the planet fades from view,
the face of the water shimmers white,

as if it were the day's tardy protector,
or a testimony, or memory
of the light yielding unto the night.
Month of the swallows flying frantically
as the sky slowly beings to darken,

with so many midges in the air,
above the manly struggle of the ferry
against the current to reach the far bank.
In its wake there's no more travelling
as bed becomes our only destination.

The Falkland Burn

Mandy Haggith

is a babbled ballad from the bens
an ingle-ingle ootle-ootling thing

it's a symphony of plops and drips
all liquid linguistic fingerings

it's a long strong song
singing of springs mingling

Granite
Ewan C Forbes

GRANITE IS A cruel stone. In summer it sparkles in the bright light of the sun. But if it's bright already, do we need it to? In winter we could use the sparkle, but in the damp and in the dark the stone offers us nothing but shades of suicide grey. Town planners of old tried to offset this effect with greenery. There was too little then to do anything but highlight the grey, and now the green is being removed. Trees do not earn money, nor can they pay to remain where they are. So the granite wins.

#

When we moved here the weather was glorious. Buildings sparkled as we drove to our new house.

'The silver city,' Paul said. I don't know if he'd heard that somewhere or if it just came to him. I agreed.

We'd been happy then, that summer. Everything was new and exciting. Summer never lasts as long as it should. It was in the autumn, when the grey consumed the green, that Paul started going on his walks.

#

Granite contains ten to twenty parts per million of uranium. This is considered an amount high enough to worry over and low enough not to do anything about. There are many things like this, so many that if you added them all together the cumulative stress generated is probably the greatest health risk. We still worry about the granite, but now we add stress to the list too.

#

'It will be better after winter.' That's what he'd said, when I could get him to talk. All conversations we started dried up quickly, leaving a bitter taste. Then Paul would go out for a walk and I'd sit and read, or watch TV. Mostly I'd think about how little I really knew Paul.

#

The last place I lived was built of soft stone. One of the things I had to get used to here was the lack of scaffolding, the buildings here are hard. They defied almost all but the most utilitarian of masonry, yielding only to occasional aesthetic flourishes and in so doing highlighting only how hard the stone was in the first place. And once it's up, it stays up.

#

Sometimes, I think I started in mid-spring, I'd follow Paul on his walks. There are some beautiful buildings in the city, but Paul never walked past them. There are some lovely parks, but at night they aren't well lit. I wouldn't want him walking through there at night, but he never did. As I trailed his steps, always behind a corner just out of sight, I'd see that we walked only through the streets that made up the bulk of the city. Nondescript houses, streets of dead or dying shops, and construction sites for uninteresting buildings yet to come. It was as if he'd taken a travel-guide and selected places to walk through based on the *lack* of merit.

Whenever I followed him, I would always leave for home before Paul. His walks would take up most of the evening and, after the initial thrill, I would soon lose interest. He'd come home and I'd ask how it had been. I never got an answer that could explain anything.

➤➤

Sometimes, I'd think of the city and imagine Paul's travels being drawn out in dotted red, like in those old films. I'd imagine it tangling and overlapping until all the least exciting places were blocks of deep and violent red. Little islands of what gives a city its character were diminished and dominated by the red. Sometimes, if I thought about it long enough, I wouldn't think about Paul. Without his dotted red line, all that was left was grey.

I liked to go into town. I liked seeing crowds and hearing the noises of the city. I enjoyed being in the shadows of buildings that, despite their stubbornly unyielding exteriors, had a beauty that Paul's city lacked. The people have come to reflect the granite; their faces are stony and unyielding. Like the granite, they are not going anywhere. But they carry with them in groups a vibrancy that is hard to see in the individual walking empty streets. There's music. It's not good, but it's there. Buskers playing easy covers: you forget you like it until it's gone. I'd say three quarters of liking a song is knowing it, you learn that when you're abroad. Then here's the bustle and interaction of people meeting each other, little bursts of recognition full of smiles and surprised hellos. It's only when other people are involved that a person's face really comes alive; without interaction, you see only the vacant stare of the autopilot. That's the only face I saw on Paul, even when we were talking.

Paul never gave off any bad signals before we married. He was a perfect gent. I never really got to know him though, not then and definitely not later. In the end, I don't think he even knew I was really there. I'd ask him why he would rather walk away his free time than spend it with me, or why he never went any place nice. He'd mumble something incoherent then walk away, not even acknowledging that I knew where he was going every day.

I left him a while after the first year. I told him I was going, but he didn't react. He never reacted properly to anything. His face, his personality, it was like the granite; cold and unyieldingly devoid of features that gave any character away. Sometimes I think of him, walking empty streets in areas where nothing interesting ever happens. I wonder what he's thinking, or even if he's thinking at all. He's as much a part of the city now as anything else, when I remember him it's as that. Like the trees that serve only to highlight the grey, he has too little left of him to do anything but get swallowed up.

Cydonia

Stewart Thomson

HIS NAME IS Rob, the mutterer with the spectacles and the *how ya goin'*. He waits with us in the morning for our lift to the school. He's worked for Roger before he tells us, good bloke, won't fuck you around. We nod, none of us really ready for conversation at such a ridiculous hour. But Rob likes to talk. He talks about travelling, hitchhiking around the country on his own, odd jobs here and there. He's passed through Katherine many times; it's a little spot he likes. We'll have to see the gorge, he tells us, Katherine Gorge, beautiful. I nod and sniff, drinking my coffee and smoking my cigarette. A moment of silence finds us. Rob takes off his spectacles and cleans them against his green t-shirt. We sit and stand, breathing in the morning. It's beautiful at this time, the sky barely blue, a star still there, the sun just starting his shift, ready to roast the coolness from the morning air. But we've got the jump on him, a few more breaths of cool before he catches us. We're tired and faced with work, but six in the morning is beautiful.

Eventually a pickup rolls by with Roger's son at the wheel, introducing himself with a grunt. We climb in the back and we're off, drifting through Katherine, the wind rushing the sleep from our eyes. Twenty minutes later and we're at the school, a great metropolis of regrettable architecture and beige. Others are gathered, backpackers like us, kicking dust and smoking cigarettes, waiting for the army to assemble. And so we join them, Rob still at our side, our new friend it would seem.

Roger eventually appears in his van with another son and enough cleaning products to erase mankind. He delivers a well-practised speech about the importance of cleanliness and teamwork, the battle against grime and time. The foreigners nod, pretending to understand. We're designated our areas and thrust weapons of mops and industrial detergent. Our group is split, I'm sent with two Dutch girls to clean windows in the east wing exterior. I imagine they speak perfect English but they don't say much, barely acknowledging my hello. They stick close together, as if wanting to be closer. One of them is a little pretty, the other not a lot. I wonder if they are lesbians.

As the sun rises higher and the morning melts towards noon the school starts to stink. It's subtle at first, a whisper of rotten flesh on the warm air, hiding behind soap and sinking black tarmac. The lesbians notice it too, I see them scrunching their noses and muttering exclusively. I clean the windows and try to ignore it. The job's not so bad really. It's outside so I can smoke cigarettes and take breaks to look around at my surroundings. Beyond the school is nothing but dust and bush, a wasteland of red and creeping poison. It's so vast and empty that the eye struggles to gain purchase, slipping helplessly around the landscape like ice.

We'd stood on Ayers Rock the day before last, or Uluru as we're now calling it. Not supposed to climb it someone had told us, an Englishman in a campsite with long dirty hair and a skinny, pretty girlfriend from Denmark with bony little toes with painted black nails. Would you

➥

climb on a cathedral? he asked before turning back to the kiwi fruit he was peeling with a Swiss Army Knife. The girl was already eating hers, nodding and slurping it down like green caviar, blasé she screamed in silence. What a couple. Let us drown in your sophisticated quicksand and be reborn as beautiful as you.

So we climbed it. Under a million burning suns we crawled to the top of that ancient rock and stood atop its peak like Cydonian trespassers. We could see forever. An unending landscape of red under a heavy blanket of cloudless blue. And all the time the great fire above burned our skin, cooking us stealthily like pink sausages for the wild dogs below. We took photographs because we had to, filling our viewfinders with nothing but dust and haze. We snapped each other, group shots and solo, smiling through sunburn and mosquito repellent, ten thousand miles from home on the top of everything. And then we crawled back down because we didn't belong there. I stole a loose red rock when we reached the ground, worrying those ancient ghosts were watching, waiting to curse me.

Lunch, and I leave the lesbians in peace to nibble their triangularly cut sandwiches as I search for my brother and Pete. I find them at the back of the school, beside the football pitch, sitting on a wall with Rob, all three squeezing sandwiches into their mouths like hungry orphans. They've been cleaning the carpets in the ground floor, dragging around Hoovers and steamers, moving furniture back and forth. Rob's closer to them now, a little further into friendship, the three of them grumbling about the rising temperature. I skim around their outskirts, feeling left out. I mention the smell but they haven't noticed it. It's in the air now I tell them, right now, smell it. They stop chewing briefly, mouths full of compacted bread and cheap ham. They sniff the air, searching for something, but finding nothing. I sit with them and eat, not saying much else. When Rob's mouth is empty he talks again, this time about his home in Tasmania. He's far away, here in the bush, but there's nothing to miss and nothing to miss him. He feels more

at home on the move, meeting new people, new roads, new beds. We nod, pretending to understand, all three of us homesick for our mothers and fathers and the familiar halls they inhabit.

Back to work and the stink gets stronger. The lesbians have been taken somewhere else. I'm left with the sun and the stink and the last of the dirty windows. I peer inside; little desks and bright walls covered in thick-brush paintings and number charts. I want to paint a picture with my hands then fall asleep at the teacher's desk. Instead I finish the last of the windows and lean wearily against the balcony railing above the courtyard playground bellow. The lesbians pass by, not so close this time, dragging vacuums with squeaky wheels and smiley faces. A longhaired Euro shuffles by quietly, struggling to light a cigarette with a gasless lighter. A French couple chase each other with childish giggles and wet sponges. A dog passes slowly, old and hot, sniffing in the air for food or friendship. He looks up and sees me standing there. His black eyes dull, his nose cracked and dry like everything else around here. He makes a noise, like a cough or a sneeze, then continues on his way.

As we gather at the front of the school with our weapons and tired hands someone finds the stink. A bin behind the courtyard we're told, something dead and rotten. We drop our arms and go to look.

Crippled in the black metal bin is a dead roo. His eye peers up from death into the departing sun that cooks his skin and hair with fire. Most of him moves under a swell of feeding grubs, all climbing and slipping and eating and burrowing like a greedy yellow army. People choke back their sandwiches with coughs and groans, fleeing back to where we started like retreating soldiers. The smell is amazingly vile but I'm more accustomed to it than the others. I take it in with sharp little breaths, revelling in its heavy power. He must be a baby, I think. Lost and abandoned in the heat with only a million mouths for company. He stares up, saying nothing, not apologizing for his stink of crying for his mother. I admire him sadly, before rejoining the others.

The next day we leave that barren place, driving north towards the sanctuary of the sea. The road is the same, silent and unchanging. It takes us where we want to go, guiding us with its scorched metal signs. Our passing is its voice, that gentle drone that tells us we're moving. Without us it is nothing. And without it we are lost amongst the spiders and the snakes and the countless other evils. But with the windows open and my brother's foot on the peddle we're too fast for the sun to heat us. I let that stolen red rock slip from my hand, returning it to the ghosts of the desert. We cruise the soft tarmac like light, our bellies fat with freedom.

Austin, My Love
Jean Rafferty

AUSTIN ALWAYS HAD a cruel mouth. I used to watch her making up for the show, in the old days, when we were still together. That was before she went off with the fat taxi driver. She started with liquid base; then she outlined her eyes with thick black kohl liner. Eyeshadow depended on whatever scanty costume she chose to wear that night. If she was doing her Nazi guard routine she would have pale brown to make her face look harder, but if she was doing the number with the snake she chose green, which made her eyes glint.

She did her mouth last. She had a wide mouth and thin lips, very finely shaped. First she would go above the natural line of her lips with a dark pencil, then she would bare her teeth in a rictus grin as she filled in with bright red lipstick, always the same classic shade. 'Hooker's red,' she called it, though she was very firm that she was not a hooker. 'I'm a dance artist, darlink,' she said. Sometimes she did let them take her out and buy her champagne, but she didn't like men much. I didn't like them at all.

That's why I was surprised when she invited me down for the weekend with her and the fat taxi driver. Gilles was his name, though everyone called him Gigi. God, what a travesty, calling that slug the same as edible little Leslie Caron. I hated him and he hated me. He knew she loved me, as much as she was capable of loving anyone. If I really wanted to annoy him I'd speak to her in a Yorkshire accent. We were the only English girls in the troupe and he didn't speak it very well, so Hull English completely foxed him, the stupid bastard.

They lived in a little village on the Normandy coast.

'You'll never survive there,' I told her that last night, when she came back from the show and started throwing her clothes into a suitcase.

'I will always find things to amuse myself with,' she said. She picked up an exquisite little heart-shaped china box I'd got for her in a junk shop, then put it back down. 'You can have it,' she said. 'I will have no use for things like that there.'

It was this final piece of gratuitous cruelty which convinced me she really was going. I begged her to sleep with me one last time, but she got more pleasure from refusing me than she would have done if we'd jumped into bed together. I'm ashamed to say I went to pieces.

'Please stay, Austin. I'm begging you.'

She shrugged. 'I have to look out for myself,' she said, as if she'd ever done anything else. It occurred to me later that she could easily have packed earlier that day and stowed her case in Gigi's cab. She simply wanted to hurt me one last time.

I went to the poxy little village in Normandy, of course. She knew I'd go anywhere she summoned me, even after two years. I wanted to fall out of love with her, hoped she'd got fat or something, now she'd stopped dancing. She had, a little, but she still looked stunning to me. And to her lapdog husband. His eyes followed her everywhere she went.

Austin looked incongruous in the little village, strutting down its one street in her high heels, draped in the chinchilla wrap that her one rich admirer had given her. Gigi didn't like her wearing it. Reminded him what a sad bastard he was, I suppose. He could never buy her anything like that. She wore it regardless. I expect she enjoyed seeing him jealous, though they didn't sleep together, I'm sure. He was twenty years older than her, and a lot heavier.

There was nothing in that village, as I expected. She took me walking on the beach after lunch on the Saturday. 'Darlink, you know you can't keep up,' she told Gigi when he acted like he might come. 'Look at Ella. She's so fit. I'm afraid she'll leave *me* behind.' She knew there was no chance of that. I was desperate to be alone with her.

The beach was white sand and stretched ahead for miles. You could see Mont St Michel in the distance, its jagged spires all spikey like some kind of Gothic hedgehog. There were only a few people on the beach walking their dogs and I turned to Austin to kiss her, but she put her hand very firmly on my chest to ward me off.

'Are you mad? I am a respectable married woman here. It's a small village.'

A wave of heat was running through my breastbone where she'd touched me.

We must have walked for three miles before turning back. It was hot and the tide was out, leaving long blisters of water in the sand. I tried to take her hand but she wagged her finger at me.

'Now, don't sulk, ma petite,' she said, in her fractured English. She had been so long in France that you would expect her to be fluent in both languages, but the opposite had happened. She could speak neither well. That's the sort of fuck-up she was.

As we were approaching the halfway mark, a horseman suddenly appeared from over the dunes somewhere. The animal was magnificent, a high-mettled racehorse who clearly had no desire to transport the man sitting on top of him. He was strong and fiery, but the man was skilled and ruthless. I couldn't see his face, only the lithe elegance of his body and a certain vicious power.

'That's Stephane,' said Austin. 'He has a racing stable at the end of the village.'

I knew with bitter certainty that she came here every day to watch him. The man forced the horse round in widening concentric circles, its hooves sending a percussive shiver through the sand towards us. In its force and precision it was like a military parade, designed to show the dominance of the man.

'Didn't you know how much I loved you?' I asked Austin. The man jerked his head in a final salute towards us and let the horse go. They galloped along the sand, the horse's mane and tail flying free.

'Of course, my dear. But Gigi *worships* me,' she said.

I couldn't sleep that night. The room was too hot and I couldn't get the window open. I kept thinking about her, lying in bed with Gigi. I knew the old grampus was too fat and breathless to be able to fuck her, but then Austin never needed that to be satisfied. It killed her to lose herself in an orgasm. She liked to be in control. When he first started driving her home from the show at nights she would mock him mercilessly. 'He was staring at my boobies tonight,' she'd say. 'When we got here I make him get out and kneel at my feet. Yes, in front of all the people.'

And she would be so excited at humiliating him that we would make love and sometimes, just sometimes, she would forget herself so far as to come. That almost made me like the fat bastard.

Not now, though. I was tormented with the thought of her twining her body round his, even to torture him. Seeing her again made me ache. The back of my neck, my breasts were drenched with sweat and I had a sick feeling in the pit of my stomach. I thrashed about on the bed imagining her naked, with me. I couldn't get comfortable, and though my head was consumed with thoughts of her, I couldn't get satisfaction.

I needed to know why, why she'd brought me here. She was wicked, but there was no name for what she did in the list of seven deadly sins. Greed, gluttony, envy and the rest, they're all sins that poison the self. Austin's speciality was poisoning other people. She knew I was lying here, longing for her, while she went through her dry fucks with him. But of course he was easy meat for her. No matter what she did to him he adored her, cringed before her like a Muslim worshipping in the mosque. It was too easy for her to make him bow down to her. She needed the stimulus of challenge, of someone who at some point in the infernal round of games and forfeits, would say, *Stop. This far and no further.* I had always colluded in her cruelty, laughing when she told me about the latest poor sap forced to degrade himself to hold her. We used his shame as a prelude, an amuse-guele to our own relentlessly curious sexuality. But I was the amuse-guele here. I was a chemical catalyst in one of her endless experiments.

I went cold when I thought of it. And yet the more I thought of it the more I was intrigued. Not just to know what she would do, but to know what I would do. I was sliding at last into sleep, when the door opened and suddenly she was there, by the side of the bed, with a bottle of wine and two glasses.

'Burgundy,' cherie,' she said. 'This wine is fabulous.'

I saw her lift the bottle to pour, but the rich liquid seemed somehow to suffuse the glass noiselessly. Perhaps there was so much blood pumping through my ears that I just couldn't hear. 'Taste, *darlink*,' she said. 'It's the real peacock's tail they talk about.'

The wine was black in the dark. I held the aroma in my nostrils, gulped it into the back of my throat. It was pungent and earthy, with a heady top note and underneath a dark, loamy strength that was almost nauseating. I nearly gagged as I drank it, I was so excited. Austin made the first move, setting her glass down deliberately on the night table and forcing me back on the pillow. The last of my wine splashed on to the cotton sheet. She kissed me as if she was angry, forcing her tongue into my throat. I could feel the new softness of her stomach and breasts pressing down on me, grinding against my hipbone. I welcomed the pain. I wanted to inflict it on her, to twist her flesh till it bruised, to whip her till her white skin was scored with red, branded, with me, my name, my love.

She was on top of me, crushing me, crushing any revolt. I felt as if my body was being crucified by her. I was stretched out in sacrifice to her, waiting for the nails. She slid her hand over my breasts, flipping the nipple with her nail.

'This is mine,' she said. 'Never forget that.'

She left then and I wept. In the morning she was bright and cheerful, as if she had not come into my room in the night, not reclaimed her territory. Gigi coughed and spluttered, his eyes watchful.

'You must give up these fags, mon cher,' she said. 'It's no good for you,' but she lit two menthol tips as she said it, and handed one to him. His cur's eyes blinked out a kind of triumph at me. I wondered if that was the only physical intimacy she allowed him.

I suppose, in my heart of hearts, I knew she must be allowing him something. He was enthralled by her, in thrall. That was what she did to people, dazzled them with her physical presence and then destroyed them. She measured out her love and fed it to them, bit by bit, and by the time they realised it wasn't love at all they were hooked. Gigi had been straightforward, a decent bloke. The exotic dancers all liked riding in his taxi because he didn't pester them or make coarse jokes. Now he seemed different, reduced. Looking at his sad mouth and sluggish body slumped in the chair, I almost felt sorry for him.

It was a hot morning and I was tired, so I took a book into the conservatory after breakfast. It was the only piece of English style in their house. She had had it brought over and it was filled with potted lilies and gardenias like something out of the gardening magazine she got in the post. The smell was overpoweringly heavy and I melted into a half-sleep, the sweet scents creeping into my dreams. In the red band behind my eyes I could see her face, then her breasts, slashed open with a wine bottle and Burgundy coloured blood flowing out. I dipped my finger into the red and licked it. It tasted delicious.

Voices woke me. I struggled at first, refusing wakefulness and trying to incorporate the sound into the dream. But it was no good.

'I can make you do anything I want,'

Austin was saying. 'Anything.'

I crept out of the conservatory and down the hall, bare feet testing the polished floorboards for creaks.

'Non. C'est pas vrai,' said a man's voice, deeper than fat Gigi's. But I could sense the thrill of submission in him, just as Austin undoubtedly could. He wanted her to dominate him, subjugate him to her will.

I leant against the wall, sick and yet excited. I wanted to call out, break the spell, but maybe in the end I was as wicked as her, because more than that I wanted to see her humiliate the man. They were in the *salon*, just a few yards further. I edged along. The boards were cool beneath my feet.

'Down,' she said and clicked her fingers imperiously.

I reached the doorway and stood, staring straight at Austin. The man was kneeling on the floor, fumbling with his belt. Even from behind I recognised him as the horseman from the beach. Austin had painted her lips dark red, a richer, more decadent colour than the one she used to wear. She stared back at me, over the wide shoulders and narrow waist of the horseman. Then she leant forward and flipped the belt from his hand.

'Down,' she said and cracked the belt on the floor.

Slowly the man lowered first his jeans, then the skimpy black underpants he was wearing. His bare buttocks were hard and muscular. He must have sensed my presence, for he moved as if to turn.

'Face the front. You don't mind about her,' said Austin. She circled round behind him and slapped him with the belt, leaving a red blaze across his backside. She stood in front of him again. 'Je t'excite, darlink?' I didn't know which of the two of us she was addressing.

I moved into the room then, to watch more closely. She clicked her fingers again and the horseman started caressing his dick in front of her. He was breathing hard and his face was as engorged with blood as his penis. You could see the muscles of his shoulders and arms moving underneath his tight black T-shirt, like the lights on a gaming machine, one after the other. Austin's voice was harsh.

'Spill,' she commanded. His buttocks clenched and bucked, as if he were on his horse. As the thick white semen oozed out and dripped on to the wooden floor I could see tears spilling uncontrollably out of his eyes. I despised him and I despised Austin, with her insatiable need to demonstrate her power. The straight people in this little village would say she was perverted and for once I agreed with them. She was perverted, not in her strange sexuality, but in her wish to rub people's noses in the shit of their own desires.

I despised myself most of all for giving her the audience she craved. It would not have been enough for her to put on this little show for Gilles. He bored her. It was too easy to make him suffer. She needed me, who put on a hard face when she hurt me, me who acted like I didn't care, me who loved her to death.

Suffocated, I turned to go, just as Gigi walked in the door. He blenched as he took in the scene, the man half-naked and kneeling, the blob of liquid on the floor, me. Austin was standing with the belt in her hand, a thin smile on her lips. I knew she thought it was funny because I knew the game. Poor Gigi didn't. I had never seen a man look so mortified.

In the old days I too would have laughed at him, but I had lived without Austin for too long. Now, even though I was a player in the game, I knew it wasn't worth this man's pain, his caramel coloured eyes melting down in distress like one of Dali's soft watches. He had a ghastly pallor and looked as if he was about to retch.

'Austin, my love,' he said.

Stephane fell over, struggling to pull his trousers back up. Then he sidled out past us all, cheeks burning. I wanted to walk out but couldn't. I wondered why I had ever loved Austin, and would I ever stop. I stepped forward.

'Austin, my love,' I said.

Creamy fells

Sally Evans

At Underley we swam the Lune,
a private pool above rapids
where Ann and I once swam too near
and were pulled by the river's
smooth force nearly as strong as our limbs.

Down in the river bed
mussels lived lives unlike ours,
and minnow and trout moved silently
while, in the air, peaceable birds
flew between river
and Barbon and Casterton fells.

Ann drew them
time and again, while I sought words for them,
the creamy fells.

Reel Iraq at the Bakehouse: March 2013

For Ghareeb, Zaher and Awazan

Chrys Salt

Zaher lost his luggage so wears
my husband's woolly hat,
He seems perplexed by my egg-cup,
likes his eggs hard boiled,
eaten like apples.

We light a Chinese lantern for Awezan.
Release it from the patio under icy stars.
It is her daughter's fourteenth Birthday.
Kurdish New Year.

Joy is not lost in translation.

Nothing and everything is understood.

Ghareeb and I swap email numbers.
Books of our poetry.

The sky was pale as shell.
Snow upon snow unmade our garden
when they came,
but under it all March's yellow daffodils.

Ten years since war unmade their land.
Now I eat eggs in the Iraqi way.

New World
Peter Mackay

A cuimhne a' fàilligeadh, dhòirteadh i
A' chiad dram dhen oidhche trup 's trup
agus chitheadh i càrn de chlaigeannan
air an t-sòfa, riabhan 's breac mar chat
a bhàsaich o chionn deich bliadhna,
agus thionndadh i ann an eagal a beatha
dha a fear-pòsta nach robh, a-rithist, an sin an sin.

Cha robh teas ann riamh shuas an staidhre
agus tha an talla a-nis dùinte le duvetan
's frèamaichean-leapa luchd-màil sgaogach,
agus tha bratan Phàislig a' grodadh san fhliche
anns an t-seòmar far an do chluich i,
aon samhradh m' òige, Dvořák dhomh trup
's a rithist, an New World Symphony a' lìonadh
an aon t-seòmair san taigh le sealladh na mara.

Agus le sin bha i a' ciallachadh na mara làn.

New World

With her memory failing she would pour
the first whisky of the evening three times
and see skulls piled up in the armchairs,
dappled and brindled like a cat dead ten years,
and turn with the fear of her life to her husband
who would be again not there not there.

They never got round to heating the upstairs,
and now duvets and masking tape close off the stairwell
with the bedframes of flitting tenants,
and the Paisley carpets fester in damp
in the room where, in a childhood summer,
she played me Dvořák over and over again,
his New World Symphony filling
the one room in the house that faced the sea.

By which of course she meant the open sea.

New Year
Nabin Kumar Chhetri

I just got up.
The half read book of Murakami's *Norwegian Wood*
is pressed under my pillow. Its pages smell of pine.
On the desk, a row of books sit against the wall.
A burnt candle, pen stand and a book marker from Oxford
bath in the dim yellow light of the table lamp.
Near my bed, the halogen heater lies under a pile of dust.
It will be winter again before I take it out.

My Facebook page has been filled with New Year wishes.
Outside my window, thick fog has covered the town.
Raindrops splash on the glass pane and falls.
At the other side of the flat, my neighbour's TV is loud.
He does not know it is my New Year.

I remember. Many years back.
How we rolled on the sand of *Rapti;*
All night, Like crocodiles.
We sailed on the wooden boat
in the pale blue light of the moon, like ghosts.
The other side of the river was pitch dark.
Even the shadows were chased out.
It was like another country, another time.
Shrieking sound of cicadas, echoed from the dense wood.
We never crossed the river.

On this side of *Rapti;* we made bonfires,
we drank all night, sang old hindi numbers.
12, 1, 2, 3 - It was timeless.
The darkness gave way to a new day. A New Year.
We woke up on the sand bed.
Hearing; the sound of waves,
Bóte Dai singing far away.
Every year, when the New Year comes.
The memory of the fire, burnt, that night.
keeps me warm.

Retirement options for tube trains: #2 Glenfinnan, Scotland

Alex Howard

Slink out the service tunnel at Finsbury Park
and up the sunken cutting
by the depot:
the moonlit mainline will lie in front of you
braided and silver
like a threat. Unite with it.
(no one will know; signals are green
at 4am for a reason.)

It'll feel strange not stopping
at all these stations;
don't worry, they say it takes a while
to fully unwind.
Soon you're a needle
stitching a luminous thread
through countryside-cloth,
ducking through the déjà-vu tunnels at Hertford
under a stretching sun.

12 hours later, you'll arrive.
It won't require any announcement.
You'll feel like the entire place –
the pugnacious hills; the satin lake;
the airbrushed banks and
artex sky – were summoned just
for you. Greater trains
have felt the same.

Open both sets of doors. (Notice
how the cows stop mid-chew
at the sound?) Scent the air
with that London smell.

You fit in perfectly: that family taking
photos of you along the viaduct
have little sense of irony.

August Nicht – Biggar 1978
Andra McCallum

the hoggs greit i the slauchterhoose pens
randie louns are haein a swallae ootby my door
the hunter's staumpin aboot the lift
shakkin his stave at the tinklin staurs

I pou the hap up owre ma heid
smouer the rattlin roarin rammie, ettlin ti sleep
til the sun wauks the flouers aince mair
ti lood-perfuim the hin-end o the nicht

Po Lin Monaster, Cheinae
Hamish Scott

We gaed roun Po Lin monaster
tho anelie like as tourists gowk
wi glaikit leuks an cameras
an coft gifts blesst bi halie fowk

We daunert yont the Peth o Wit
The Sutra o the Hert, its en,
wis kervit on lang, thin widden steles
in Cheinae leid we didna ken

Rab, Jean wis no that bonnie O
Hamish Scott

Ye wrate hou bonnie wis yer Jean
Weel A hae seen hir picter O
Tho aulder than, she's grugous seen
Rab, Jean wis no that bonnie O

Fae Davaar tae Valhalla

Helen MacKinven

THERE WIS NO way I could afford to pay tae transport his deid body 137 miles. I was scunnered that I'd let him doon. Duncan's insurance policy didnae cover extras like carting him fae Glasgow tae Campbeltown. But I took him hame like he'd asked, all the way tae the "wee toon". Duncan was adamant that he wanted tae end up beside his *real* family. And he wanted tae return tae the island, Davaar Island, at the mooth of Campbeltown Loch. It wis where him and his wee brother had played wi stick swords, afore the boy died of leukaemia when he wis thirteen. Duncan never really got o'er that and wis always sayin that there wis nae where else in the world that he felt happier than oan that island. I kent taking him back to Davaar wis the right thing to dae. And then there could be nae come back aboot no obeying his wishes. I'll no have anybody bitchin aboot me behind ma back.

Duncan's original idea was jist daft though. There was no way me and the boys could launch a deid body intae Campbeltown Loch, especially inside a replica Viking longboat and huv flaming arrows fired at it. We'd get arrested for sure. And I cannae chance another conviction. I'd promised Duncan that Cornton Vale wisnae gettin the pleasure of ma company ever again. He wis proud of me staying clean. So I changed his plans a wee bit and anyway, he'd be none the wiser now he wis deid.

But why could he no have jist huv asked for the usual funeral stuff? A scattering of ashes would've been nae bother at all, apart fae the four hour journey, and the 40 minute walk across the shingle causeway tae Davaar. But I didnae grudge him that. I'd no problem with that, even though it ruined ma guid sandals. Well, a wanted to make an effort, y'know?

Naw, ma problem wis with all the other palaver he'd requested in his will. It wisnae really a will like ye see them posh lawyers reading oot on the telly with aw the family gathered roond to see whit they were gettin. Ma Duncan had left nothing that anybody wid fight fur. There wid be naebody that wid want his second haun claes or his Sydney Devine records. But he still had a will. He'd written his final wishes doon oan the back of an auld broon envelope. And he'd sellotaped it to a DVD of his favourite film, *The Vikings*. I bought it fur his birthday years ago at the Scouts' Car Boot sale. And I'd regretted spending the 50p ever since.

I knew the film better now than I ever wanted tae. When he'd had a few pints of Kestrel, it was always his first choice tae stick on the telly, and then if he stayed awake long enough, he played *Braveheart* and sometimes even managed tae get through *Gladiator*. But that didnae happen very often. It was usually jist *The Vikings* before he'd be snoring and farting in his sleep.

The final theme tune always stuck in ma heid for days, '*...da-dahhh-da da-dahhh-da, da-da-da-da-da-da.*' And nae matter how many times I'd seen it, I always ended up greetin when Tony Curtis stabbed Kirk Douglas. Duncan loved the fight scene tae and I caught many-a-time sniffin back snotters when Kirk got a Viking funeral with the longboat set oan fire. Every time we watched it, he'd make me promise that when his time wis up, I'd dae the same thing for him. I used to wonder if he'd remember asking me when he was sober, cos there was never a witness tae his request. But he must've minded efter aw cos he wrote it doon so I couldnae ignore it. Ma man wanted to be chosen by the god, Odin and join other Viking heroes who'd died in combat and end up in Valhalla, Odin's home and a Viking heaven fur warriors. Duncan was never a soldier but tae be fair, he did battle against an army of demons aw his days. I had to dae the right thing by him. I owed ma warrior that.

But this was never gonnae be a one woman joab. So I asked a couple of his pals fae doon the social club if they'd gie me a haun. They wurnae surprised at his request, he wis known as being a bit of an eejit. But they loved the big man like he wis a brother. They made a fool of his teuchter accent and the way he'd ask them, 'Hoots hepnnin?' and they knew the Campbeltown answer was to reply, 'Nathin!', they played along cos it was aw jist a bit of fun between them.

Geordie agreed to make the longboat cause he tellt me he'd got an 'O' level in Woodwork but a didnae mind him be in school long enough to pass an exam. He even went tae the bother of getting his laddie tae order a model boat kit off the internet. Geordie said ye can get anything these days aff eBay. Even a Viking longboat. It was a cracker. The model had a red and white stripy sail, wee oars and everything. Duncan would've loved it. It seemed a pure shame to set it oan fire. It took Geordie three weeks to make it cause he suffers fae the shakes maist days. I was fair chuffed when he showed me it even though the glue had run doon the side, but it was gaun up in flames anyway.

The longboat never made it to Davaar. It only got as far as Inverary. Geordie had got a len of his laddie's souped up Corsa and we invited Chalky and Tam along for the run to join in the ceremony. The motor roared like a tractor and it wis a crush in the back sittin next to Tam but it wis better than getting the bus fae Buchanan Street. Tam was desperate fur a piss so we stopped at Inverary. There's nae other reason to stop there unless you want tae buy a tartan travel rug or a 'See you Jimmy!' hat. The place is full of shite and Tam wasnae talking aboot the public toilets. He jumped intae the car but forgot tae shift the balsa wood longboat. He said he was picking splinters oot his arse for weeks. It was just lucky I had Duncan's ashes in a wee urn on ma knee, I wanted to keep him close to me fur as long as a could. Geordie wis pure raging but it was like a pile a matchsticks so we chipped it oot the widnae once we were back on the A83.

The banter was great though, Duncan would've loved the drive and before we knew it, we were speeding doon the road past Tayinloan and only 19 miles fae Campbeltown. But we stopped to let Tam have another piss in a layby, the man jist cannae haud his water. Tam blamed the excitement of the trip but it was mair like the three cans of Special Brew he'd slugged since we left Inverary. The atmosphere wis hairy though cos nane of us really knew whit we were daein and how we were gonnae pull off Duncan's plan.

Before we could even think about getting oer to Davaar though, we needed a new longboat. The shops in Campbeltown stocked everything you'd ever need, if you were living in 1975. There wisnae a toy boat to be had anywhere in the wee toon. But Chalky came up with a great idea. We drove along to Tesco's and bought a big tub a Flora, scrapped oot the marg and hey presto, a boat. It wid dae the joab and that's aw that mattered. Tam said that gaun tae Tesco wis a guid chance to stock up oor carry oot so we'd be able to toast Duncan. And we bought a copy of the *Campbeltown Courier* to wrap roon the arrows fur when we set them on fire, it wisane worth a read first. The paper's headline wis ridiculous, '*Ka-taštrophe*' aboot a wee Ford motor crashing intae someone's front gairden and narrowly missing the hoose. That's headline news in the wee toon.

Chalky's no as stupid as he looks with his missing front tooth and his gammy leg cos he minded to check the timings for the tide gaun in and oot to Davaar. The last thing a wanted wis to get stranded on an island wi nae pubs and wi they three mad bastards. There wis a blackboard outside the Tourist Information

Office oan the pier and we were jist in time tae make the walk while the tide wis low.

Geordie drove us east of the toon, tae a layby beside the start of the causeway. Chalky had asked aboot timings at the Tourist Office and they said that we'd three hours to get there and back again. And they tellt him that the causeway wis known as the *Dhorlin*, as if Chalky wid need the info fur his next appearance oan *Mastermind*. But we still had time fur a can of lager each before we started walking. We followed the tyre tracks fae a farmer's Land Rover and took turns tae carry the cross bow. Tam had got the cross bow fae Victor Morris's shop years ago when he wis bothered wi foxes sniffin aboot his pigeons. Duncan gave up his doocot cos of foxes. One night he left the door open and when he got back fae the social club, it wis like a scene fae a horror movie. Blood, feathers and deid birds everywhere so ye cannae blame Tam for fighting back, although Duncan said the crossbow wis aw for show. Tam's always fancied himself as Rambo although the only likeness I can see is that he's got twa eyes, a nose and a mooth.

The crossbow wis heavier than I thought it would be. Geordie's a gentleman and tellt the boys that I didnae need tae take a turn. Chalky took the Tesco bag with the carry oot and I had Duncan's ashes in the wee plastic urn I picked up fae the crematorium at Daldowie.

Ma sandals were letting in water but nothing wis gaunny spoil the day. It minded me of the Sunday school trips we went on when a wis wee. The sun wis poking its napper oot between the clouds and the only thing we should've brought wis a picnic rug, we should've thought aboot that at Inverary. Tam started singing,

'Now Campbeltown Loch is a beautiful place,
But the price of the whisky is grim.
How nice it would be if the whisky was free
And the Loch was filled up to the brim.'

We were aw pissing ourselves laughing and joined in at the chorus,

'Campbeltown Loch I wish you were whiskey,
Campbeltown Loch och-aye!
Campbeltown Loch I wish you were whiskey,
I would drink you dry.'

Duncan would've been fair chuffed and I jist hoped it wis aw true aboot the afterlife and he wis watchin us marching across the sandy wet pebbles. The mood wis great, the lager helped and we took nae time at aw tae get tae the island. There wis lots of goats runnin aboot and Tam said he wis gonnae take one oot with the crossbow. I didnae ken if he wis kiddin or no but Geordie grabbed it aff him and tellt him tae grow up. We aw went a bit quiet fur the next wee while. That's how aw the fights start between them, joking one minute and cursing the next and I jist hoped the atmosphere wisnae ruined. But we were soon pissing ourselves laughing again when Tam slipped oan fresh goat shit and landed oan his arse. Chalky said it usually took a session with a "lock in" at the social club afore Tam couldnae staun and called him a lightweight. Tam laughed. I wis fair relieved. Geordie gied him a haun up and we were back on track.

Davaar wis nicer than a expected, I wis the town mouse and Duncan wis the country mouse. He could never get me tae move back with him; it was far too quiet for me doon here. But in small doses, I did like the calmness of the place, away fae traffic and the screamin neighbours next door. All I could hear wis the sound of seabirds; even the boys seemed to be enjoying the peace. The island made me breathe slower. And Duncan would've been pleased aboot that. His pals walked ahead with Tam whistling an Andy Stewart tune. I stopped to pick up a piece of green beach glass. I felt the smooth edges of the emerald oval. I wondered where the glass had come fae, wis it once a fancy wine bottle emptied by rich folk oan a yacht? Or wis it a Buckfast bottle that one of the local neds had tossed intae the Loch? It didn't matter where the glass had come fae; it was a thing of beauty noo, like one of Liz Taylor's jewels. I pocketed it, a keepsake fae Duncan's final journey.

Geordie said we shouldn't go too far roon. It wis enough that we'd got oan tae the island withoot takin chances aboot getting hame again. I sat on a boulder and waited. The boys didnae seem to know whit tae dae next either.

>>

Eventually, Tam got got oot his arrows for the crossbow and tore aff the front page of the *Courier*. I dug into ma handbag fur the ashes and the Flora tub.

Geordie asked me if I wanted to say something first but Duncan wis no a big yin fur speeches so I said we should maybe jist hae oor ain private thoughts. The boys seemed relieved. Efter a couple of minutes and once we'd finished the can of lager Chalky passed roon, we moved closer to the water's edge. I'd decided to keep the wee urn, it would look good oan the mantelpiece so I tipped the ashes into the Flora tub. Tam got the crossbow ready. And that's when we aw realised that we'd nae matches.

We aw used to smoke but we're mair health conscious these days. Duncan would've found it funny cos he wis the only one of his pals tae still smoke Capstan Full Strength right up tae the end. There wis nae chance of a light aff him this time. Duncan always joked that if the fags didnae kill him it wid be the booze. He'd never a thought that the Number 32 tae Shettleston would get there first. Flattened he wis, still haudin a fag on his way hame fae the social club.

There wis nothing else fur it. We launched the Flora tub and let it drift oot tae the Loch withoot the flaming arrows. The only problem wis it kept comin back with the tide. Chalky said that the big man wisnae ready to leave us yet. But we couldnae staun there aw day or we'd get stranded oan the island. I wis takin nae chances but I could see Geordie's face go pure white when a hurled a boulder at the tub. A missed. I explained tae the boys that we should try and sink the tub or the ashes wid be floatin back tae us aw day. They didnae look too keen at first but soon got stuck in and efter twa or three goes each the tub tipped and Duncan was a circle of grey ash, drifting oan the water, until he slipped underneath the surface oan his way tae Valhalla. I squeezed the piece of beach glass so tight that even the smoothed edged dug into ma palm. I wanted it tae hurt. There wis nae other way I could think of tae feel the pain of missing ma Viking warrior.

The Sneeze
George McQuilkin

IT WAS JUST a sneeze. He sucked in his cheeks, tried to hold his head steady, closed his eyes and let go. Oooosssss......!! Good! Except that he was driving a car approaching a main road, and the rider of a blue-striped racing bike travelling at speed and expecting the car to stop, was surprised when it didn't. The bike bounced once on the car bonnet, then crumpled against a tree on the far side; the rider, sailing over the car, crashed hard on the stoney pavement where he lay unmoving.

The car behind pulled around the accident, and the driver, a woman in her early fifties, kept going to an appointment which turned out to be disastrous because she was haunted at having left the scene of an accident; the sale of her long distance trucking company did not take place as the other party quit the meeting early, mistaking her distraction for a change of heart about the deal they had discussed at such great length over previous months.

However, the associate physics professor walking along to his university class, saw the accident and did stop, cradling the rider's head in his arm and waiting until the ambulance arrived; this resulted in him being thirty minutes late for the lecture which, when he walked through the door, he found had been adjourned by the Pro-Vice-Chancellor of the University who had been asked to review certain faculty members performance as a result of a demand for budget cuts within the University. A report was lodged over the associate professor's third late attendance, resulting in him being certain he would be passed over for promotion; his partner, a brilliant mathematician, who had warned him repeatedly about his lack of punctuality, decided she'd had enough, and left him to join her life with another mathematician in her department who recently had been paying her a lot of attention.

As a result of the lecture not given, the associate professor's prize pupil, a young man who was on track to becoming the most outstanding high-speed particle physicist that Scotland had produced in a generation, wandered down Byres Road with time on his hands; at the coffee shop where he was drinking a mocha and making intricate calculations in his head, he was approached by Heather Huntley–Brown, an admirer of all things scientific and of scientists in particular. Subsequently they adjourned to her flat where a child was conceived on her roommate's bed; the prize pupil forever now missing the chance to further a romance between himself and the shy Doreen McDougall, who sat next to him in class and was another gifted physicist. If tested their combined DNA would have shown that had they married and had children their first daughter, possibly named Hilary, would have had the potential to combine the mathematical insight of Einstein with the necessary perseverance of Darwin, and she would have been able to discover the formulae for the elusive and long sought-after Unified Field Theory, explaining the relationship of everything to everything else.

The associate professor fell into a deep depression over his partner leaving and the lack of promotion prospects at the university, and he refused to speak at a conference in Zurich to lobby for the second Large Hadron Collider being built in Scotland; his actions resulted in a decision being reached in favour of a site in South Africa which eventually caused the resignation of the South African president for having promised too great a portion of the cash resources of his country in which one half of the population live in poverty. However, his resignation did encourage a young man of the Sotho tribe, who believed that his destiny was to speak up for the dispossessed, to lead a protest movement which eventually swept throughout all of South Africa, resulting in his widow being elected the first female president of the country, where she instigated radical pay reforms requiring women to be paid equal to men for the same work, and that the highest paid in any company could not exceed 20 times the lowest paid.

At the clattering sound of the bike hitting the car bonnet, a young boy playing on the verge looked up sharply, his ball bouncing unattended into the street where it was popped by a passing city lorry whose driver, deaf from loading bins all day, didn't hear his mate shout a warning. The boy, who was to develop a lifelong fear of round objects exploding, started to cry and a bearded man who was passing by and came over to comfort him, was soon accosted by the boy's mother who had quickly arrived on the scene, and as she thought he was the cause of the tears, called the police who took the man in for questioning. A subsequent search of the man's house revealed a hand gun and bullets with the name of various public officials written on them, though his wife, when interviewed by the press, said in her time living with him she found him '...a good, caring man.' This was unfortunately not sufficient to keep him out of jail where during the second year of his incarceration he stabbed two correctional officers and then killed himself with a knife he had crafted in the prison workshop from a bar of steel.

The ambulance attendant who, when the emergency call arrived, was forced to interrupt a phone conversation in which her boyfriend was claiming he felt he was not at fault for the events in the restaurant the previous evening, attempted to call her boyfriend again in the ambulance on the way to the hospital to no avail; however, the momentary distraction of the call caused her to attach the wrong tag to the injured cyclist, so that the young emergency doctor performing his first solo shift thought the patient had a toxaemic metatarsal and sent him off to surgery where the large toe on the right foot was mistakenly removed. In the follow up hospital investigation, the emergency doctor was put on notice and subsequently left the profession, discovering a lucrative new career as a consulting internet doctor dispensing advice at £50 a session.

The ambulance attendant, working her way through university, was suspended from the ambulance service though she subsequently sued them for sex discrimination; her colleagues and friends thinking 'something was fishy about the whole episode,' demonstrated solidarity with her by walking through campus carrying dead fish from a nearby stream which had suffered chemical pollution. The lawsuit took a toll on the former ambulance attendant's health, and as she was the first in her family to go to university, her decision to drop out pleased no one except her younger sister who since the age of five had been envious of her accomplishments and now, just as the younger sister was about to start cohabiting with a heroin addict named Zack, saw an opportunity to excel in the family narrative; instead of living with Zack she applied to the University to study psychology where she was accepted and excelled, graduating with First Class Honours with praise heaped on her dissertation entitled *Family Dynamics As A Determinant Of Social Outcome;* later she was to become the Chair of the School of Psychology at Oxford University.

The memory of his sneeze and the subsequent accident haunted the driver of the car. One night, when his wife tried to arrest his flailing arms by climbing on top of him, their flimsy bed bought in a local charity shop, collapsed with a bang, waking the woman living in the flat underneath who, thinking it was a mortar explosion of the same kind that had driven her into exile from Iraq, immediately donned her white robe and called her son in Baghdad to whom she hadn't spoken for over three months, asking if he was all right; he replied that he welcomed the opportunity to tell her that he and his long-term girlfriend had decided to get married and the wedding would be in two weeks; this resulting in her the next morning visiting a travel agent and booking a last minute ticket to Baghdad. In twenty-four hours she had packed and was on the plane, where she sat next to a man going to his own daughter's wedding in Baghdad, and when they discovered it was their children marrying each other they talked for the next six hours, deciding just before landing in Dubai that they had so much in common that they would join their own lives together, thereby announcing to their surprised son and daughter who met them at the airport that a double wedding must be planned.

On the same plane, an Indian businesswoman returning home from America witnessed the couple's increasing intimacy, and on hearing the man's shout of joy, 'She's accepted me!' decided that love was what she needed now, and reaching her family home in Uttar Pradesh, she sent a message to a man with whom as a teenager she had a shy romance, once kissing passionately in the deep shade of a banyan tree. The man, having never been able to touch another woman because the memory of her was so strong, hurried over and, leaving his sandals on the porch, entered to encounter the woman of his dreams; though as they talked and finally lay in a bed together, he found that after the initial excitement his anxiety caused his penis to go flaccid and the moment was never consummated.

Unnoticed by him as he hurried over, one of his soft sandals flattened a large red ant (*Yavnélla indica*) which had been working all morning pulling the carcass of a cicada into a pavement crack. The ant had its remaining life squeezed out by subsequent walkers and was left to deteriorate in the heat until an unexpected monsoon washed it into a drainage ditch where by coincidence it was reunited with the offending sandal which had been carried off

from the porch and abandoned by a feral dog. The ant and the sandal rode the crest of a wave together through the drainage ditch, eventually emerging out to the sea where the ant was consumed by a passing dogtooth tuna and the shoe was left to float until washed up many kilometres down the beach where it was picked up and examined closely by a policewoman conducting a missing person inquiry. Despite their disappointing sexual encounter, the Indian businesswoman and the man were married, but the first incident set the stage for the wife's later infidelity with a computer mogul of national prominence, a relationship which continued for some time until discovered by the mogul's wife who successfully ordered a contract killing of her husband, inheriting afterwards a vast fortune. Meeting the Foreign Minister of India in a 5-star hotel on the South Indian coast, the wife married again in a sumptuous wedding on the banks of the Ganges. The craft industries of India underwent a surprising growth spurt when she featured at a state banquet, table clothes, place settings and utensils handmade by the poorest Indians, and over the next few years ten million Indians became employed in self-financed craft co-operatives, several of them becoming the largest privately owned businesses in India.

Eventually, the cobbled pavement where the cyclist landed after passing over the bonnet of the car was planted in grass with councillors on the south side of the city concurring to a safety review of all city owned land, as long as they received a favour in return, namely votes for a new 50,000 sq. ft. addition to the city's conference centre.

The cyclist returned home after a two week stay in the hospital, walking with a cane and coming to terms with the fact that he would never fulfil his dream of competing one day in the Tour de France. His wife at first expressed sympathy, but eventually became distant, finding that she could no longer contemplate his injury without bitterness as her mother had nursed for years her invalid father 'wasting the best part of her life' she had said, and the daughter had vowed at an early age never to

➡

be held hostage to anyone in a similar way.

After the divorce, the cyclist used his hospital compensation payment to take a two year bicycle tour around the world, where in passing through South Africa over a flat sandy plateau which was once the proposed site for a Large Hadron Collider (and was now an extensive housing project for low income workers), he met a female cyclist from Burkina Faso who had left her home where most of her village had turned to craft work taught to them by a visiting Indian expert. In Pretoria they were briefly stopped in front of a five star hotel by a security guard who as a former policewoman in India had once found a sandal that she incorrectly attributed to the perpetrator of a double murder, an error for which she was forced to resign and later felt it necessary to leave the country and come to South Africa.

On returning to Scotland the cyclist and his new companion, now his life partner, rode past the site of the original accident which he pointed out to her, though because of the changes made by the city engineers, it was barely recognizable and he didn't bother to stop. They were just in time to catch a major bicycle trade show, the first to be held in the new extension to the conference centre. Squeezing past them at one mini-session on urban bikeways, was the driver of the car who had hit the cyclist, but the driver was late because of having to console his unhappy young son who had fallen and bruised his knee, and thereby the driver missed an opportunity to talk to them and possibly discover their connection to one another. Afterwards over coffee at tables set out on the conference floor, the cyclist and his partner initiated a conversation and eventually agreed to go to work for an older woman sitting next to them who after several failed attempts had recently sold her trucking company, and was now starting up a foundation promoting safer bikeways in urban areas throughout the country.

The first crack
Ross McGregor

They took our neighbour off the branch ae the tree
By the bowlin green wall
Yer brother called me a cunt just for wantin
To look one last time

We pushed each other about
On the way home, fallin
Into some bushes where we fought
Quietly for a while

A pair ae scabby stuckies
Rustlin about in the leaves
Nearly diggin a hole for ourselves
But I left him there, another one

When I walked home I felt cleaner
Even among the stench ae damp
Trees, dirty hands and trousers
Clingin tae ma legs, achin

I knew ye'd be waitin for me
Yer hungover smokin sleepy limbs stretchin
Ower the sheets in the pink and grey bedroom
Lit with the first crack ae mornin sun

Raven in Winter
Nalini Paul

Draw back the curtains to shadows.

Colour might appear
even as the raven flies
or tries to shape the landscape.

Blue emerges, like a moon mask.
A few pieces of rust cling to branches.
The roads shine with frozen rain
as Raven returns the sun
to light.

But his favourite shade, the night,
flits about rooftops and hops fences
like an indecision, until
   hillsides slumber
   windows dim
   rivers chatter, nervous.

Something far too distinct to call my own
follows close,
not death or even a ghost
but an imprint—
   blackened fingers
   loch-blue eyes.

Ash starts to stir...
a featherbed fellow
with pointed beak and sheet-white skin
flies straight back

surfaces black.

The quiet of white on white

Larry Butler

...no whiteness (lost) is so white
as the memory of whiteness... William Carlos Williams

the quiet of white on white
the crunch of white under boot
the weight of white on branches
the wheesh of white under sledges
the light of white on white ridges
the shape of white on stone dykes
the smooth of white on roof slates
the change of white in clouds
the blue of white in shadows
the stage of white moonlight
the magic of white in dreams
the struggle with white on a page
the triumph of white off the page
the black on white of a full mind
the white fear of a blank mind
the trouble with white when stained
the white when lost in white-outs
the grey of white in a thick fog
the white moon in a blue sky
the white wash over bad news
the wish for white when all is black
the quiet of white on white on white

Markings
William Bonar

in blazing starlight
we stop late
on the Oban road
pee on frost

scented vapour rises
tincture
of animal
of stardust

Northern Entropy
William Bonar

our sun seems
to keep its distance
grows sear and dim
in winter

we light decoys
to lure it home
sacrifice
to keep them burning

Final Scene
Kathrine Sowerby

There's no traffic on the road apart from a man on his motorbike
filmed from behind like the Italian film director Nanno Moretti

in his film *Dear Diary*, weaving through the streets of Rome, black t-shirt,
white helmet to the soundtrack of Algerian musician Khaled singing Didi

Or the man in the photograph on his moped taken en route to the Warhol
museum in Slovakia, his striped t-shirt holding in folds of flesh

and the road full of geese. We were looking for wooden churches like the
Armenian churches in the film *Calendar* by Atom Egoyan. Locked down

long takes of his apartment, and his wife who leaves him for their driver.

Ae Circle o Aul Stanes
George T Watt

(Inspired by ae short story frae Jorge Luis Borges, *The Circular Ruins*)

A crept intil the rickle o stanes, lyin like a nest o haird biggin
while the caul blast birlt aroun, abune ae wash o sterns filled the lift,
the temperature wuid faa muckle furder.
Atho a chittered awaa A happit masell beist a cuid,
an laid ma tousled forfochten heid apo ae clump o rash
an fell intae ae wanrest sleep.

A dreamt aince again A wir ae strappin loon,
heid strang an gallus, nae wise or quick witted wi ma mauchty weicht,
the timmers brunt awaa an aa the greetin wuidna douse the flems,
A wir inept, A haed nae wordiness,
ainly my fail neives an bluided braken banes.

A gaithered ma streingth an wi ae bit cruik
hobbled intae the tully whuar a cuid bide hibbled aneath the birks an braken
till the factor an his sudger billies haed finished thair murdrous darg.
Ma injuries mended but ma hert wis sair lamented
an A oathed masell niver tae return tae the airt o ma bairnheid,
but that wis lang syne.

A cairriet ma thochts an illtemper ower mony ae furrin laun,
tuik fowk oot ower the Prairies in covert wagons,
herded kye frae Rio Grande do Sul ower the braid Pampas,
focht in the jungle agin fowk faa held dear fit A haed lost
an fit ae traitor A felt fan a thocht aboot it,
so A jyned thay bleck cheils an wis hated by baith as ae turncoat.

A panned fur gowd an fun ae chuckie o it but the siller did nocht fur me,
A delved wi hoors o the basest rank, drank oot ivry saloon an hostelrie A cuid find
an scaittered ma wits in the Chinese opium dens.
Ainly fan A haed blew it aa an fun masell clartit an mingin in the sharn an gutters
did A find the wull tae cairry on.

A gaed awaa tae the heichts o the Fuar Aist in thair in secluded temples
A fun ae kin o peace, straunge Goads brocht silence tae ma ragin thochts,
stilled the edderpyson that coursed throu ma veins,
an fur aince A cuid sleep wi an innocence A haedna kent
since A wis ae bairn bedded doun in the neuk o the aul hous.

A aipened ma een an luikit oot ower ae wurld virginal an cours,
but in ma neb A cocht a hamely reek,
A peered asclance an oot the corner o ma een A spied
ae fire wi ae pot o purridge an ae beaker o milk.
Fit kin o fowk haed duin this fur me A cuidna tell
fur thay maun hae sleed awaa fan A roused.
A jaloused it wis the fairy fowk faa bide ablo the aul dun,
we wir aye warned niver tae pley thare as bairns.

A ate wi gusto, sic ae braw meal as iver A'd tasted
thou A'd ate in the tap hotels aa ower the wurld,
sang an drank wi Italian tenors in Rome,
an spent mony a thochtie while in busy Parisian restaurants wi aa kin o airtists,
but gin a cuid gang thare noo,
A'd raither bide here in the cranreuch wi ma hamely fair.

Sated A laid doun an slept mair while the wund whined ower ma heid
an the snawdrift laid athwart ma beil.
A dreamt o ae loon braw an sturdy faa crossed the haich bens
an doun the braid straths, an in his van
wir aa the displaced fowk camin hame tae reclaim thair ain.
Thay haed aa thair baests wi thaim, hauncairts fu o aa thair wares,
thare wir beehives an seedcorn an aathin thay wuid need tae aince again
mak the glens provide fur thair weelbein.

Thay brocht the aul sangs the wummen wuid sing at the waukin
an the auler men wuid sing at the milkin, queans were lauchin wi joy
an the young loons wir castin slee ees at the ains faa tuik thair fauncy.
Thare wir bairns runnin roun an the burnies ran and pleyed wi thair chatter
while abune the sun shone bricht an cheerie.

An haich in the passes the sudgers sloped thair airms,
the lairds wheezed an coughed but naewan bid thaim ony heed
fur thair dey wis ower. Nae langer
wuid thay rule ower thay glens frae afar, nae langer
wuid thay haud the deer o the bens an the fush o the rivers abune the fowk
faa belanged thare afore thir kin ran rochsheen ower aabiddie.

A slept fur forty deys an forty nichts while the winter blast blui ower,
the bonfrost turnt the grun iron, yet a niver felt the caul thou ma claithes wir gae thin. A
thocht lang an haird aboot this.
Fit wey cuid A endure this caul that wuid fooner ony ither biddie?
It was then A jaloused wi ae thocht that dirled ma heid,
wis A nae mair than ae straiggled quair, in somewan elses dream?

Night Shift at the Cessnock Psychic Centre

Andrea Mullaney

HIYA PAL!

Héllo, would you like me to cut the cards?

Who's that? You're no Stuart, I asked for Stuart.

No, I'm Phil, sorry. Stuart's left, I'm afraid.

Where's he gone?

I think he gót anóther job. So, do you want a reading?

Wéll... aye, okay then son.

Divide the pack into three, offer the caller a choice of A, B or C, place the chosen pile on top and start laying out a three card spread. Very basic layout, not as interesting as the Celtic Cross variation that he'd use if he were just reading for himself, but the guidelines are to keep it simple.

Phil is an anomaly at the Cessnock Psychic Centre because he actually knew how to read Tarot cards before he got the job. Most of the readers only had 30 minutes training before they were put on the phones for the first time and most of that was about what you could and couldn't say to the callers:

No personal information

No sétting up private readings – a sackable offence

No absólute promises or ftatements – keep it vague

Never predict a death or serious illness

Never remind them of the time, or the coft after the initial ftatement of rates

Keep it light but never make a joke of the cards, or the service, or them

He'd seen the job advertised at the Jobcentre, of all places. Usually that kind of vacancy notice only provokes people to moan to the Adviser that there are never any real jobs on the board, not for people with any qualifications or experience. But Phil had actually paused after the obligatory laugh. He'd picked up the Tarot from books and given enough readings to mildly tipsy girls at parties to know that he could do it. It turned out to pay a bit more than working in a bar and he doesn't have to cold-call anyone – they call him, drawn in by the classified ads in the Evening Times. The lines are only open after dark, so he gets the days free.

And it is a funny job to have, it is funny to tell people that's what you do – because it is so obviously not what he really is. It's just temporary. Phil is actually a qualified librarian with a post-grad degree, but there aren't many openings in libraries just now because of the cuts.

In fact, the notice stays up in the Jobcentre all the time because, like most call centres, staff turnover is pretty high. About a quarter of the readers are men but they are in the highest demand, because nearly all the callers are women. The most popular readers are those gay men with identifiably camp voices, like Stuart who'd just stopped coming in suddenly – that happens a lot – or Mikey the supervisor, who'd given Phil his desultory training on the first night.

Right, here are the cards you've to use.

Actually, I've gót my own, if you don't mind. The Ryder-Waite deck's a bit simpliftic, I prefer the Hermétic—

Yeah, actually, you've gót to use these. Keeps it consiftent. This lift télls you what the cards all mean, you just look it up. But don't say it straight out, dress it up a bit. These ones are the court cards.

The Major Arcana—

Whatever.

Phil doesn't sound very camp and he isn't gay, as it happens, so he has chosen to take on the role of slightly flirtatious nice-guy, the one that women don't really fancy but like as a friend. It doesn't work with everyone. A lot of the older women have no time for it and just want a reading, no messing, as if they'd put it on their shopping list between oven chips and Brillo pads. But it works for some.

Aw Phil, I mean I just don't know where I'm going wrong!

Come on, you're not going wrong.

I am, I let him walk all over me. I've packed the kids off to their da's and he's no even phoned to say he's no coming! It's like, no again, you know?

Angéla, listen. I can tell you're a very trusting person, your cards show you always see the best in everyone. Your first card here is the Queen of Cups, it's a card of nurturing and empathy. But you need to maybe stand up for yourself a wee bit. In the second position you've got the Seven of Wands, it's about overcoming obstacles, so I know you're a very strong person underneath.

Oh aye, I've had to be. I've had to be.

Yes, I can see that. You've had hard times. But you're a great mum, you're a special person...

Now, Phil knows, obviously, that what he is doing is ethically challenged. He is encouraging women on pretty low incomes to spend 60p per minute to confide in someone about their problems with their boyfriends, or their kids, or their general frustration and disappointment in life, when they could call their friends or The Samaritans for nothing. But think of it this way. They're probably not going to call The Samaritans, are they, and their friends might be bored of listening or give them bad advice. They could spend that money on fags or a bottle of vodka to cheer themselves up, which wouldn't really do them any good in the long run.

Phil is not a counsellor, clearly, but he does his best: he tells them that they shouldn't let men treat them like crap, by sleeping with their friends or borrowing money off them or hitting them. They definitely shouldn't ever let men hit them. He tells them that they are great, when perhaps no one else does, and he tells them to go to the Citizens' Advice Bureau if they've got debts. Also, he sometimes tells them he's got to go on a break, even if he doesn't, if they've been on for ages and he's worried about their phone bills. These women would probably not take advice from a 26-year-old librarian normally, but if it's good advice, does it matter if it comes via the random shuffle of picture playing cards?

Just by being himself, or the flirtatious nice-guy version of himself, he is reassuring them, at some level, that there are men out there who are better than what they've had. Not him necessarily (Phil has cheated on his girlfriend three times over five years, most recently last month with another Psychic Centre reader whom he now suspects is phoning his house late at night and hanging up when his girlfriend answers), but, you know. Out there, somewhere.

Anyway, it's not as if he doesn't believe in it, sort of. Surprisingly, given the obvious fraudulence of the 30-minute training session, everyone working at the Cessnock Psychic Centre does. Probably only Phil has heard of the Order of the Golden Dawn or read Crowley's The Book Of Thoth, but they all accept that the Tarot has a mystical connection to the spirit world and applied for the jobs because they 'always knew they were a wee bit psychic'.

If pushed, Phil has a pseudo-intellectual justification for it, which involves Jung's theory of the collective unconscious, the cultural significance of the 'People's Bible' in pre-literate societies, the benefits of archetype visualisations in cognitive therapy and, if necessary, reference to WB Yeats, Timothy Leary and Italo Calvino. He will often explain some of this to tipsy girls at parties while drinking red wine from plastic cups, but to be honest, they would probably prefer it if he said, "It's just a bit of fun, isn't it?"

➛

It's not that Phil is always trying to get off with these girls at parties. Firstly, he doesn't actually go to that many parties and besides, three one-night-stands in five years is not that many, especially as the first one was in the very early days of his relationship and it was with his ex-girlfriend whom he hadn't exactly broken up with yet (they lived quite far apart), so if anything, it was *more* legitimate, in a way.

Phil's current girlfriend is called Bethan and she is also a librarian who cannot yet get an actual job in a library, so she is working in a youth café project which technically holds some books for loan, as well as a much larger number of computer games. This will sound a lot better on an application form for a real library job than Tarot Reader at the Cessnock Psychic Centre.

Bethan does not believe in the Tarot as such, but she likes to make up stories about the pictures and she thinks it's interesting that the High Priestess card was once called The Popess and can be interpreted as a reference to the apocryphal Pope Joan.

When she goes on holiday with her friends – Phil doesn't like holidays – she hunts round the shops of strange cities to find him unusual decks of cards. In New Orleans once, she bought him a beautiful gothic set that is so elaborate you can't really make out the pictures, so it's not much use for readings, but it was a nice thought.

It's not that he doesn't love her.

But he likes the attention, the flirting, the boost of having someone take him at face value rather than knowing those rotten bits he doesn't like to think about. He likes the novelty of a fresh body, a new set of moves, or at least getting a genuine laugh for his oldest anecdotes. He likes making people like him.

Okay, the first card represents who you are now, the next one is about your underlying influences, what's made you who you are, and the third one is about the future, where you're going.

Can you tell me what's going to happen, but? Am I gonna get aff?

Hang on, sure... there's The Sun, that's a very positive card. There's someone supporting you, a great support.

That'll be my mammy. She's stuck by me all the way.

In your past, I can see there's been a bit of chaos, a bit of darkness maybe. We've got The Tower here, that's a card that means things falling apart, but also making the wrong decisions.

Yeah... definitely. I'm trying to kick it but. I'm on the programme.

I can see that, your referent card – that is, where you are now, it's the Ace of Swords, that means fighting a battle. But it also means a fresh start, so you can do it, it's saying you can win the battle.

Dae you really think so?

Yeah, definitely, I really do. Yeah.

The readers are allowed a ten-minute break every two hours. Phil doesn't smoke, but he goes outside anyway. They work in a unit on an industrial estate so he needs the air. He sees Kerry, who he slept with last month after a drunken night out. God. What was he thinking? Kerry is small and has a jaw a bit like a bulldog. She is a lot harder than Bethan or the girls Phil went to university with. When she's not on a call, she hangs around with Mikey the supervisor, talking in corners. Phil is sure that they are the ones phoning his flat and hanging up when Bethan answers. Bethan has been a little upset by these mysterious silent calls and her friends have advised her to buy a whistle and keep it by the phone. Phil has asked Kerry to stop and she denied it and told him to fuck off. He has no proof.

He walks past Kerry as if he is going to the 24-hour shop but when he gets there, he hasn't got his wallet with him, so he has to do a stupid mime of "oh, the precise kind of crisps I wanted to purchase aren't here and nothing else will substitute, so I'll just leave it after all". He goes back to his desk and the minute he sits down, Mikey puts a call through, even though he hasn't had ten minutes yet.

...

Hello? Are you there?

Yes.

Em, so, have you had a reading before?

Oh yes.

Good, well, I'll just cut the cards then. Do you want A, B or C?

Téll you what, don't do a three card spread, do a Céltic Cross.

Really? Okay, that's, that's no bóther, that's great. Give me a minute. What's your name, by the way?

It's me Phil, do you nót know me?

Oh – yes! Sorry, I didn't recognise your voice there. Sure, of course.

He doesn't recognise it. Well, you can't, not all of them – you get to know the regulars who call a couple of times a week, but not the occasional callers. It's easier if you get to know them, of course, because then you know what they want to hear. You'd think he'd remember though, because it's an odd voice, husky and echoey. Probably a tranny on a bad line.

Okay, in the centre of the cross representing your present, we've gót the Magician card, that actually represents knowledge, wisdom and pótential.

Does that mean I'm quite a wise person, Phil?

Em, yes, it can mean that, yes definitély. Now, do you have a question you want to concentrate on? You don't have to say it out loud, just kind of hóld it in your mind.

Mm hmm.

You don't have to téll me, but is it a question about love, or work, or money, or— ?

Yes.

Yes? It's about money?

It's about all of them.

Right, so they're all linked, that's fine. So we'll look at the immediate challenges going on in your life, we've gót a Two of Pentacles—

He's not getting much to go on. Sometimes you get these callers who want to test you, so they make you do all the work. Pretty stupid, it's their money – as long as he keeps them on the phone, the Centre doesn't care if they believe or not. But it is annoying when they don't go along with it. He's just trying to do his job.

That's a funny card, it's about change and flexibility, things that can go either way.

A bit like you Phil, eh?

Ah, aha-ha, my reputation precedes me! Em, wéll, you've also gót the Moon here, which is showing that you often have moments of insight,

you're quite intuitive aren't you?

Yeah, I am Phil. I'm sensing sométhing about you.

Ah. He should have realised it was one of *those* calls, where they string you along for a while and then yell, "It's total bullshit!" and collapse laughing with their mates. Phil doesn't really mind, it's fair enough in a way and he still gets paid, after all. He readies himself for the jibe.

Right, go on then.

I'm sensing that you are at a crossroads in your life, Phil.

Em, okay.

I can téll that your overlying intentions are good, but underneath there's a lack of confidence, isn't there? There's a conflict going on inside you, so much pótential but so much doubt.

Listen, I'm supposed to be reading you, you know, my boss might be listening in—

You just have to hang in there, don't make things harder for yourself. You'll gét a proper job eventually and it might nót work out with your girlfriend but it'll still be okay, in the end. One way or anóther.

Are you taking the piss, a wee bit? Wait, is this Mikey? Is— is that you, Béthan?

You know who it is, Phil.

I—I don't think— this isn't how it's supposed to go—

Yeah, this isn't really you, right? It's just temporary. I understand, you know. You're worth more than this. Don't séttle for being like this. Who you are now, who you've been, where you're going, it's all in the cards. But it's how you read them. How you interprét things to make a story for yourself. Otherwise they're just pictures, meaningless pictures of cups and swords and princes and jésters.

I've read your cards Phil, I've been where you are. I just wanted to say, it'll all be all right. Bélieve me. And don't be too prétentious, it's just a bit of fun, isn't it?

Phil finishes his shift at 3am. The sad, the lonely, the drunk and the mental, that's who phones a psychic call centre at that time of

➥

night. He wraps up his cards in a silk scarf of Bethan's and goes home in a taxi. As usual, she half-wakes, asks about his night, falls back to sleep. It's hard to go straight to bed after a night shift, so Phil lays out his cards on top of the duvet, by the moonlight, in a simple three-card spread.

The Four of Cups: a contemplative figure sits under a tree, with three cups at his feet; an arm appearing from the sky offers him a fourth cup. A card representing a period of self-absorption, of dissatisfaction, of ambiguous opportunities, of blended pleasure.

The Two of Swords: a young woman, blindfolded, holding two crossed swords. A card of choices, of indecision, confusion and denial, but also of truce or stalemate.

The Fool: an innocent young man stepping off the edge of a cliff. A card of potential, of new beginnings, of taking risks, of dreamers.

West Island Echo

Fiona Worthington

Westislandecho.co.uk
Saturday 20th October 2012

Fish Farm Stink

By Charlotte Kingfields-Blake

YESTERDAY, I WAS privileged to land for the first time in a small aircraft at the airport on the Isle of Kilbar. Privileged, because the island boasts the only runway in the world to be washed twice a day by the tide, as the airstrip is located on a beach. An island of natural, unspoilt beauty, as we came in to land I could see a handful of people bent over picking cockles from the beach, a local source of nutrition and employment for centuries. But although it would seem that not much has changed here for generations, this fragile economy is under threat by a new development that has split the community and could pose catastrophic, irreversible damage to the environment. I am referring to the recently launched fish farm, "Iasg", located in Snog Bay on the East coast of the island.

Local MP the Rt Hon Seamus Campbell, has long been campaigning for a full investigation by the Farming and Fisheries Commission into the long term effects fish farming may have on the region. He met with the head of "Iasg", Mr Jim Greer, after requesting a meeting with him to discuss some of the concerns raised by islanders about the safety of his use of various chemicals in coastal waters.

From his home in Kilbar, the Rt Hon Campbell, known locally as "Gunaim", issued the following statement: 'Concerning the matter of the "Iasg" fish farm and the concerns of local residents about the effects of the fish farm on other fish, crustaceans, people's health, future employment and the ecology of the whole area, I have spoken with Mr Greer himself about this and the effects. It is a matter that concerns me and those of many other islanders. I welcome the employment that the fish farm has created locally, but we must be vigilant and realistic in assessing the full impact the chemicals used in the fish farm will have on all of us locally. The local fishermen are concerned the pollutants and pesticides will affect local fish stocks and in the future there will not be enough fish in the area to fish, so losing their only means of employment in the island environment. I understand also that some people have become unwell on eating local seafood that up until now was harmless.' He then went on to add, 'Rest assured, I will be doing all I can to bring the matter to the attention of the relevant authorities, and, hand on heart, I will personally be involved in this matter and its concerns until I am satisfied that an answer has been reached.'

Local Councillor, Angusina MacCleod, has also put pressure on various authorities to look into the possible consequences that fish farming will have on the island. 'This is something that all islanders should do something about. The more of a voice we have, the more they will have to listen and take note of what we are saying. I urge everyone to get involved and sign the petition I have placed in the post office, the

➥

Co-op, the bank, the butcher's and the church. With one voice we will proclaim: "*Mach a'seo!*" "Get out of here!" Thank you.'

Mr Greer was unavailable for comment at present, but I was able to talk to one of the fish farm workers who dismissed any suggestion that there was anything harmful in what they were doing. He pointed out that there are many fish farms in many other locations, with no known side effects on human health or the environment. He also highlighted the fact that the fish farm has created employment and stability at a time when the fishing industry is in decline as a whole.

In an interview with the resident island doctor, Dr Fickle, I asked if he was aware of any changes in the health of the population since the fish farm had been founded. He stated that a significant number of cases of nausea and allergy had arisen in the past few months. However, he did say that this could not directly be attributed to the new fish farm, but he would welcome an impartial review of the situation.

Having spent the day speaking with many of the islanders, I am keenly aware of how sensitive and important the outcome of any investigation will be. They will continue to raise awareness of their concerns together with the backing of their MP, as someone commented, 'with "Gunaim" on the case how can we lose?' Any economic decline in the island would be a disaster for the whole community, with people having to leave and seek employment elsewhere, on a possible scale that has not been seen since the clearances. But the determination of the islanders to muster on in the face of adversity can be summed up in the words of the Rt Hon Seamus 'Gunaim' Campbell, 'You can't change the weather, but you can change the sails.'

COMMENTS POPULAR NOW | NEWEST| **OLDEST** | MOST REPLIED

Blueface21 says: 4 hours ago
Another example of colonial rule and all the more reason for our independence

AngusOgg says: 4 hours ago
They want us out

Flo says: 2 hours 37 minutes ago
Too right

Bongo says: 4 hours ago
My bro works on a fish farm

Tina22 says: 4 hours ago
Where is this??

Blueface21 says: 3 hours 14 minutes ago
Isle of Kilbar, God's own residence. West Scotland heaven.

Theplankman says: 3 hours ago
at least they have jobs lol

Gingertips says: 3 hours ago
Does anyone know how to make scottish tablet?

MairiNT says: 3 hours ago
Don't think she – journalist – speaks gaelic. Doesn't 'Gunaim' mean useless?!

Neilboy says: 2 hours 44 minutes ago
Aye it does. And he is.

KisimulRising says: 3 hours ago
Typical bloody English. We were here first. We're back, long live independence.

Blueface21 says: 2 hours 33 minutes ago
Wa hae Scots! Time to fight.

Tricialove says: 2 hours 25 minutes ago
Have you guys actually read the article?

MairiNT says: 3 hours ago
And it's Snoc Bay!!!!!!!!!!

MairiNT says: 3 hours ago
Has anyone signed the petition yet?

Thelochman says: 1 hour 26 minutes ago
wtf no way. Ma jobs ma job.

Tina22 says: 2 hours 53 minutes ago
There's a good recipe for tablet at sweettooth.com

MoragAnn says: 1 hour 43 minutes ago
My rash is still there. They should be shot.

Thelochman says: 1 hour 23 minutes ago
Dr Fickle shud be shot. shit stirrer.

BennyLop says: 1 hour 20 minutes ago
What's happened to our beautiful island?

Thelochman says: 1 hour 16 minutes ago
an shoot Gunaim an Angusina.

Bettyboo says: 1 hour 10 minutes ago
If you have allergies try yoga – seriously it works. It worked for me.

Uighguy says: 1 hour 8 minutes ago
Fishings fucked.

Thelochman says: 1 hour 3 minutes ago
your fucked

➥

Uighguy says: 1 hour 1 minute ago
COMMENT REMOVED

Fudge44 says: 45 minutes ago
I went to Kilbar once. Didn't see much, the mist lasted two days. Would go again tho.

Sugardumpling says: 43 minutes ago
Blueface21, if ya let yer sheep in ma wee garden again I'll punch ya. Get RID OF EM

Calumthebrave says: 37 minutes ago
Anyone interested in reading more at fishfarmsthetruth.com?

Now Here
Jane Alexander

THIS TIME, I'VE remembered to check the map. I know where I am, in relation to where I need to be. And the sun is out, distant but clear, and the blackbirds are singing and I'm distracted by the flirtatious yellow of the daffodils, the feel of spring on my face, and so I walk for a while eyes dancing with gold, ears nose skin all dizzy with spring, and then—

Then— this is not—

This turning, surely—

There should be— shouldn't there be—?

Ridiculous! I laugh at myself, uncertain. I laugh because I'm not lost, not yet. It's just that I've come too far. Or not far enough.

I make my choice. Instead of walking shrinking circles, wearing a path in the pavement, I push on in pursuit of the next corner, chasing the brow of the hill, where surely the city will open before me.

I push on, and streets repeat themselves. The sun has edged behind a cloud, refusing to help. The daffodils are no use as signposts, all the same blunt yellow. I turn, and the world swings, too much and unpredictably. I'm unaligned: my straight lines are zigzagged. Each street, road, alley starts in hope and ends in disappointment.

Once again, I'm lost. Once again, I've failed.

But it's amazing the things they can do nowadays.

The chip itself was a speck of a thing. Dr Ramsay showed me, tilting his cushiony fingertip so it caught the light. I leaned in close, close enough to see the gridlines on its silvered surface, and the altitude lines of his fingerprints. Tiny, but sharp-cornered; I was relieved to hear it would sit just under the skin at the base of my skull. There, it would pick up signals from GPS satellites.

The something they would put into my brain had no such sharp corners. It was soft. Microscopic. Alive. A bio-engineered single-cell organism, programmed to feed data from the receiver chip to my parietal lobe. Too small, too living to sit on Dr Ramsay's finger. He showed me a picture instead. The cell was oval, like a tablet; a mottled purple bug.

'It's really a minor procedure,' he said. 'Minimally invasive.' I wondered if he practiced that voice: deep and calm. I'd tried to be deep and calm when I told you I'd made my mind up. I'd repeated the doctor's phrases, word for word.

'It's like a faulty electrical connection,' I'd said. 'Inside my brain. And what this does is, it compensates for that bit of loose wiring.'

You winced. 'It's just the idea of putting something into your brain...'

'I know, sure; it is a bit yeuch. But in every case so far, it's been a complete success. And before I had my eyes done, remember I was squeamish? – the lasers cutting the lens; all those stories about how you could smell the burning – and now: ta-da!' My hands made sunbursts, miming enlightenment.

You'd narrowed your own eyes, letting me know you weren't convinced. You couldn't see why I'd take any kind of risk to solve such a trivial problem. To you, my absent sense of direction was part of me: frustrating, occasionally; amusing, frequently. Endearing, you'd once said. Little girl lost. But it wasn't you needing your hand held, going through life like a child.

'You won't be able to feel it,' said Dr Ramsay, 'once it's in.'

It would be inserted during a neuroendoscopic operation. I'd be up and about the next day. Really, they scarcely needed to knock me out.

They did, though – they knocked me out. Jesus, of course they did. This was my actual brain.

I woke up crying. I always cried after general anaesthetic. Tonsils; teeth; appendix. A chemical thing. There was no pain. Just a tenderness at the base of my skull, and a patch of wadding and gauze.

By the time Dr Ramsay arrived at my bedside to tell me how smoothly the op had gone, I was more or less composed.

'When does it start to work?' I asked, wobbly-voiced.

'Now. Straightaway. Give it a go, if you feel up to it.'

'Don't I.' I coughed, tried again. 'Don't I need to go outside?'

He shook his head. 'Not necessary. You'll find it's extremely sensitive. It should work fine, even where the signals are faint.'

'How do I...?'

'Just think of a place. Anywhere.'

I thought of you, at home, waiting.

'Oh!'

Dr Ramsay's lips curved with professional satisfaction.

'It's like – that's amazing. I just thought of home, and it *knew* – I knew.'

'Try somewhere further afield.'

For some reason I thought of Germany. And there it was, massed off to my right. Berlin, I thought, and the sensation tightened, narrowed. The flat we'd rented last year in Prenzlauerberg. It tightened again.

'So what's happening, you see, is that the brain – your brain – is responding to the stimulus...'

As he spoke, I was swamped by a fresh wave of tears. Nothing to do with what he was saying, or Prenzlauerberg, or the tightening in my brain. The anaesthetic. A chemical thing.

'... in effect creating its own navigational software...' Dr Ramsay stopped.

I closed my eyes, covered them with my hand. 'It's just, sorry. It's so bright.'

Dr Ramsay murmured something about rest: I heard retreating footsteps; a closing door. He'd left the lights on. I turned my face to hide in the dark of the pillow.

Through the next hours I floated in and out of sleep, in and out of tears, as the anaesthetic worked its way through my system. Each time I woke I tested myself. Orkney. Piccadilly Circus. The Sahara desert. I knew them all. A web, unbreakable and thin as air, stretched round the globe with me at its centre. And like the spider knows the arrival of a fly in its web – a tug, a tension, an almost weightless weight – I could think North, and I felt it. Could think Edinburgh Castle, and I felt it. Think James's house, think Kazakhstan, think Sydney Harbour Bridge – and I felt it. My web was the size of the world, and my world was changed.

The first check-up, post-op. Dr Ramsay stood behind me, hands on my skull. His fingers were cool on the stubbled patch around the tiny scar. 'That all looks fine,' he said. 'All working okay?'

'Well – it's amazing,' I said. I would have told him all the things I'd told you: how in the mornings, first thing, I took a bus or a train to somewhere I'd never been, and walked like a cat straight home. How I walked all day, farther than I ever had before, through streets that appeared and intersected exactly as they should – like the city was building itself around me; like I was imagining it into being. How I'd started to drive alone, and the driver's seat no longer felt like the wrong side of the bed. And more: how the first time I'd picked up my guitar, after the op, every note, every chord I reached for was there, in precisely the right place. Pitch, tone, duration. How I no longer had to shape the music, it was shaped for me. The notes perfectly spaced, waiting for me to happen across them. But he was already back at his desk, updating something onscreen.

'Honestly,' I said instead. 'Life-changing.' I hesitated, and then, 'What's funny though, is – I know it's my imagination – but it's like, sometimes, I can feel it.'

'Ah.' He smiled. 'That's, as you say, your imagination, of course. When you open your eyes in the morning, do you feel a tingle in your occipital lobe? No, of course you don't. It's really exactly the same. The same kind of sensory processing.'

I lifted a hand to the back of my head. Ran my finger round the soft stubbled circle. 'Sure,' I said. 'I know that. Of course.'

It was by accident, that I started to mess with it. I was striding north, swinging round each correct turn, and I thought of you. It was the weekend you went to London, and I was thinking you'd be on the train, still, but just about to pull in to King's Cross. As the chip pinpointed those north London suburbs – Tottenham, Finsbury Park – 300 miles at the back of me, my step slowed slightly. The feeling was like being watched, by someone who's behind you. There was the same urge to turn, to be facing the 'right' way. I held that picture of you, and increased my pace. At the back of my head, a pulse twitched. The faintest flicker. As if – as if the bug didn't like it.

It was meant to be my final check-up.

'Healed nicely,' said Dr R. 'Hasn't it? And no problems at all?'

I took a breath. 'I want it out.'

I could feel surprise through his fingertips. When he moved round me, back to his desk, his face wore a rumpled look. But his voice was deep and calm as ever. 'What's making you feel this way?'

So I told him about last week; the night you'd waited up for me. How I'd slept in the car, worn out from driving, because every day I drove further and it was never enough. How I'd yanked out the car radio because the music was like a war inside my head, the notes so imprecise, misplaced so painfully in space and time. How the sky was a single massive eye that

never ever blinked; how my web was the size of the world, and I was trapped in its centre. How the bug knew where I was and pinned me there: always, exactly, and only – *there*.

All the things I should have said to you, when I got home at 4.23am and you asked me where I'd been – instead of screaming at you to get out of my head, and you walking away, and telling me I was too mental to talk to, and I had to go back to the doctor.

When I'd finished, there was a deep calm pause.

'Well,' he said eventually, 'we can do it with a local. We can do it right now.'

It wasn't until he'd numbed the back of my head that the question struck me.

'How can you get it out like that?'

'It's a small incision; the chip's right here, right under the skin—'

'No. It. The bug.'

'It's not— it's just a chip, you remember the one I showed you?'

'But inside. The—' I couldn't find the word. I dropped my voice. 'The living thing.'

'Oh no. That won't come out. It doesn't need to. You can imagine, with its information feed removed, it has no function. It's inert. Just a tiny part of you. It's just a cell.'

The final appointment, I had to fight for.

Dr Ramsay's voice was no longer calm, and nor was it quite as deep. 'There's nothing,' he said, 'over hundreds of successful operations – nothing at all to suggest the kinds of problems you seem to be experiencing.' His gaze shifted from his screen to the clock on the wall behind me, until finally he met my eyes. 'I can assure you,' he said, 'it's quite impossible.'

Impossible that I could really feel it. A deep, buried itch, alive, like a virus. Impossible for it to be active. To be growing. To be steering me.

'But – has anyone else had it reversed? Had the chip taken out?'

'As far as I know,' he said carefully, 'yours is the only implant to have been removed.'

'So then – you wouldn't know. If it could carry on working.'

➥

'It's impossible. There's no data feed.'

I felt my mouth tug down, and bit the inside of my lip. I couldn't trust my voice.

'Have you been sleeping alright?'

I shook my head. Wanting to explain: it's the bug, all night it keeps me half-awake. tugged every which way through the night.

'Loss of appetite? Lack of energy?' He jabbed at his keyboard, making a note. 'I'd recommend you speak to your GP about the treatment possibilities.'

I sat silently as Dr Ramsay washed his hands of me.

'He, or she, might suggest a low dose of Prozac, which is a very effective anti-anxiety medication... or it might help to get away for a bit, if you can...'

But I couldn't. I couldn't get away.

I'd thought, somehow, the sea might confuse it. On the ferry, on deck, I'd let the wind pull my hair horizontal, let it batter me about. But when I thought of you, I felt an easterly twitch; I thought of the island, and it pulled to the west.

Today I climbed the highest peak on the island. The bug kept tugging me, making me climb as the crow flies, so I found myself sliding on scree, grabbing sharp handfuls of gorse. At the summit the sky was huge and the bug was stronger than ever. The day before, I explored the caves at the base of the cliffs. I clambered and crawled as deep as I could inside the rock, but the itch was always there.

It's a little better now: at night, in the pitch black. Sitting outside the cottage, under a sky that's solid with cloud, and studded, invisibly, with satellites. Everything unseen: owls, mice, bats revelling in the dark. Me, pinned to the earth.

Even under the ocean it will know where I am. Even under the soil.

What I've realised is that I'll have to be burned, become multiple. I will become a cloud, in all directions at once, the million million specks of me irretrievably lost in the world.

I find I am looking forward to it.

Confused?
Seth Crook

The first word of this poem is the,
but the second is the first.

MYTH AND MYSTERY AT THE EDGE OF THE WORLD

Call of the Undertow
Linda Cracknell

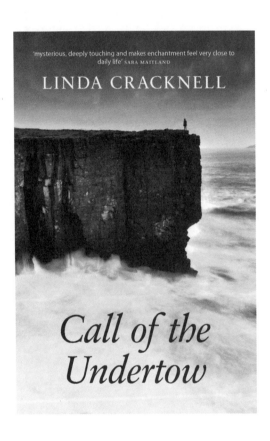

'mysterious, deeply touching and makes enchantment feel very close to daily life'
Sara Maitland

'...seductively pulls the reader into the deeper more dangerous currents of the human heart. Emotions ebb and flow along with the tide, in language clear and crisp as sea air.'
Cynthia Rogerson, author of
I Love You, Goodbye

**Released: 14th October
RRP £8.99**

**FREIGHT
BOOKS**

Pre-order now from:
freightbooks.co.uk

Contributor Biographies

Jane Alexander is a writer, creative writing tutor and literature development freelancer living in Edinburgh. Her short fiction has most recently been published in *Take Tea With Turing* and *New Writing Scotland*. Find her at bestorder.co.uk

Janette Ayachi is an Edinburgh-based poet with degrees from Stirling and Edinburgh Universities. She has been widely published in over forty literary journals or anthologies, shortlisted for Write Queer London and a Lancelot Andrewes Award. She is the author of *Pauses at Zebra Crossings* and *A Choir of Ghosts*. Loves straight rum, new cities and olives. janetteayachi.webs.com

Fran Baillie's whole family had a degree except her and the cat. This was remedied in 1989 with an English/French (Hons). She then enjoyed working for 12 years as a lecturer at Dundee College in the Special Needs Department. After retirement in 2001 she got a place on the life-enhancing MLitt course at Dundee and will never not write. She enjoys writing in Dundonian/Scots.

William Bonar's pamphlet, *Frostburn Steel*, was published in 2004 by Dreadful Night Press and his poems have been published in a variety of newspapers, magazines and anthologies. A short sequence, *Visiting Winter: A Johannesburg Quintet*, published in *Gutter 06*, was chosen as one of the Best Scottish Poems of 2012. scottishpoetrylibrary.org.uk/poetry/poems/visiting-winter-johannesburg-quintet

Stephanie Brown is a student on the Glasgow University Creative Writing MLitt programme. She has previously been published in *Gutter*, *Tip Tap Flat*, and *From Glasgow to Saturn*.

Paul Brownsey has been a journalist on a local newspaper and a philosophy lecturer at Glasgow University. He has published about sixty short stories in Scotland, England, Ireland and North America. His story *Comin Thro' the Rye* appeared in *Gutter 07*. He lives in Bearsden.

Larry Butler was born in the USA and has lived in Glasgow since 1981; he teaches tai-chi in healthcare settings, leads life-story groups at the Maggie Cancer Care Centre and facilitates writing groups for Lapidus Scotland (creative words for health and wellbeing) lapidus.org.uk. Recent publications include *Butterfly Bones* (Two Ravens), and *Han Shan Everywhere* (Survivors' Press). He edits pamphlets for PlaySpace Publications.

Ron Butlin has an international reputation as a prize-winning novelist and is also the Edinburgh Makar. *The Sound of My Voice* was included in *The Guardian's* list of '1000 Books You Have To Read' (between Butler and Camus!). His poetry and fiction have been translated into over ten languages. He lives in Edinburgh with his wife, the writer Regi Claire. ronbutlin.co.uk

➤→

Nabin Kumar Chhetri is an upcoming student at the University of Oxford. He graduated with an MLitt in The Novel from the University of Aberdeen. He is a member of Scottish PEN. He has received awards from Italy, Israel and Nepal for his writing. His work has been published in more than 30 international journals.

Regi Claire is a Fellow of the Royal Literary Fund and a creative writing tutor at the National Galleries of Scotland. She is the author of four books, most recently *The Waiting*, a novel. She has twice been shortlisted for a Saltire Book of the Year Award. One of her stories has been selected for The Best British Short Stories 2013.

Juliet Conlin was born in London in 1970 and grew up in England and Germany. She holds an MA in Creative Writing from Lancaster University and a PhD in Psychology from the University of Durham. She works as a writer and translator and lives in Berlin. Her debut novel, *The Fractured Man*, was published in July 2013 by Cargo Publishing.

SMJ Cook grew up on a farm in the north of Scotland, studied law at Edinburgh University then worked as a lawyer in London. She now lives in St Louis, Missouri with her brewer husband and two children. This is an extract from her first novel, *Time Laid Up In Store*, set in a fictional Scottish village.

Frances Corr has been a new writer for about twenty years now. In an earlier life she wrote plays which made it to the stage and over the years has squeezed out some short stories and poetry which have made it to print. She is also an artist and is currently contemplating the combination of art and words.

Seth Crook taught philosophy at various universities before deciding to move to the Hebrides. He does not like cod philosophy in poetry, though he does like cod, poetry and philosophy. His poems have started to appear in *Snakeskin*, *Other Poetry*, *The Rialto, Open Mouse, Ink, Sweat and Tears, The Journal, Northwords Now, Antiphon, The Interpreter's House, Message in a Bottle, The Passionate Transitory, Streetcake* and *Gutter*!

Andrew Crumey's latest novel is *The Secret Knowledge*. He teaches creative writing at Northumbria University and is a mentor for Scottish Book Trust; formerly he was literary editor of *Scotland On Sunday*. He won the Northern Rock Foundation Writer's Award for his novel *Sputnik Caledonia*, which was also shortlisted for the James Tait Black and Scottish Book Of The Year awards.

Martin Donnelly is the singer and songwriter for Scotland's least hardworking band, The Savings and Loan. He lives in Leith with his wife and baby daughter. songbytoadrecords.com/artists/the-savings-and-loan

Sally Evans is known for book-length poems as well as being Editor of the long-lived broadsheet *Poetry Scotland*. Recent work has appeared in Stirling Castle writers exhibitions, anthologies such as *Starry Rhymes* (on Ginsberg) and Split Screen, in which she has performed in Manchester, Callander and Pitlochry.

Jim Ferguson is a poet and prose writer based in Glasgow. Born in 1961, Jim has been writing and publishing since 1986 and is presently a Creative Writing Tutor at John Wheatley College in Glasgow's East End. His collection *The Art of Catching a Bus and Other Poems* is published by AK Press. His novel *Punk Fiddle* is published by Whirlpool Press. His website is excellent: www.jimfergusonpoet.co.uk

Ewan C Forbes lives and writes in Aberdeen, Scotland. He has fiction forthcoming in the anthology *Ominous Realities*, and in Eggplant Literary Media's *Transdimensional Library*. His work has previously appeared in *Daily Science Fiction*, *Sand Journal* (as Ewan Forbes), and in *Digital Science Fiction* (as E C Forbes). Ewan C Forbes said to say hello and to wish you well.

Graham Fulton is a poet from Paisley. His most recent major collection was *Full Scottish Breakfast* (Red Squirrel Press). Previous collections include *Humouring the Iron Bar Man* (Polygon) and *Open Plan* (Smokestack Books). Full-length collections are to be published by *Smokestack Books*, Red Squirrel, Roncadora and Salmon Poetry. *Reclaimed Land: A Sixties Childhood* is due out in 2013 from The Grimsay Press. He runs Controlled Explosion Press. grahamfulton-poetry.com

Andrew F Giles has work in *Ambit*, *Magma*, *Equinox*, among others, and edits online literary arts journal *New Linear Perspectives*. He is currently researching poetry & poetics at the University of Bristol.

Harry Giles grew up in Orkney and is based in Edinburgh, where he helps to run the spoken word events series Inky Fingers and the live art platform ANATOMY. His pamphlet *Visa Wedding* was published by Stewed Rhubarb in November 2012. Credits, videos, recordings and writings about art and politics and anxiety can be found at harrygiles.org

John Glenday's first collection, *The Apple Ghost*, won a Scottish Arts Council Book Award and his second, *Undark*, was a Poetry Book Society Recommendation. His most recent collection, *Grain* (Picador, 2009) is also a Poetry Book Society Recommendation and was shortlisted for both the Ted Hughes Award and the Griffin International Poetry Prize. He was a judge for the 2011 National Poetry Competition.

Rody Gorman lives on the Isle of Skye. He edits the annual Gaelic anthology *An Guth*. Latest collection *Beartan Briste/Burstbroken Judgementshroudloomdeeds*, Cape Breton University Press, 2011.

Jen Hadfield's poetry and visual art has been heavily influenced by Shetland's landscape and language. Since her second book, *Nigh-No-Place*, won the T.S.Eliot Award in 2008, she has worked primarily as a poet, creative writing tutor, and classroom assistant, but walking, and gathering wild food and materials for her visual art-works, are as important in her creative life as her language-based practice. Her third poetry collection, *Byssus*, is due to be published early 2014.

Mandy Haggith has two published poetry collections: *Letting Light In* (Essencepress, 2005) and *Castings*, (Two Ravens Press, 2007) and a non-fiction book, *Paper Trails: from trees to trash, the true cost of paper* (Virgin Books, 2008). In 2009 her first novel, *The Last Bear*, won the Robin Jenkins Literary Award. Her second novel, *Bear Witness*, has just been published by Saraband, and with them she is also editing an anthology of tree poems, *Into the Forest*, due out in autumn. This summer she will be Poet in Residence at the Royal Botanical Gardens in Edinburgh. She lives on a woodland croft in Assynt.

Irene Hossack writes poetry, short stories and reviews which have been published in British, Australian and American journals. She studied at Monash University, writing her doctoral dissertation on the poetry of Geoffrey Hill, and teaches Creative Writing and English Language at the Open University. She was shortlisted for a New Writers Award 2010/11. Some of her work is available at: irenehossack.wordpress.com

➤➤

Alex Howard is poet, screenwriter and PhD candidate at Edinburgh University. He has read at the Edinburgh International Book Festival, and has had work published in *The London Magazine*, *Aesthetica* and *The Cadaverine*. He has won the Red Cross International Writing Prize, and his sitcom *Big Bad World* is under development having been shortlisted by the BBC.

Andy Jackson is from Manchester but lives in Fife. His debut collection *The Assassination Museum* was published by Red Squirrel in 2010, and he edited *Split Screen* (Red Squirrel, 2012), an anthology of film & TV poetry (a sequel *Double Bill* is due in 2014). *Whaleback City*, an anthology of Dundee poetry co-edited with W.N. Herbert, was published in 2013.

Vicki Jarrett is a novelist and short story writer from Edinburgh. Her first novel, *Nothing is Heavy*, was published in 2012. Her short fiction has been widely published, broadcast by BBC Radio 4, Radio Scotland and Radio Somerset, and shortlisted for the Manchester Fiction Prize and the Bridport Prize. She is working on a short story collection and a second novel. vickijarrett.com

Màrtainn Mac an t-Saoir: Ùghdar, bàrd is sgeulaiche a tha air a bhith ri a chiùird fad deannan bhliadhnachan a-nist. Ann an 2003 bhuannaich *Ath-Aithne*, cruinneachadh de sgeulachdan goirid, Duais na Saltire airson Ciad Leabhair is chaidh an dà nobhail a lean sin, *Gymnippers Diciadain* agus *An Latha As Fhaide* a chur air a' gheàrr-liosta airson Leabhar na Bliadhna. Nochd a dhàin ann an *Dannsam Led Fhaileas* ann an 2006, agus ann an 2007 chaidh Crùn na Bàrdachd a bhuileachadh air. Bho 2010, tha Màrtainn air a bhith na 'Shore Poet'.

Martin MacIntyre: An acclaimed author, bàrd and storyteller, Martin has been working across these genres for a number of years now. In 2003 *Ath-Aithne* - a collection of short stories - won the Saltire Award for First Book and his two subsequent novels *Gymnippers Diciadain* and *An Latha As Fhaide* achieved short-list placings for their Book of The Year Award. His poetry was published in *Let Me Dance With Your Shadow* in 2006, and in 2007 Martin was crowned 'Bard' by An Comunn Gàidhealach. Since 2010, he has been an Edinburgh 'Shore Poet'.

Peter Mackay is a writer, broadcast journalist and academic. Originally from the Isle of Lewis, he is a lecturer in Literature at St Andrews, and is the author of *From Another Island* (Clutag Press, 2010) and *Sorley MacLean* (RIISS, 2010).

Rob A Mackenzie was born and brought up in Glasgow and lives in Leith. He has published two pamphlets (with HappenStance and Salt) and two full collections (both with Salt), the latest of which, *The Good News*, was published in April 2013. He is reviews editor of *Magma Poetry* magazine.

Helen MacKinven writes contemporary Scottish fiction and was a mature student on the MLitt Creative Writing at Stirling University, graduating in 2012. Several of her short stories have been published and she is currently working on her third novel. She lives in a small rural village in North Lanarkshire with her husband, two sons, two dogs and eight hens.

Nikki Magennis is a Scottish writer and artist. She has written two erotic novels, dozens of short stories (erotic, literary and otherwise), and her poetry pamphlet is forthcoming from Red Squirrel Press next year. Read more: www.nikkimagennis.com

Iain Maloney is a widely-published writer of fiction, non-fiction and poetry. Originally from Aberdeen, he now lives in a relatively safe part of Japan. He has an MPhil in Creative Writing from the University of Glasgow and a novel, *Dog Mountain*, available to a good home.

Andra McCallum has made a career out of not having a proper job. He writes poetry to help while away the time, smokes forty fags a day, is partial to good Kentucky sippin' whiskeys, is on the verge of clinical obesity, and has taken to making 'old man noises' when hauling himself out of chairs. Life has treated him well.

Marion McCready lives on the west coast of Scotland, her poems have appeared in a variety of journals and magazines. Her poetry pamphlet collection, *Vintage Sea*, was published by Calder Wood Press (2011). She is a recent recipient of a Scottish Book Trust New Writers Award.

Ross McGregor writes poetry and fiction. His poetry has appeared in *New Writing Scotland*, *Gutter* and Tramway's *Algebra*. He lives and works in Ayrshire.

Carol McKay won the Robert Louis Stevenson Fellowship in 2010, and in 2012 her story *Flags* won the inaugural Booktown Writers' Competition. Her e-book *Ordinary Domestic: collected short stories* is available from Pothole Press. Carol teaches creative writing through The Open University and writes reviews for *Booktrust* and *Northwords Now*. She blogs at carolmckay.blogspot.co.uk

Paul McQuade is a Scottish writer now living in Ithaca, New York, after several years in Tokyo. His most recent work includes commissions from the Scottish Arts Council and publications in *Numéro Cinq*, *Little Fiction*, and *Specter*. He is currently working on his first novel in between translating books about Marxist polar bears.

George McQuilkin is an American who came across the water to Scotland so long ago he has started to feel like a stranger in his native land. In a previous life he made documentary and television films, but now writes short stories and novels (well, a couple) for children and adults. His story, *A Monkey in the Garden*, appeared in *Gutter 07*.

Andrea Mullaney is a writer, journalist and tutor based in Glasgow, who was previously published in *Gutter 05*. As the Europe & Canada region winner of the 2012 Commonwealth Short Story Prize, *Granta's* New Voices section included her as among "the most exciting emerging talents in the world" (no, really, they did). More info at www.andreamullaney.com

Niall O'Gallagher's first book of poems, *Beatha Ùr* (Clàr), was published in the spring. Also forthcoming in 2013 is *Saoghal air an t-Saoghal* (Clò Ostaig), a collection of essays on Scottish Gaelic writing, edited with Pàdraig MacAoidh. Ten sonnets with Irish versions by Eoghan Mac Giolla Bhríde will appear in pamphlet form later this year. He lives in Glasgow.

Roy Patience was born and brought up in the Highlands. Since graduating from the University of Aberdeen, his poetry has been published in *Causeway/Cabhsair* and *Magma*. A keen volunteer at the Scottish Poetry Library in Edinburgh, he divides his time between Edinburgh and Aberdeen.

Nalini Paul's first poetry pamphlet, *Skirlags* (Red Squirrel Press, 2009) was shortlisted for the Callum Macdonald Award. She was George Mackay Brown Writing Fellow in Orkney (2009-10), and has collaborated on a number of projects. Recent commissions include the script for Ankur Productions' *Jukebox* (Tron Changing House) and poetry for Glasgow *Film's For All* project (both 2013).

Mary Paulson-Ellis has published fiction in anthologies and literary magazines including *New Writing Scotland* and *Gutter*. She has an MLitt in Creative Writing from Glasgow University and is both a Hawthornden and a Brownsbank Fellow. She likes to write about the murderous side of family life.

Gillian Philip's books include *Crossing the Line*, *Bad Faith*, *The Opposite of Amber* and the Rebel Angels series – *Firebrand*, *Bloodstone*, *Wolfsbane* and *Icefall*; she also ghostwrites for *Beast Quest*, *Darke Academy*, and Erin Hunter's *Survivors*. She has been nominated and shortlisted for awards including the Carnegie Medal, the Scottish Children's Book Award and the David Gemmell Legend Award. Her home is in the north-east Highlands with her husband, twins, three dogs, two cats, a fluctuating population of chickens and many nervous fish.

AP Pullan was born in Yorkshire but now lives in Ayrshire. He has had poems published in various magazines and online. Andrew is a teacher working with pupils in crisis.

Jean Rafferty is the author of *Myra, Beyond Saddleworth*, a novel 'compelling and disturbing in equal measure.' (Deborah Orr, *The Guardian*). An award-winning journalist, she has written on everything from sport to Satanic Ritual Abuse. She only had the nerve to submit this rather strange (but true) story because the distinguished American novelist Edmund White told her he 'loved it.'

Elizabeth Reeder writes fiction, lyrical essays and for radio, and has two published novels, *Ramshackle* (Freight) and *Fremont* (Kohl), both of which have received critical acclaim. *Ramshackle* was shortlisted for the Saltire First Book of the Year Award and longlisted for the Author's Club Best First Novel Award. She teaches on and convenes the Creative Writing Programme at University of Glasgow.

Mark Russell's debut poetry pamphlet will be published by Tall-Lighthouse later this year. He has poetry published or forthcoming in a variety of journals and anthologies, including *The Frogmore Papers*, *Poetry Salzburg Review*, and *Bliss* (Templar), and was shortlisted for the Bridport Prize in 2012. He has an MLitt in Creative Writing from the University of Glasgow and is a St Mungo's Mirrorball Clydebuilt poet.

Chrys Salt is an award winning writer, The Literature Convener for The Dumfries and Galloway Festival, Artistic Director of The Bakehouse and author of five poetry collections. A poem in her fourth collection *Grass* was selected as one of The 20 Best Scottish Poems 2012. chryssalt.com and thebakehouse.info

Hamish Scott was born in Edinburgh in 1960 and now lives in Tranent, East Lothian. His poetry has been published in various outlets including *Lallans*, *Poetry Scotland*, *Open Mouse*, *Ullans*, *Anon*, and *Northwords Now*. His first collection, *Kennins*, was published in May 2013 and is available as a printed pamphlet from www.scottish-pamphlet-poetry.com and as an e-pamphlet from Amazon.

Kathrine Sowerby is a Glasgow based poet with a background in fine art. In 2012, she was a runner up in the Edwin Morgan Poetry Competition, commended in the Wigtown Poetry Competition and received a New Writers Award from the Scottish Book Trust.

Judith Taylor comes from Perthshire and now lives and works in Aberdeen. She has had poems published in a number of magazines and is the author of two pamphlet collections, *Earthlight* (Koo Press, 2006) and *Local Colour* (Calder Wood Press, 2010).

Mary Thomson, curator and art critic from Yorkshire, now lives in Glasgow. Of her three pamphlets one was shortlisted for the 2012 Callum MacDonald Memorial Award. She has performed one and two-woman shows at the Ilkley Literature Festival Fringe in 2010 and 2011 and in London in 2012. Two poems have appeared as Poems of the Day in *The Herald*. www.marythomsonbooks.com

Stewart Thomson graduated from the National Film and Television School in 2008 then returned home to bask in the simplicity of the Glasgow underground system. He has since been nominated for two Scottish BAFTA awards, had his first television commission and has a feature film in development with BBC Films. He is currently working on his first novel.

Samuel Tongue has published poems in numerous journals and anthologies including *The Red Wheelbarrow*, *Anon 7*, *Northwords Now*, *North Light: The Anthology of Clydebuilt 3* and *Magma*. He is the current holder of the Callan Gordon Award as part of the Scottish New Writers Awards (2012/13) and convenes a course on The Media Bible at Glasgow University.

Kate Tough's novel, *Learning to Fall* (working title), is out in 2014 with Cargo Publishing. katetough.com

George T Watt was born in Clydebank, raised in Edinburgh and now lives in Dundee. He started his working life on the Island of Islay and on farms in the north east of Scotland. Graduating from the Open University with 1st Class honours in Literature in 2006, he writes in Scots and English and is published in *Lallans*, *The Ileach* and *New Writing Scotland*.

Crìsdean MacIlleBhàin/Christopher Whyte's fifth collection, *An Daòlag Shìonach*, containing new poems 2002–2007 and uncollected poems 1987–1999, will appear in September, in Gaelic only. A book of Tsvetaeva translations, *Moscow in the Plague Year*, covering the period from November 1918 to May 1920, is due out from Archipelago Books of New York in April 2014. He currently divides his time between Budapest, Venice and Glasgow.

Colin Will, an Edinburgh-born poet and publisher with a background in science, lives in Dunbar. He has chaired the Boards of StAnza and the Scottish Poetry Library. His sixth collection, *The Propriety of Weeding*, was published by Red Squirrel in 2012. His own publishing house, Calder Wood Press, specialises in poetry chapbooks.

Kevin Williamson was founder and editor of Rebel Inc, is one half of Neu! Reekie! and co-editor of *Bella Caledonia*. He lives in Leith, dreams of volcanoes, and of a Scotland fit for everyday heroes. His first collection of poetry *In A Room Darkened* was published by Two Ravens Press.

Fiona Worthington currently lives in Glasgow with three of her four sons. Previous places she has lived are as diverse as London, St Petersburg (Russia) and the Isle of Barra in the Outer Hebrides. She is a professional artist, specializing in landscapes, and has exhibited her work in various locations in Scotland. In her spare time she writes fiction.

'...as now I think, said Austerlitz, that time will not pass away, has not passed away, that I can turn back and go behind it, and there I shall find everything as it once was, or more precisely I shall find that all moments of time have co-existed simultaneously, in which case none of what history tells us would be true...'

WG Sebald, *Austerlitz*